Barefoot Bodyguard

Charleston Series Book 5

Sue Langford

Copyright © 2024 White Sand Romance Publishing

All rights reserved.

ISBN: 978-1-7381095-8-6

To the lovers of small towns, the addicts of billionaires, the love of spicy romance and to the readers who inspire .

"There's something about you I can't explain. But whatever it is, it makes me want you in ways I can't even describe." – A. Zavarelli

Chapter 1

"Faith, while I can appreciate that you want to leave. Right now, it's not happening. There's a massive storm headed here. They told us to stay off the roads. We're staying at the beach house."

"Ridge, you're trying to make a move. If you're gonna make it, just make it already. I've..."

He leaned in and devoured her lips.

"That all you've got?"

******

Faith had a luxurious life. One that most people could only dream of. She owned her company, she had real estate all over the world, but there was one thing that she wanted that money couldn't buy. She had been single for years, having short-term relationships that never mounted to anything. Nobody could handle a woman that had money. Nobody could handle the woman who had the looks and the power. She was almost 5 foot 8, chestnut brown hair and green eyes. A look that most of the guys that she'd dated considered her a vixen. She loved her beach house, and the fact that she had the best house on the block, in her opinion of course. All she needed was an assistant to help her out with the day to day. The business ran itself most days, which gave her time to concentrate on her other love – being at the beach.

She'd intentionally bought the house where her mom and dad had re-met. It wasn't really her style, but after the money she put into the remodel, it was beautiful. The only thing missing was someone to share it with and make new memories with. The only thing. The fact that her house was beside that spot that her folks loved, gave her a little bit of hope. It had worked for them. She'd hoped that someday she'd get that same moment.

"Miss Faith, I understand that you really hate the thought of this, but you do need security. Actual security. Someone has to be there to keep an eye out. There are a ton of situations that you could end up hurt," the business head of security said.

"I get it. I don't want security, nor do I need it. I have houses all over the place. I don't need to have a personal security guard."

"You have security in each location. Either you get some personal security, or I'll get it for you."

"Why," she asked determined to get her way as per usual.

"Because a threat was made. I can't sit here and watch you risk your life," security said.

Faith shook her head. "Fine. Get some names. I'm going to the beach house for a couple days." Her head of security nodded.

Faith headed out. She needed space, and another hit of the fresh salt air. She went back to her big house, got a few things together and went to leave. "Miss Faith, would you be alright with me driving you over," her security guy said.

"I'm fine. I'm just going to the beach for a while. Why would I actually need security?"

"Because there have been threats. Your parents were also worried."

"I'm fine."

"Understood, but would you at least let me drive you over? I can get the new guy to follow us in the sportscar." Faith shook her head.

"Fine, but he gets one ding on that car, and he's fired."

Faith watched out the windows, like she had when she was a kid. She watched the live oaks, the palmettos and the palms all blending in together. She opened the window to take in a breath of the fresh air as they made it past Angel Oak and made their way down the small highway and out to the other bigger highway to get her to Sullivan's Island beach house. It was within walking distance of her mom and dad's beach house, but far enough away that she had privacy. She needed it.

When they pulled in through the front gates, she smiled. It was way past being her happy place. It was the only place that she had any solace. She headed in, seeing security there waiting on her. "What," she said.

"Your mom popped over. She said for you to come by," her security said.

"Yep," Faith said as she walked up to her spacious bedroom. She slid into shorts and a tee and walked out to her balcony, looking out at the water. At the waves making their way to the shore of pristine white sand. She closed her eyes, inhaling the salt air.

It had been a favorite place since she was little. Every year, her folks would come over to that little spot by the house that she'd now bought. There was a little plaque there, that they'd put up when she'd bought the house. Every year, they'd come down there and Faith would smirk, seeing her parents kissing. It was what felt like a picture-perfect moment. The longer that her mom and dad were married, the more she imagined a love like that. The kind of love that meant having someone who would always be there. Even when her dad had done events, he'd called to check on her and her mom. He'd send flowers just because. He'd come home to what always seemed like a long hug and kiss from her mom. She remembered attaching herself to her dad's leg until he picked her up and included her in the hug. If she could ever find a man like that, she would hold on. They just didn't make them like her dad anymore.

When there was a knock at the door to her room, she turned around. "What's up," Faith asked.

"Your car is here. Locked up and in the garage. Did you need me to pick up any groceries," the housekeeper asked.

"It'll give me something to do. Thank you though."

"Will do. Your wine is in the cooler. I put extra towels outside in the towel bin for you if you're up for a swim. Just let me know if you need anything."

"Thank you," Lily said.

"Most welcome," her housekeeper said.

Faith went back to looking outside. How could she really be in danger? At the beach? Never.

She curled up on her oversized chair outside and grabbed her laptop, going through work emails and seeing 10 resumes sent over for her new personal security. She picked one, seeing a photo. He was alright in the looks department, but she didn't want to have to have that much security. It was ridiculous in her eyes. The fact that he looked like a childhood friend, made it a little easier. If it was the guy that she thought he was, him being around her might just be a few more fireworks than she would be expecting.

She finished her emails, sent one off to her dad that she was at her beach house and went to walk down to the beach when her phone went off. "Hi Dad," Faith said.

"Is there anything you need me to get to in the office," her dad asked.

"Nothing for my part. Everything's done with the book stuff. Mom's newest is doing really well. I think there are a few events that we have to do, but we're good. How are you two doing?"

"Good. We're flying out to LA for her signing and for the promo. Do you need anything?"

"Thanks, but no. I'm good. I'm gonna hang out here. Security keeps saying that I need to have a personal security person. You know how I feel about that."

"Do it. I know that you aren't happy with the idea, but you need it. Your mom and I have one too."

"I get it. I found one out of the pile they handed me. I'll see if I can handle him."

"Just keep mom and I posted," her dad said.

"I will. Have fun. See you when you're back," Faith said as they hung up.

Her dad was so old-school, it was almost funny. She knew what he meant. She also knew that if this security guy was the guy she thought, there would be a lot more fun in her life. She looked out at the water, sliding her phone in her pocket, and walked down to the beach, walking out to the water. She wandered as the waves caressed her feet. The salt water always felt so good. Even when Faith was little, she loved running in the waves along the white sand beach. She'd loved it as a kid, and it was even better now, carving out a little space for herself. The downside was that she didn't have anyone to share it with. When she heard the notification on her phone, she looked at her phone seeing that Ridge was coming within the hour for an interview. She took a deep breath, ran her fingers through the sand and made her way back up to the house, sliding a t-shirt over her bikini.

She came inside, freshened up a little and her security from the house came over and mentioned that her appointment had arrived. Faith smirked and sat down on the sofa.

"Miss Faith, sweet tea," her housekeeper asked.

"Please," Faith said as her housekeeper handed the glass to her and put a second down for Ridge.

When he walked in, Faith almost laughed. "Ridge Sams is here to see you," her property security said.

"Show him in I guess," Faith said as she tried to stay professional.

"Miss Faith," Ridge said as he walked in.

"Come have a seat," she said. One look at him and she knew. He was the same guy that she'd known as a baby. She knew the look.

Ridge Sams was the son of her mom and dad's friends Carter and Addison. He was ex military, muscular and 6 foot 3. The dark brown hair and hazel eyes were sexy as all get out. Even his tattoos were hot. He had a golden tan, giving away that he loved the beach as much as Faith did. The slight facial hair was even sexy. She could tell with look that he was one and the same.

"You know that you're here to interview to be my security yes?"

Ridge smirked and nodded. "Yes. Honestly, I'm a little surprised that you even need it," Ridge said.

"Well, thanks for that. How available are you with being able to be around at all times?"

"If you want me to stay with you, okay. Not an issue. I have a rental that I can get out of if you need it," he said as Faith couldn't help looking that hot specimen of a man up and down.

"Why security," Faith asked.

"I've always been the protector. I figured that with all the training I had in the military, I could do that for a living."

"You have references right," Faith asked.

"How many did you need," he replied as she caught him looking her up and down.

"Can we start with three," Faith asked.

He handed her three names and numbers. "Am I allowed to ask you a question," he asked.

"Sure," Faith said.

"You've known me since we were kids Faith. Why didn't you just call me and tell me that you needed security?"

Her heart started pounding in her ears. "Honestly, I wasn't sure if you were the same Ridge," Faith replied.

"If you need me, tell me. I'll take the job. At least I know how sneaky you can be," Ridge teased.

"I'm not sneaky."

"Yeah you are. Did you forget me helping you jump back into your bedroom window when you tried to sneak out?"

"That was the sunroom window."

"Because it was near your bedroom," he teased.

It was definitely the same guy. The last time she'd seen him, they had graduated high school together. Almost 10 years prior. "Ridge, this is a real job. They're kinda making me get security. The least I can do is find someone that I know is good at their job."

"And what else could you possibly need other than me?"

"Someone to keep me safe."

"I'm here if you need me."

"No funny business either."

"Funny as in making you laugh or funny as in trying to do what I tried prom night," Ridge said quietly.

That night, he'd tried to get her away from her friends and saw her head outside alone. He came up behind her and was about to try and kiss her when her boyfriend of the week came outside. He'd blown his chance then. He wasn't about to blow it now.

"You're not funny. He almost kicked your butt," Faith said.

"Does this mean that you're gonna let me have the job?"

"You good with the pay?"

He nodded. "This mean that I get to hang on the beach," he teased.

"You're security."

"So occasionally," he joked.

Faith nodded. "They want me to have security. I don't think I need it, but the security at the office says I do."

"Why?" Faith shrugged and got up, walking into the security office that she had at the house and handed over the information, scanning it and sending it to the business security letting them know that she'd chosen Ridge.

When she came back out to the living room, he was looking outside to the view. "I still can't believe that you bought this place," Ridge said.

"Meaning what?"

"You didn't know that a guy who hated your folks lived here? I remember hearing stories about it."

"And the little plaque down there by the bottom of the steps is what I did for their anniversary. If this house wasn't here, they wouldn't have bumped into each other," Faith said.

"At least you have that," he teased as he sipped his sweet tea.

"Next time something happens that you need security for, just call and tell me."

"I haven't talked to you since high school Ridge. How would I have even known," Faith asked.

He smirked and pulled out his card from his wallet, handing it to her. "How long do you need me here for?"

"Not just here."

"Full-time?" Faith nodded. "This will be fun," he said sarcastically.

"If you don't want to, tell me now," Faith said.

"I'll do it, but don't get mad when I say you shouldn't do something." Faith shook her head and walked back down to the beach. He followed, seeing her run around in the waves like she had as a kid.

They talked, laughed and talked business then headed back to the house. "So, what's the big problem that they say you need security for?"

"Obviously something that they aren't telling me," Faith said as they came up the steps and headed back inside. He walked her inside, and his phone went off with a call from her office.

"Sir," Ridge said.

"Faith has chosen you to be her security. Can you come in tomorrow morning to discuss what's going on," her head of security said.

"I gather that I'll be bringing Miss Cartwright with me?"

"No. We will discuss it tomorrow." He hung up with them and looked at Faith. She had no idea that people had been hiding things from her. He shook his head and looked at her.

"What," Faith asked.

"You're not gonna like it."

He sat her down and told her what he'd been told on that call. "Seriously," Faith asked.

"I'll know more tomorrow."

"Promise me that you'll tell me?" Ridge nodded. She was irritated, angry and even livid at that point that someone in the company had kept secrets. She wondered if her parents knew. If that was why they'd pushed so hard for her to get security. He took a deep breath. "You can stay if you want," Faith said.

"I'm gonna head off and get the condo paperwork done. Where do you want me to stay," he asked.

Faith smirked and walked him upstairs to the extra bedroom. "That work," Faith asked.

Ridge nodded and they headed downstairs. "Alright. I'll see you tomorrow," he said. Faith nodded and watched him leave. He put his jacket in the truck and headed off.

Faith shook her head. He was hotter than she remembered. The man showed in jeans and a suit jacket to the interview. He was almost too hot. She shook her head, trying to wipe the vision of him from her head. He was her security. Her personal security. She couldn't be drooling over him when it was supposed to be business. The one thing she did know, was that if they did go beyond that boss and security relationship, she'd be screwed.

She took a deep breath, walked back outside and slid her shorts and tee off, diving into the warm salt water. She needed it. She needed to feel like the world wouldn't blow up without her. That she could take time that she wanted. She swam, dove under the water and surfaced to see someone standing outside her house staring at her. She swam in and the closer she got, the more she realized that it was the security at the house.

"What," Faith asked.

"There's a call on your cell phone. They've called twice already," he said as he handed the phone to Faith.

"Yes," she said.

"I was thinking. How crazy would it be if I asked you out tonight," she heard.

"Holden?"

"Who else would it be," he replied.

"I'm not even dealing with you today," Faith said.

"Yes or no? We can go to the boathouse."

"Holden, I said no then, and I'm saying no now."

"One dinner."

"Holden."

"I'll come get you. You're down at the beach, right?"

"Seriously Holden."

"I'll be there in 30." When he hung up without her saying no yet again, she shook her head. She walked inside, had a quick shower and did her hair, slid into a tank and a pair of blue jeans, slid her sandals on and came downstairs.

"Miss Faith, where are you heading so we know," her security asked.

"Dinner with Holden," Faith said rolling her eyes. She put her things into her purse and just as she slid it over her shoulder, she heard the doorbell.

Faith shook her head as security went and answered. "Hey," Holden said as he handed her some flowers.

"Thank you," Faith said.

"Welcome. You ready," he asked.

"Sure," Faith said as she wrote down where they were going. He got her door, helped her into his truck that was way too oversized, and they made their way to the restaurant.

"So, how have you been doing," Holden asked.

"Good. Taking a break for a long weekend. How have you been," Faith asked trying to play nice.

"Good. I got another dealership. That makes 3, I think plus my IT business. If you ever want to get something other than the SUV and the sportscar, just tell me. I'll get you a deal," Holden said trying to play the big shot.

"I appreciate that," Faith replied questioning why she ever got in his truck.

When they pulled into the restaurant, she swore she saw Ridge's truck. They went inside, walked out to the patio and he got them a table. They sat down and almost instantly; he was ordering them shots.

"I'm good. I'll just have a sweet tea," Faith said.

"Girl, one drink," Holden asked.

Faith shook her head. "I'm good," she said. The waitress came back and gave Faith her sweet tea and Holden his two shots and double Jack and Coke.

"What can I get y'all for dinner," the waitress asked. Faith ordered her favorite salad and some shrimp, and he ordered what had to be the biggest plate on the menu.

"So, really though, what have you been up to? I've been trying to call you. Every time it goes through to voicemail," he said as Faith caught herself looking around to see if Ridge was there.

By the time they got through the food, Faith heard footsteps coming towards them. "Holden," a male voice said.

"What on earth are you doing out here? Long time no see buddy," Holden said as he got up. Faith looked and saw Holden giving Ridge a guy hug. "Come sit," Holden said as Ridge pulled a chair over and sat down beside Faith. "You remember Faith right?"

Ridge looked Faith up and down with a smirk ear to ear. "Yep, I remember this one. She started way too many fights in high school."

"And how did I manage to do that," Faith asked.

"You just looked too sexy. That's all," Ridge said as his arm slid to the back of her chair.

She finished her sweet tea and without even saying a word, Ridge got her a second. Before Ridge showed, she was about to bail on the date altogether. Now, as long as he was there, she was staying. They hung out, talked and when Faith was staring to get antsy, Ridge offered to drive her home since Holden was already drunk. "Please," Faith said. She thanked Holden for dinner and they headed out. When Ridge held her hand as they walked through the restaurant, she smirked.

"What are you doing here with him anyway," Ridge asked as he helped her into his truck.

"He sort of cornered me into a date. I don't know that I even had a chance to say no," Faith said.

"Quick talker. He always has been. That's how he got me down there too." Ridge said as she smirked.

"You do know you didn't have to drive me back, right?"

"Yeah I did. I didn't want him driving you after he was drinking like that. The man was already drunk before he even got there. I can guarantee that," Ridge said.

"Well, thanks for the save superman," Faith teased.

He smirked. "If I have to keep doing that, you're gonna have to take me with you from now on."

"Where," Faith teased.

"Funny," Ridge joked ad they pulled back into her driveway.

"Did you get the condo stuff figured out," Faith asked.

Ridge nodded. "He sort of knew that I wouldn't be there long," he joked.

Faith smirked. When he parked the truck, she turned to look at him. "What?"

"The arm on the chair? Really?"

He nodded. "That's what happens around you. I almost felt like I had to keep you safe from him," Ridge said.

"And did you?"

"Considering that three or four girls were staring a hole in him when we walked out, yes," Ridge said as he hopped out and got her door.

"Ridge."

"Faith," he said.

"I guess I'll see you tomorrow," he asked.

Faith nodded. "I'll be out here," she said as he gave her a hug.

Barefoot Bodyguard

He wanted to kiss her. Hell. He wanted to devour her lips until her legs curled around him and carry her up to that massive bed. He had to stop. He let go and she headed inside. He got into the truck, noticing that he was way too hot and bothered. "Down. She's the boss. Not you," he said as he calmed down enough to drive back to the condo and pack his stuff into a suitcase.

He walked into his condo and called his mom. "Baby. How are you doing," his mom asked.

"Good. Got a new job."

"And? Who are you guarding this time?"

"You'll laugh."

"Tell me it isn't Lily and Emerson's daughter."

"Mom."

"About time you two bumped into each other again. I don't know why you didn't ask her out in high school. You should've."

"Because she was dating someone. Just keep it quiet. You know that Dad's gonna have something to say about it," Ridge said.

"Baby, he asked if we'd talked. He was at the office with Faith's dad today. I'm sure he already knows."

"And are you two alright?"

"Yes. We're actually going to a movie premiere. It's gonna be in New York. If you want to come home and hang out, you're welcome to. You still have the key," his mom said.

"I do. I'll pop over before I head to meet up with Faith."

"Alright baby. See you tomorrow." He hung up with his mom and shook his head. His dad already knew, which meant that Faith's Dad did too.

When Faith came inside, her phone went off. Half-expecting a drunk Holden on the other end, she answered. "Hello," Faith said.

"Are you sure that you want Ridge to be your security," her dad asked.

"Honestly, he knows me well enough to know the stupid stuff I get myself into. I'm more comfortable with him instead of your ex-military crew that you and mom have."

"You're 100% sure?"

"Yes. Why does it matter," Faith asked.

"Because he has paperwork to sign."

"Dad, I need to know. Why is everyone so uptight and determined that I have security?"

"You're single, you're the head of the part of the business that could get dangerous like it was when your mom and I re-met."

"And," Faith asked.

"Baby."

"Dad, just say it."

"Someone made a threat with photos and sent it to me."

Faith's jaw hit the floor. "Who," Faith asked.

"I don't know, but the guy that irritated your mom and I before we got married is out. It could be him; it could be anyone. If you're comfortable with Ridge, fine. Just don't try to outrun him."

"Yes dad."

"I get it. I'm going overboard, but I don't want you getting hurt and either does your mom. Just stay close to Ridge."

"Dad, tell me the whole story. All of it. I need to know."

"There are other issues than just that idiot. There were threats from one of the former owners of one of the businesses I took over years ago. He is still irritated that I gave you the publishing end of the business. Your brothers got security as well, but they let me take care of hiring for them. I knew you wouldn't be as easy."

"Dad, while I appreciate that, I think I'm good with Ridge. It doesn't look as obvious with him being security. I promise. It'll stay professional. I'll be fine. Don't worry," Faith said.

"Alright baby. We'll give you a call when we're back. You're welcome to come to the beach house if you want to."

"Thank you. Give mom a hug for me. Enjoy the vacation. Love you guys," Faith said as she hung up.

She looked out at the water, watching the moonlight reflect on the waves of her little piece of paradise. If what her dad said was really happening, maybe Ridge wasn't enough. Maybe she did need more. When she got a text from Ridge, she smirked.

"Hey," Faith said as she called him.

"Hey yourself. So, I got the information. It's a lot more than I thought," Ridge said.

"Meaning what?"

"Meaning if you want me out there, I'll come now. There's nothing on TV anyway."

Faith smirked. "And the TV would be different here?"

"Beach view. Something to actually do. We can hit the ground running in the morning."

"Whatever you want Ridge. I'm just chilling here."

"Mom says hi by the way."

Faith smirked. "If you talk to her, tell her I said hi back."

"See you in a half hour," he replied.

Faith took a deep breath, let the security staff know he was coming and went upstairs. She grabbed a hoodie and came downstairs. "Miss Faith," her housekeeper said.

"Yes," she said.

"I made up that extra room for him. It's the one next to yours right," her housekeeper asked.

Faith nodded. "My folks are determined that I have security. That'll have to do," Faith said.

"And the other house is set as well. The room beside yours."

"Thank you," Faith said.

Ridge showed a half hour later with a bottle of Jack, a bottle of the wine that she'd always liked and a sweet tea from Sonic in hand. "What on earth did you do," Faith asked.

"If I'm staying, it's coming with me." Faith took the bottles, putting them with the other alcohol in the bar and showed him to the bedroom. "At least I'm nearby in case you need something," he teased with that grin. That sexy grin. The one that made her think more about him making a move instead of doing his job.

Faith headed back downstairs, and Ridge couldn't stop watching her walk away. She was sexy. A lot sexier than usual. Her legs were hot, tanned and he could just imagine how it'd feel with them wrapped around his hips. He tried to take a breather and calmed himself then headed downstairs. When he saw her walk outside, he shook his head, poured two glasses of Jack and walked outside, handing one to her.

"How'd you know," Faith asked.

"Because it's the cure for just about everything. What's wrong," Ridge asked.

"I had no idea that all of it was going on. Not even a clue," Faith said. He walked out to the beach, and she came with him as he sat down on the sand. She smirked and sat down with him. "What," Faith asked.

"Whatever it is, breathe. Nobody is getting near you. I just got a freaky feeling when I talked to your dad's security team. I didn't want you here on your own tonight."

"What was that bad," Faith asked.

"I don't think they..."

"Ridge."

"They had photos of you in the water, on the beach, outside and when you got here. It's not safe. Leave it at that. I'm doing a full sweep tomorrow. If it means me taking over for the property security I will."

"It's not like I'm gonna be here for a month. I'm just here for the weekend."

"Faith, while I appreciate that, I don't want you out here solo either. Not with everything that was threatened. Just give me a chance to fix the security stuff. Seriously, it'll be like we were roommates. That's it," Ridge said as he took a gulp of his drink. She drank the entire thing down and walked into the house. She put the glass in the sink and walked upstairs to bed, leaving him on the beach solo.

"Alright Ridge. Behave yourself. You want her, fine. Keep it to your damn self. No more reacting because of how damn sexy she is. She's off limits," he said silently to himself as he finished his drink. How in the hell she downed a half-glass of Jack without batting an eyelash, he'd never understand. He headed inside and locked up, talking to her security.

"Sir," the security said.

"We need to do a full sweep. Make sure that there aren't any hidden cameras. Nothing. They have photos of her on the beach and on the porch. Even in the water. We need to eliminate any hidden cameras. I don't want them getting more photos. I don't want inappropriate photos coming either."

Security nodded and got to it while he locked everything up and went upstairs to his room. He knew that she was irritated. Frustrated even. He also knew that her being frustrated meant that she was not gonna be able to sleep. Hell. He could've made sure she slept like a damn baby. He'd lose the job, but that feeling he had at that moment would've gone to good use. At least he wouldn't have needed his second cold shower of the damn day.

Chapter 2

Faith woke up at 5am. She couldn't sleep. The Jack helped, but not enough. She pulled her workout shorts on, slid her sports bra and tank on and freshened up, opting for a run on the beach. When she got to the main floor, Ridge was sitting at the countertop with a coffee. "What are you doing up," Faith asked.

"Couldn't sleep. We going for a run," Ridge asked.

"Whatever," Faith said.

He looked at her. "Faith, I get it."

"No, you don't. Everything was fine until everyone freaking tells me that the world is blowing up in my face. You don't have to live that," Faith said as she grabbed her water.

"That's why I'm here Faith. So you don't have to worry about it."

"I do."

"I know. Hell. I was worried all night too. I couldn't sleep either."

Faith shook her head. She went to walk outside, and he followed, running with her. When it turned into a contest, then a race, then the two of them laughing, he knew she was alright. She needed the release. The endorphins. She needed to get the frustration out. In his eyes, she needed a damn gym and a punching bag. "What," Faith asked as she stretched out on the steps.

"Didn't realize it was a marathon race," he teased.

"Ridge."

"Where are you heading after this weekend?"

"Home," Faith said.

"Good. Do you have a gym?"

Faith nodded. "Full one and a tv."

"You need one."

"Right," Faith said as she walked inside. She went to make breakfast and her housekeeper swept her from the kitchen, making Faith and Ridge breakfast. "I can cook," Faith said.

"And you don't need to be in my kitchen. Out," her housekeeper joked.

Faith sat down on the chairs at the island, and he looked at her. "What?"

"Nothing," Ridge said.

"Then why are you looking at me like that?"

"Because. What are you doing today," he asked as Lily wanted to roll her eyes.

"Relaxing, hanging here, walk on the beach and maybe head back to the house so you can get settled."

"Done," he teased.

"Ridge."

"I don't take long to get unpacked.

"Funny," Faith said. He shook his head, and her housekeeper gave them their breakfast. "You went seriously overboard," Faith said.

"I had it prepped. Enjoy," the housekeeper said.

They had breakfast and Ridge got a grin ear to ear. "What," Faith asked.

"If I keep eating like this, I'm gonna end up needing a 2-hour workout," Ridge said as Faith smirked.

"And now you know why I do that run in the morning when I'm here."

"And when you're home?"

"Full hour workout every morning plus yoga outside when it's nice."

He smirked. "Then I guess I'll have to help you out with the workout too," he joked.

"Ridge, you'd be surprised."

It had been a while. He had no idea how strong she actually was. "And how surprised are we talking," he asked.

Faith shook her head. Just as he was about to get up, her phone buzzed. "One sec," she said as she walked into her office and answered.

"Yes," Faith said.

"A call came into the office for you. It's a little bit odd, but it was for you. They're determined."

"And who is it," Faith asked her assistant.

"I'll forward you the voicemail," she said.

"Thanks. Anything else that looks fishy that you need me to look at," Faith asked.

"A few. I'll send them to the house for you. Do you need anything from the office?"

"Not yet anyway. I'll be in on Tuesday."

"Alright. Enjoy the long weekend."

"Will do," Faith said.

She got the email with the message, slid her AirPods Pro into her ears and listened. "We need to talk. I know you know who it is Faith. Did you think that you having a guy around was gonna make me leave you alone? Nice try. By the way, nice bikini." Faith shook her head and almost dropped her phone.

Not two seconds later, Ridge was at the door of her office. "What's wrong," Ridge asked. Faith replayed it for him. "Who," he asked.

"Cameron Fairchild. A guy who was determined to get a second date when he barely made it through one."

"Where does he live?"

"Honestly, no idea and I don't care to know either," Faith said.

"You alright," he said as he noticed her hands a little shaky.

"He was worse than Holden. Way worse. Honestly, I don't want to have to see him."

"Up," Ridge said.

"What?"

He gave her a hug. "I'll handle him alright?"

Faith nodded. "I can handle him. Punching him and knocking…"

He hugged her again. "That's what I'm here for," he replied. Faith shook her head, brushed her tears away, being the tough woman, and walked upstairs. "Faith."

"I'm fine."

She walked into her bedroom, closed the door and walked into her main bathroom. She shook her head. "He doesn't get to screw with you. Breathe," she said to herself as she turned on the shower. She got undressed, stepped in and washed that feeling away. That one that Cameon had given her when they'd gone out. He was exactly like the guy her mom and dad hated. Pushy, obnoxious, demanding, bossy and stalking her. She took a deep breath, washed her hair and finished getting washed up. She flipped off the water, stepping out and wrapping herself into a fluffy robe. That's how she was calming herself. She walked into the bedroom, grabbed her bikini and shorts from the closet, got dressed and was about to go do her hair when there was a knock. Lily slid her hair from the towel and opened the door.

"What's up," Faith asked as she stood face to face with Ridge.

"We're heading to the house. I know you wanted to be out here, but after the photos and that, you're not safe here. You alright with that?"

"I guess," Faith said.

He was shirtless. Hot, and shirtless in nothing but shorts and aftershave. "Can we get your car taken to the house?"

"Already heading over I'd assume."

"Leave in a half hour?"

Faith nodded.

"I'm keeping you safe. I promise you," Ridge said as he looked her up and down and almost drooled.

"I appreciate it. I'll get my stuff together," Faith said as he went into his room.

Within the hour, they were heading back to the house. He'd talked her into driving with him, for safety reasons, and when they pulled into the house, he was in awe. "This is where you live? Seriously," Ridge asked.

"Mom and dad have the other house. This one is a lot more my style," Faith said as they hopped out and she grabbed her things. He grabbed his bag, and she showed him inside.

"This makes your beach house look like a shack," Ridge teased.

"Come on. I'll show you around," Faith said.

She showed him the main floor, the gym, the theater room, the wine cellar and then showed him the upper floor. "This is a guest room? This is bigger than my condo," he said.

"Why such a small place then," Faith asked.

"Because I'm never there. I'm always working," he joked.

"Well, for now, here you go," Faith said.

He shook his head. She went and got settled then headed downstairs. He watched from his room. Something was off with what he saw. She wasn't being herself. He came downstairs and saw her walking into her office. He walked downstairs and went and talked to security, realizing that now that he was there, they were only there for the premises and not Faith. He shook his head, made sure that he had any information about intruders or anything at the house and went her office, knocking at the door.

"What's up," Faith asked as he came in.

"I need to talk to you for a minute," Ridge said.

Barefoot Bodyguard

"What's wrong?"

"Well, there's a little situation. I just found out some interesting info. The security you have is only taking care of the houses. Not you. That means that no matter where you're going, I'm gonna have to go with you. What events do you have coming up," he asked.

Faith made a list. "Can't cut them down a bit?"

She shook her head. "Most of them are work, then I have a few that are family stuff that I have to go to since mom and dad are going away."

"You gonna be okay with me coming with you?"

Faith nodded. "I'll just email them and let them know."

"You sure you're okay?"

"So long as I don't have to say what's going on..."

"Then tell them I'm your date. Friends."

Faith looked at him. "Date?"

"At least nobody will question me being there."

Faith shook her head. "And see it on the front page of the paper in the morning?" He shook his head.

More than anything, he wanted to kiss her. He'd wanted to since he first saw her. He'd dreamt about it. The fact that they were one room apart from each other was slowly killing him. He looked at her. "You sure that's what you want to do," Faith asked.

"We kinda don't have a choice. I'd rather not have people know I'm your security. Makes it easier to blend in."

"If you think so," Faith teased.

She sent an email to her secretary to make sure that she had a plus one set up for the events coming up. "What else do you have on," he asked.

"Nothing. I was gonna hang at the beach at my place or my mom and dad's. That's all I had planned," Faith said.

"Then we sit down and go through things."

"Okay. Do you think we can go to mom and dad's beach house tomorrow?"

He smirked. "I guess," he said.

"I just need to clear my head. Whatever is going on at my place…"

"They're getting rid of the hidden cameras that nobody knew about. Those pictures weren't exactly good. There were photos of you in your bedroom there. They're gonna be removed and fixed this weekend. That's why I didn't want you to be in the middle of it."

Faith shook her head. "I've had that house for years."

"And those pictures didn't start until recently. Faith, while I'm sure there are lots of guys out there that would love them, hiding cameras to take photos isn't exactly a good move. Whether it was the guy who owned it before you, or someone being an idiot, I'm getting rid of them. You deserve your privacy."

"So, you saw the photos?"

"Unfortunately, yeah. Faith, you don't want to see them. Leave it at that." She looked at him. "No," he said. She nodded, silently saying that she wanted to see them. "I'm not doing it Faith. You don't need to see them. Leave it at disturbing if it's the guy after your folks."

"Let me see them."

He shook his head. Faith got up and walked upstairs, walked into his room and saw the folder, grabbed it, and walked into her bedroom. She sat down and went to open the folder when Ridge took it out of her hands.

"Did nobody ever tell you no? I said don't look at it. That you'd just be upset." When she tried to grab it from his hands, two of the photos fell out.

She watched them fall to the floor like a feather from a pillow mid pillow fight. When she saw it, Faith's jaw dropped. "How," she asked as Ridge grabbed them before she could see the other one.

"Like I said. Hidden cameras. Faith, I get that you didn't think you even needed security, and that you didn't want security. I told them to screen the house for hidden cameras. They should've done it long ago."

Faith shook her head. "How long ago," Faith asked.

"Meaning what?"

"How long ago were they taken?"

"Within the past month."

Faith shook her head and slid to the floor. "Why? Why would someone do this," Faith asked.

He helped her to her feet and sat her on the chair. "Tell me what you want me to do," Ridge said as he held her hand. Faith took a deep breath, and he shook his head. "Faith."

"I can't believe that nobody even bothered to look for them when I bought the house. I sent them in to do a security check of the entire freaking beach house. How did they not know," Faith asked.

He shook his head. "Leave it at you probably need better security."

Faith shook her head. "I can't," Faith said.

He helped her to her feet and gave her a hug. "Tell me what's gonna make you feel better," he asked.

"Mom and dads."

He nodded. "When are they heading out?"

"Tomorrow."

"Then we go tomorrow afternoon. I messaged a couple of my military buddies to come take care of the cameras. They do security now anyway. When you need people who are actually gonna do their job, those are the guys." When Faith nodded, he shook his head. "You alright," he asked.

"No."

He wanted more than anything to kiss her and get her mind off all of it, but he had to try to stay focused. He looked at her. "Tell me what you want me to do," he said.

"I need a drink."

He smirked. "I know, but realistically, since it's before lunch time, what do you want?"

"I need to get away from here."

"Where?"

Faith shook her head. "Anywhere."

He nodded, walked downstairs and saw the housekeeper. "Sir," the housekeeper said.

"Ridge. I'm taking her to Hilton Head for the day. What can I use for a picnic," Ridge asked.

"I'll get something together. Give me a half hour."

Ridge nodded, thanked her and went upstairs. He contacted his buddies, mentioning that she was gonna need better security. When they all replied back with a sold text from both of them, he went into his room and called her dad's security.

"Ridge," he said.

"The two guys doing security at the beach house are pointless. There are hidden cameras all over the house that nobody got rid of. They have photos of Faith. Am I allowed to eliminate them?"

"I'll handle it. Thank you for letting me know."

"I'm taking Faith to Hilton Head. Probably Hunting island. She is getting space and breathing room to cool down," Ridge said.

"Understood. I believe her mom and dad are leaving around 2pm. I can get the house ready for her to come," her dad's security said.

"I just want her calm. That's it."

"Understood. Let me know when you're on the way."

"I will. I have two guys that I do security with that are ex-military removing the cameras and patching the walls at her beach house. Am I permitted to get them to watch the house?"

"Send me their information. We can discuss."

"Thank you," Ridge said.

He went and grabbed his swimsuit, threw it into a bag and grabbed two beach towels and a beach blanket. When he heard Faith crying, he knocked on her door. "Faith."

"I'm fine."

"No, you aren't. Not if you're crying."

"I'm fine," Faith said again. He shook his head, got his things into his bag and she came out of the bedroom in shorts and a tank with a hoodie overtop.

"Faith."

"What?"

"The cameras will be gone by the end of the day. We can go out to Hunting Island and then head over to your mom and dad's beach house. We're away from all the drama."

Faith nodded. "Okay."

He took her hand, her housekeeper gave him the picnic basket, and they went to head out. "We can take my car," Faith said.

"My old pickup. Nobody will suspect."

Faith smirked. "Did you ever get the air conditioner to work?"

"You didn't mind when we were driving here," he teased.

Faith smirked.

They got on the road and headed off to Hunting Island, determined to get her mind off of everything that he could. They laughed, sang music and reminisced the entire way out there. He found a quiet area for them to relax, and they hung out and enjoyed the sunshine for a while. Within a few hours, both of them were starved. He opened up the picnic basket and gave her a drink, taking the food out so they could eat. Just as they were finishing lunch, Ridge noticed the sky getting dark. "Crap," he said.

"What?"

"Look up," Ridge said as he started packing everything up. He slid her phone and his into his pockets and they made a run for the truck. Just as they got in, the first raindrop hit the windshield. "Maybe we should've checked the weather?" Faith nodded. They both started laughing. "Fine. Maybe we can beat it back to Isle of Palms." Faith shook her head and laughed. The first laugh that she'd had in days.

They got on the road and started making their way up to her mom and dad's. "You sure you want to go up there?"

Faith nodded. She needed the comfort of home. The home that she'd lived in until she hit 21. When they finally got there, the storm had just started. They made their way in, saying hi to security. They went and dried off a little and Ridge went and made a cup of tea for Faith, grabbing himself a glass of Jack. When Faith came downstairs in a t-shirt and shorts, he smirked.

"Stealing your mom's stuff or dad's?"

"Mine," she teased. He handed her the cup of tea, and she opened the sliding door to the porch. Just as she did, the lightning started then the storm hit.

The rain was coming down in buckets and within a half hour, the power was out. Security had made sure the house was secure then headed to the other house to make sure it was safe, leaving Ridge and Faith there alone. "What," she said.

"Nothin," Ridge said as he opted to start a fire in the fireplace like they had during Christmas break years ago. She watched him make the fire just like her dad did when they'd come out to the beach before the holidays. Like he'd taught Ridge himself.

"What," Faith said when he caught her watching him.

"Are you gonna actually close the sliding door?"

"No," Faith teased. He got up and closed it halfway, then walked her over to the fire. She grabbed the blankets from the sofa, grabbed the pillows and opted to talk for a little while.

"What," Faith asked as he looked at her.

"I remember holidays here with my folks and yours. We always had so much fun."

"You mean until my dad started getting overprotective and refusing to allow boyfriends," Faith joked as she laughed.

"Oh, I remember. I remember my mom trying to get us together a few times. The last time was when we were like 16 I think," he said.

"20. Nice try though," Faith teased.

"What?"

"Graduation. Your mom tried talking me into it when she came to help me get ready for prom."

He shook his head. "See, she never told me she'd said that."

"Ridge, nobody told anyone anything. My brothers even remember when they tried getting us together."

"And why did we never go there?"

"Because we were best friends. We were practically family Ridge. I was 2 days old when you were born."

"See, I always did like an older woman," he joked.

"Meaning what," Faith asked.

He shook his head. "Nothing."

"Ridge."

"We were friends, but I did kinda have a little thing for you."

"Had?"

"I mean, I haven't exactly seen you since high school."

"Until now," Faith said.

"Still."

She looked at him then got up. "What?"

"Do you think we should head back," she asked.

Ridge took a deep breath and checked his phone. "We can't exactly head out. The road is kinda swamped. The weather station says to stay off the roads." He knew the reaction she'd have. She was starting to feel trapped in. He knew that she wanted to leave, and his only option was to distract her.

"Ridge, I don't want to end up being stuck here. We need to go."

"The storm is headed straight here Faith. We can't do anything about it. We have to stay put."

"Food?"

"We have some left from the picnic and there's food still in the fridge. It's fine."

Faith shook her head and went upstairs. "What," Ridge asked as he followed her.

"I can't stay in this house."

"We don't have a choice, Faith." She walked past him and went back downstairs with her pillow from her old bed.

"Did you seriously have a king-sized bed when you were living here?"

"They upgraded it when I hit 15. Stop distracting me," Faith said.

He took her downstairs and sat with her. "What," Faith asked.

"We're fine. You know we are."

"I hate not being able to go anywhere."

He shook his head. "I get it, but it's not like we're in a tunnel somewhere. We're fine. We're warm, we have a fire, and we have food. We don't need anything else except maybe power," Ridge said.

"Go figure. Always seeing the freaking bright side," Faith replied.

He shook his head, and they curled up. "Cards?"

Faith looked at him. "Nope. If there was ever a power outage here, we just hung out and went to bed or had a bath or something," Faith replied as he saw her starting to feel uncomfortable. He pulled her over to him and they hung out. When his arm slid around her shoulders, somehow, she felt better, but she knew he was up to something.

Seeing her all worried was something he was used to, but seeing her like she was at that moment, seeing her curled up with him, feeling her body against his was starting to get him all hot and bothered again. "Ridge, you're trying to make a move. If you're gonna make it, just make it already. I've…"

He leaned in and devoured her lips. "That all you've got?" He shook his head.

"You gonna kick my butt," he teased.

She looked at him. "What was that?"

"I wanted to do that when I saw you at prom."

She turned to face him. "Ridge."

"What?"

"What was that really?"

Barefoot Bodyguard

"Distracting you."

"And?"

He looked up at her. "You gonna kick my butt?" She shook her head, and he kissed her again.

When she shook her head the lightning hit the sand outside the house and she almost jumped into his arms. "And here I thought that you were the tough guy," Ridge joked.

"I am. That was just too close," Faith said as she turned and looked at him.

"What," he asked.

"Did you..."

He smirked. "What," he asked again. He leaned towards her and kissed her again as he felt her arm slide around his neck. That one kiss became the two of them making out like he wished that they had in high school.

He leaned her into the pillows as they watched the fireplace crackle. Just as she was about to pull off his shirt, his phone went off. He grabbed it and answered. "Yep," Ridge said.

"Are you and Faith out at the beach," his mom asked.

"Yeah. She was a little freaked about the house, so we came to her mom and dad's. Why?"

"You didn't look outside then," his mom said.

"Torrential rain. What," he asked.

"Just stay inside. I talked to Lily. There's stuff in the cupboards that don't need heat. Your dad said he could come down if you need him to."

"I thought y'all were leaving to go away," Ridge said as Faith shook her head.

"We are. I wanted to make sure you were alright."

"Mom, I love you, but go. Your flight's gonna be late anyway," Ridge said.

"We're flying with Lily and Emerson. Just be safe alright," his mom asked. Ridge finally got off the phone with her and Faith couldn't stop laughing.

"Yeah. Mom has crap timing," Ridge said.

"You seriously had a crush on me?"

Ridge shook his head as Faith sat up. "Yeah. I still might," he said.

Faith shook her head. "Ridge, why did you actually sign up to do security?"

"I talked to one of the security guys and they suggested I talk to you about it. I did."

Faith shook her head. "What?"

"Nothing," she said. When the fire crackled, he smirked. He got up, grabbed a few things out of the cupboard and brought it over to Faith. Like they were having a picnic by the fire.

"Nice," Faith said.

"Thankfully, your folks stock up the cupboards. You alright," he asked as he checked the fire.

"Back to what we were talking about."

"What," Ridge asked as he sat back down by the fire.

"Ridge."

"What?"

"Where did all of that come from?"

"What," he asked as Faith moved closer.

"You know what."

He took a deep breath and looked over at her. "I wanted to take you on a damn date most of high school."

"We were friends all the way through school. We were practically brother and sister. Why did you wait so long," Faith asked.

"Because you always had a guy around."

She shook her head. "Nice excuse," she said as the lightning cracked and the rain fell that much harder.

"Should we have stayed at the house?"

"Probably, but we're good," he said trying to get his mind off of the tanned silky legs beside him. The dark brown hair making him hot and bothered. The woman who'd lived in his dreams for years. He tried not to look, but when she got closer, he shook his head.

"Ridge."

"What?"

"Finish what you were saying."

"Faith, leave it."

"You had a crush on me that long?" He nodded. "Why are you so quiet Ridge?"

"Because I'm not saying anything else that is gonna get me in trouble."

"Who said you were in trouble." He gulped.

He knew that the longer they were alone, the better the chance that he was going to make a move that he couldn't possibly take back, and he'd never be able to get her to forget. He looked at Faith and she smirked. "What?" She looked at him. "Just kiss me already," Faith said as she smirked. He knew that was her way of giving him permission.

"You're still my…" She kissed him and slid her legs across his lap as his arms instinctively wrapped around her and pulled her closer. He knew that he was messing with fire. He knew that one screw up and he'd be gone from her life all over again. That one kiss, turned back into making out.

When they came up for air, she smirked. The fire was finally going out and she grabbed water. "What are you doing?"

"Putting the fire out," Faith said.

"Why?"

"Because. I thought we could go hang upstairs."

He had to stop himself. "We can wait for the embers to go out," he said. Faith shook her head.

She walked over and slid back into his lap. The woman was way too tempting. He would've got her naked right there if there weren't suspicious people around taking photos. "We can't do this here."

"Upstairs," Faith said.

He shook his head. "I'm your bodyguard, not..."

She kissed him and he shook his head. "Two minutes," he said.

"What?" She slid out of his lap, and he got up, drawing the shutters so they had privacy, then made sure the doors were all locked.

"What on earth are you doing," Faith asked.

"Making sure that the house is secure and that we have privacy."

Faith shook her head. "What were you planning to do," Faith teased.

"Doesn't matter. I don't want whoever started with those photos catching you and me."

"Doin what," she teased with a smirk as she curled up in the pillows.

"Faith, quit. I'm trying to keep you safe and away from the stupid cameras."

She motioned for him to come closer. "What," he asked.

She kissed him. "Come sit with me." Ridge shook his head and sat down beside her.

"What?"

She kissed him again and his arms slid back around her, pulling her tight to him.

"Better," Faith said.

"I thought that we were behaving?"

"Totally over-rated."

"Faith."

She shook her head. "What?"

"You realize that I'm supposed to be your bodyguard."

"You sort of are," she teased.

He shook his head. "That's not exactly what I meant."

She kissed him. "Do you want me," Faith asked.

"You're taunting," he said.

"Teasing. Yes or no?"

"Faith."

"It's not a difficult question Ridge." He kissed her with a kiss that gave her goosebumps and made her heart start to race.

"Good enough answer," he replied as his hands slid down her back.

"Nope. I need words," Faith teased.

He shook his head. "Yes," he replied.

She smirked. "I had to do all of that just…" He kissed her again and leaned her head into the pillows, pulling her legs around him as they started making out all over again.

He knew he'd kick himself for it. When it came time for him to really protect her, he'd be in a relationship with her. He let her up for air and she tried pulling his shirt off.

"Faith."

"Off."

"Why," he asked as she pulled it right off.

"Because I said so," Faith said as he shook his head. He kissed her again and slid her shirt off.

He kissed her, deepening the kiss until she was going for his shorts. He stopped her.

"Why," she asked.

"Because we're not…"

She kissed him again and he pinned her to the pillows. "Why," she asked.

"We're not doing this when we're in a beach blackout. If we're doing this, we're doing it the right way," Ridge said.

"Which is what," Faith asked.

"You'll see. I just don't want to do this curled up on the damn floor."

She kissed him.

"What?"

She shook her head. "You sure?"

"If you were anyone else, I would. It wouldn't matter. It's you Faith. I'm not gonna treat you like a hookup. I never would."

She kissed him again and he shook his head. Part of her wanted to swoon. He really thought of her that way? When she thought that he wasn't like all the other guys she knew, she was right. He wasn't. He was better.

"And what are we gonna do out here all alone," Faith asked.

"How long have we been friends?"

When Faith realized it had been 28 years, she almost questioned herself. "28 years," Faith replied.

"Friends."

She looked at him and kissed him. "Fine, but when we get back to reality, we're talking about..."

He kissed her. "I just don't want us jumping that far ahead."

"Ridge, it's sex. Not running to the chapel."

He shook his head and kissed her as her legs slid around his waist. "We're not going there. Not tonight," he said.

Faith shook her head, and he devoured her lips until he knew more than anything that she wanted him. Just as she went for his shorts again, the power came back on.

He smirked. "See? Even the power company agrees," Ridge joked.

She kissed him again and flipped the light off. He shook his head and got up.

"Where are you going?"

"Checking to see how the roads are."

He looked outside and the roads were still a little flooded. Who knew how bad it would be trying to drive back to her place. They had no choice. They had to stay. When he came downstairs, the lights were off and there were candles.

"Faith."

"What?"

"I know what you're doing."

"Are you worried that they're gonna show up and ruin the mood? Trust me. They won't. I'm an adult," Faith said.

He shook his head and Faith took his hands and led him back over to the fireplace. "You're just determined."

Faith smirked. "You want to wait, fine. I get it. I kinda like the idea of just sitting here and hanging out. What's wrong with that?"

"Besides the fact that you're determined to take advantage."

She kissed him. "Just sit."

Ridge sat down and she looked at him. "What," she asked.

"You're making it really hard to be your security."

"Which part?"

"Faith, I'm being serious."

"What if I just said that for tonight you aren't?"

Ridge got up and went and got himself a beer. He needed to dump an ice bucket worth of ice into his shorts, but it would've been too obvious. Knowing Faith, she'd be just as bad. She'd taunt him even more. "What are you doin," Faith asked.

"Breather and beer," he said as he heard Faith grab a soda from the fridge. He went and looked outside, watching the waves crash against the sand. It was beautiful, and the way the lightning lit the sky into shades of blue and pink. It was gorgeous. It was solitude. When he felt arms slide around his waist, he turned. "And what do you want," he teased.

"Are you really that determined to behave?"

Ridge nodded. "Like I said, if that's gonna happen, it's gonna be somewhere that isn't your mom and dad's house."

She shook her head. "Then we run back to my place."

He shook his head. "Not in this," he replied staring back out at the storm. "We could end up here for two days. The storm isn't letting up."

He pulled up the weather on his phone and she was right. Luckily, her folks and his had headed off before the storm hit.

"We can take the candles upstairs," she teased.

"Faith."

She kissed him, got the candles and went upstairs to her old bedroom. He grabbed the others, putting them onto a plate or two and followed her up the steps. She went and grabbed the pillows, throwing them back on the sofas, making sure the fire was completely out, and came back upstairs. He was staring out her bedroom window, still watching the waves.

"We haven't had a storm like this in forever," Ridge said.

"Would you sit down and stop staring out the window," Faith said as she closed the shutters.

"Determined?"

"If we're gonna be stuck here, then you have to actually sleep," she said.

"Give me two minutes." He left the room and went downstairs to ensure the alarm was on. When he saw that it was, he almost didn't want to go back upstairs. She wasn't the kind of woman that you sleep with and never talk to again. She never was. He also knew that if he did sleep with her, it would change everything. He made sure a second time that the house was locked up and secure and went into Faith's bedroom to see her going through emails.

"Anything interesting," Ridge asked as he leaned on the door frame of her bedroom door.

"A couple from the security at the house. The guys you got to come fix the house found more," Faith said. Ridge shook his head and went into his emails:

> *14 cameras hidden and removed. Doing a full scan of all the walls in all the rooms. Honestly, I don't know how she lived here knowing those were there. You alright? I heard something about us staying on and doing security with you?*

Ridge smirked. Telling her how many cameras they found wasn't in the cards. All she needed to know was that the house was clear. When he found another few messages from old one-night stands, he deleted them. He didn't need that drama. When he went through the rest of his emails, there was only one that wasn't spam:

> *Hopefully you two stayed at the house. I heard the roads were flooded. Let me know that you two are alright. By the way, if you decide you want to date Faith, I'd love it – Mom.*

He shook his head. "What," Faith asked as she watched him.

"I got a really fun message from my mom. An email actually."

"Yeah, I got one from my mom too. She said she's okay with us dating," Faith said as he almost laughed.

"I swear the two of them really need to quit," Ridge said.

"They've been trying to get us together since we were little," Faith said. When he looked at her, Faith got up and walked over to him.

"What," he asked. She motioned for him to come closer. "Faith." She went up on her tiptoes and kissed him as he picked her up and wrapped her legs around him. When he leaned her onto the bed, she knew. She was getting her way.

Chapter 3

"You were saying," Faith asked as she slid her shirt off.

"What? I never said we were doing…"

She kissed him. She reached for something in her drawer and handed it to him.

"What's…. Faith, we…"

She kissed him. "What?"

"First off, nice try. Second, we aren't…"

She nodded and kissed him. She slid her shorts off and he shook his head. "I know what you're doing," he said.

"I know. Why are you so dang worried?"

He shook his head and her legs tangled around him. "Faith, I'm not doing this. You want to do anything else, fine. Not that," Ridge said.

"What's wrong with me then?"

He got up. "I can't."

"Ridge."

"I'm supposed to be protecting you. Not screwing you."

He walked back downstairs, noticing that the condom was new. He shook his head, sitting down on the sofa. He was past being turned on. He wanted her so badly that he could taste it. He just couldn't do it. He couldn't sleep with her knowing that she'd whoop his backside to the moon if he did something that she didn't want. She was lonely. That's all it was. He wasn't fixing that by screwing around with her. He laid down on the sofa and tried to get at least a nap in before the next morning.

"Are you seriously gonna avoid me and sleep down here? We're not kids Ridge," he heard when he woke up.

"What?"

"Are you that determined to stay as far away from me as possible?"

"I'm not doing it. You deserve better."

"Stop being an idiot," Faith said frustrated as all get out. She walked over to the sofa he was on and looked at him.

"You seriously think that," she asked.

"Yeah I do," Ridge said, determined not to let her any closer. When she sat down on the edge of the sofa beside him, he took a deep breath, determined not to let her notice that the closer she got, the more turned on he was.

"Really? Seems to me that you want me," Faith said.

"You do realize that bossing me around isn't gonna work for you right?"

"Just admit it," Faith said.

"Doesn't mean that I'm gonna act on it," he said as he got up, cooled off and managed to get away from her just long enough to calm his body down.

When he opened the sliding door just a little to get some fresh air, she shook her head and went over to him. "Just come upstairs. At least you'll sleep in a decent bed instead of the sofa," Faith said.

"I know what you're trying to do Faith. Leave it. We aren't sleeping together. We're keeping this professional." She sat on the counter, and he shook his head.

"Down," he said.

"Make me," Faith teased.

He knew what she was doing. "Fine. Stay up there. Sleep up there if that's what you want," he said.

Barefoot Bodyguard

He closed the sliding door, got his phone, slid his backup battery on the back and went and curled back up on the sofa. "Seriously?"

"Managed to sleep last night. Why now," he asked.

"Because we're stuck in the dang house. The roads are flooded. I wanted to say something yesterday and didn't."

"So, you hired me because you liked me?"

"Because I know you're good at your job, and because I know that you are someone that I can trust. The fact that I'm a little shocked how much you'd changed was just a bonus."

"Meaning what Faith?"

She hopped off the counter and walked over to him. "Fine. I was attracted alright?"

"If that's the real reason..."

She kissed him. "Come upstairs."

"No."

"Come. You feel so damn strongly about it, you can sleep in the damn guestroom."

"I'm fine."

Faith shook her head. "You're that determined to stay away from me?"

"That determined to not be something for you to pounce on in the middle of the night," he teased.

She kissed him and grabbed his pillow. "What," he asked.

"You want a pillow, walk upstairs."

She walked upstairs and put the pillow on her bed. He shook his head. She was frustrating, annoying, irritated and he was now turned on all over again.

He walked upstairs, walked into the guestroom and saw that there was no bed in there. He took a deep breath. He walked into her room, and she smirked. "What," Faith asked.

"You're ridiculous. You know that right?"

"He finally turned it into her writing room?"

Ridge nodded. "Pillow."

"Not unless you're sleeping in here."

"If I do, stay on your side of the bed."

"Scared," Faith teased. He shook his head, pulled his shirt on and sat down on the opposite side of the king-sized bed from her. She shook her head and they both nodded off.

When he woke up the next morning, she was asleep in his arms and her arms were wrapped around him. He shook his head and went to get up when she stopped him. "Where are you going," Faith asked.

"Downstairs. Making sure that everything is in one piece."

"Would you just sit?" He shook his head and got up, heading downstairs. He freshened up a little in the kitchen and looked outside. The roads were still under water. It's not like he minded, but he wanted to get out of that house. He shook his head. At least his truck was above the pool of water. He looked and came up with an idea. He grabbed some fresh fruit, made breakfast and coffee for them both and walked upstairs.

"And," Faith asked as he walked in.

"I can carry you out to the truck and we can head to your big house if you want," he said.

"And the bridges won't be flooded?"

"Or your beach house."

"Sort of like damned if we do and damned if we don't," Faith said.

"I'll call the guys and see how the roads are over there."

"Just eat first," Faith said as she took a gulp of the coffee. He had his breakfast, texting the guys. When his phone went off two minutes later, he got up and went into the hall.

"Well, we got the cameras out, patched up the walls and we're repainting. Beyond that, we're good. We're good on water as well. Just up past the top of my feet," his buddy Calvin said.

"We were gonna head back over. It's halfway up the tires over here."

"Just be careful. Honestly, I'd tell you to head inland, but I doubt that I could talk you into it let alone her," Calvin teased.

Ridge smirked. "When y'all are done, let me know. As long as it doesn't look like anything's changed, we're fine."

"There was a package delivered this morning. No idea how, but it has her name on it. Is that the same Faith that you were crushing on when we were..."

"Goodbye," Ridge said almost laughing.

He came back into the bedroom and saw Faith with a smirk. "And?"

Barefoot Bodyguard

"They have your beach house almost finished. They're re-painting. What if we headed to your place," he asked.

"Beach or the other house?"

"Inland and away from the flood."

Faith nodded. "Fine, but I have one request first."

"No, we aren't going to Starbucks."

"Ridge, come here."

He walked towards her. "What?"

She went up on her tiptoes and kissed him. "Sit."

She pushed him to the bed, so he was sitting on the edge. "What?"

"We're having a date."

"You're still my boss," he said.

"And?"

Ridge shook his head. "Cut it out Faith."

He got up and she pushed him back onto the bed. "What?"

"Do you still like me?"

"I told you already. We're not doing this here."

"Yes or no?"

He nodded and she kissed him. "Good."

She took his hand and walked him into the massive shower.

"What," he teased.

"Shower."

"I can when we get to the house."

"Ridge."

"Not happening." She pulled his shirt off and he shook his head. "I'm not doing it. We talked about…" Faith kissed him and went for the drawstring of his shorts. "Faith."

"It's not like I haven't seen one before. Shower," she said.

He shook his head. "Go ahead. When you're done, I'll have mine," he said determined to not get naked anywhere near her.

He went into the hall, closing the door and called one of his friends that lived out near Faith's house.

"What's up," his friend Conner asked.

"What are the roads like?"

"Wet, but not flooded. You heading back up this way," Conner asked.

"Taking Faith back to her place. I just wanted to check. Isle of Palms is kinda flooded a little."

"The houses dip a little. That's it. If you can get out of the garage, you're fine heading up here. I just make a Starbucks run."

"Thank you," Ridge said.

"Welcome. Come by the house, okay?"

Ridge hung up with his buddy, grabbed his shirt and went downstairs, cleaning up and putting the clean dishes away. When Faith walked downstairs in jeans and a t-shirt, he smirked. "Good. Actual clothes," he teased.

"Go and shower then," Faith said.

"I'll shower when we're back."

"We're going to the house?"

"Yep."

"Why can't we just go back to my…"

"Because they're re-painting. Trust me. You don't want to see where the cameras were."

"Fine. Whatever."

She was irritated. More than irritated. Why he couldn't just give in for a second and have fun being stuck in the house together, she didn't know. She knew that he had more respect for her than that, but it didn't stop her thinking about it all night. It didn't stop her missing having someone who craves her. Having someone who seduced her until she gives in. Partially, she wondered if he really did want her. The fact that he didn't push her away was at least a step. She just kept questioning whether he even wanted her around.

He shook his head, walked back upstairs and went in and showered. He was past hot and bothered and had been all night. The only reason he'd tried to push her away was because they were in her parents' house. He wanted them on their home turf. If he'd walked her into that beach house and she'd seen the holes in the rooms, she'd never feel safe there again. He finished his shower and stepped out to see a warm towel on the counter. He shook his head, dried off and got changed. When he stepped out of the bathroom in his jeans and shirtless, she looked at him. "What," he teased.

"Nothin," she said as she got her things and came downstairs.

They headed out a little while later and when he held her hand in the truck, she smirked. "What," he asked.

"How many cameras did they find?"

"More than two. I didn't want you freaked out. That's the only reason why," he said.

"How many," Faith asked.

"Promise you aren't gonna snap?"

"Ridge."

"22," he replied.

Faith's jaw hit the floor of the truck. "What?"

"Like I said." He held her hand a little tighter. By the time they got back to the house, they were both starved and feeling a little better.

"I still can't believe that you had to carry me to the truck," Faith said.

"I wasn't gonna let you get soaked for no reason. Luckily, I didn't get soaked either," he teased. Faith smirked and they went inside. Her security was there and happy that they were back in one piece. When she went upstairs, Faith walked into her bedroom and saw the packages had been delivered. When Ridge came upstairs, he threw his things into his room and his phone buzzed with a text:

Come into my room.

He took a deep breath, slid a different shirt on and knocked on her door.

"Come on in Ridge," Faith said as he walked in.

"What's up?"

She closed the door. "Now that issue that you were having at the beach house. Still a problem?"

"I told you that I wasn't doing anything until I'm ready. What's wrong with you and all your raging hormones? It's like you're a horny teenager."

"Around you," she replied.

"Faith, seriously though."

"What do you think," she asked, showing him her new lingerie.

"You can stop now."

"You sure you don't want a fashion show?"

"I think you need to have a really cold shower," he said.

Faith looked at him. "Still nothing."

He shook his head. "I have work to get done," Ridge said.

She shook her head, and he went to leave.

"Come here," Faith said.

"What?" She grabbed his hand and pulled him to her. "What?" She kissed him.

When she felt him pick her up and wrap her legs around him, she was almost stunned. He leaned her against the wall and when they came up for air, he slid her to her feet.

"What," Faith asked.

"Like I said, I'm not doing anything. I'm supposed to be protecting you. Let me do my job Faith."

She shook her head. "And if I came home with someone else?"

"Go for it," Ridge said. Faith looked at him. "What?"

He headed out of her room and walked downstairs to go through the security paperwork and emails. When his phone buzzed again with an update from the guys at the beach house, he was paying more attention to that. When Faith came downstairs, he could hear how irritated she was. "What's up with Faith," the other security guy said.

"She's just a little frustrated. Nothing out of the norm," Ridge said. Faith went into her office and Ridge heard her door close.

He shook his head and tried to get work done when he got a call from the guys at the beach house. "What's up," Ridge asked.

"Well, we got everything patched and repainted, but we found a couple hidden microphones. We're eliminating them and tracing where it came from. We got one idea, but she's not gonna like it. Her security should've found it," they said.

"Crap. Okay. Scan it all. Keep me posted."

"Will do. Let me know what she says about us doing security."

"I will. Thanks," Ridge said as he hung up. He shook his head, got up and walked over to her office door, knocking.

"Ridge, wasn't it enough to humiliate me?"

"I got an update about the beach house."

Faith shook her head. "What," she asked as he came in and shut the door.

"They found bugs. I don't know how many, but they found them when they were clearing up this morning."

Faith shook her head. "I never should've bought that damn house," Faith said.

"I know why you bought it. The memories your folks have with that house, even with all of the dang issues, that it means something special. It always had. Now, it's just gonna be safer and more secure. It'll be safe from a billion and one issues. It'll be secure by the time the guys are done. I promise you."

"Ridge, what is wrong with me that you're determined not to be near me?"

"All I said was stop trying to make a move. I get what you want. I feel you. Just give it a break Faith. I never said I didn't like you. That I didn't want to have you around. I just said, let me do things in my way and in my time."

"And if I don't want to wait until you're..."

He kissed her. "I said time. Period. You want to go out and screw some random idiot, go ahead. Just remember who your damn bodyguard is. I'm gonna be standing right there." He walked out of her office and went upstairs.

He got his clothes unpacked and sat down. Why he'd even agreed to be her security was starting to be on a loop in his brain. She was stubborn, a pain in the backside, and more than annoying. He wanted her, but he wasn't doing anything until he was ready. If she couldn't understand that she could find someone else. Her crap security she'd had prior to him, would get her life put in jeopardy in 3 seconds flat. He slid a different shirt on and went through the settings they had to keep the house secure, and the rest of the paperwork he'd got from her dad's office.

When his phone buzzed 10 minutes later, he took a deep breath. "Yep."

"Where are you," Faith asked. "Upstairs. Why," Ridge asked.

When he heard the phone disconnect, he shook his head. He knew it was a matter of 14 steps before she barged into his room. She walked in without even a knock. "What," he asked.

"So now you're allowed to barge out of my office," she asked.

"When you're being an overgrown child? Yes. You want something that you can't have, you throw a damn tantrum. Just because I said not right now, doesn't mean it can't happen at some point. It means I get to choose. You want to screw someone, go ahead. You want me to leave, fine. Say it."

"Why? What's wrong with me that you aren't even slightly attracted," Faith asked.

"Faith, stop. For once, just stop. Let me be a damn man. I'm your security Faith. That means I work for you. You can't just keep trying to make me look like an idiot. You want to get laid, fine. I'm not doing it." Faith looked at him. "What?" He could see her eyes turning that bright green. The same green that had drawn him in with every one of her breakups. "What," he asked again.

"I had a crush on you. I never did anything, but I always wanted to. You showed up and it was like I got my life back. I just wanted, for once, to feel wanted for me and not because of my money."

"Then stop pushing Faith. Try remembering that I knew you when you were a kid. When we were babies, my mom used to tell me that you and I were gonna get married."

"I want you in my life," Faith said.

"I'm right here," Ridge said.

"I dated the wrong guys most of my dang life. For once in my damn life, I made the first move, and you shot me down Ridge."

"All I said was that I didn't want to in their house. That I wanted to wait. It's called being a damn gentleman."

"Then stop being a gentleman for 5 damn minutes."

"It's gonna take longer than that," he said as he got up. When she was speechless, he kissed her. "About time."

She shook her head. "Not exactly what I meant," she replied.

"Now you know Faith. I'm not gonna have my way and walk off. That's what idiot guys do that don't actually care. We practically grew up as brother and sister."

She looked at him. "You were my first crush."

He looked at her and shook his head. "Then give me a chance to do things my way. Please?" She nodded. "No more mouthing off either. I get that you want to be a boss, but stop yelling at people," he said as he sat back down. She walked over to him and kissed him again. "What?"

"Can we go to a movie?"

"When you have a home theater? Why?"

She shook her head and almost laughed. "Come watch a movie?"

"Maybe," he replied as she gave him a hug.

She finally left his room, and he shook his head. He finished going through the papers when he got an email:

> *I was never sure of her security. Thank you for keeping me posted. I trust you to handle hiring replacements. Thank you for keeping my daughter safe. – Mr. Cartwright.*

Ridge smirked. At least that was something. He went through the backgrounds for all of her security and none of them were as qualified as his team was. He went through a plan of where they were needed, got references from them and then decided on planning out a revamp of the security at her beach house. When it got to 6pm, his stomach was growling so loud he figured that Faith could've heard it. He walked downstairs to see her making grilled shrimp pasta. "What are you doin," Ridge asked as he watched her.

"One of my easy recipes. I gave the housekeeper the night off. Doors are all locked up and we have the house to ourselves somewhat. Wine?" He saw the bottle, and the half-glass that she'd already been drinking.

"Soda maybe," he said.

"One glass won't kill you," Faith replied.

"On the clock. Soda." She shook her head, handed him a ginger ale and a wine glass, and went back to finishing making dinner. "Why are you trying so hard," he asked.

"I'm not. It's an apology dinner," Faith said as she plated it for them both and handed him one of the plates.

"Thank you I think," Ridge said. They sat down and had dinner in peace and quiet. "I get that you want someone with you. I do. Faith, you had your choice of guys since we were kids. What happened," Ridge asked.

"I dated and ended up with bad people. When I decided that I was staying single, you walked in wearing the jeans and..."

"The jeans? That's your reason?"

"Ridge."

He shook his head. "You're serious? Me showing up to talk to you about your dang security and all you saw was the jeans?"

"Distracted me."

He shook his head and finished the last of his pasta. "You made an amazing dinner. I still can't believe that all it took was the jeans."

"Ridge."

He smirked and got up and cleaned up the dishes. "What," he teased.

"You do know that I can do the dishes right," Faith asked as she came up behind him and helped. "Least I can do after you cooked," he teased.

They got everything cleaned up and Faith went and grabbed dessert from the fridge. "What," he asked.

"Peach pie," Faith said.

"I'm stuffed. Honestly, I couldn't eat another bite," Ridge said noticing that her security was out of sight.

"Where did everyone really go," Ridge asked.

"I gave the housekeeper the night off, some of the security is still here. Why," she asked.

"Because it's too quiet."

"It's called a normal night. We're off in the middle of nowhere. Big security gate, lots of actual cameras outside. We're fine."

He nodded and went and made sure that everything was locked up tight. "What," Faith asked, watching him run all over to make sure that everything was secure.

"I'm not a fan of everyone disappearing," he said.

Faith smirked. "All I was doing was giving everyone a break. You and I both know that I'm safe here."

"The question is, why is someone sending those photos and who sent them? Faith, we eliminated them accessing anything from within the house. They can't get photos unless they're inside. Doesn't change anything. I did a full scan of the house here. Luckily, there was nothing, but I still need someone else here with us."

"Ridge."

He looked at her. She'd made dinner and given everyone a night off to apologize for how she'd acted. When she was trying to push him into being with her. It wasn't to make her even more anxious about being in the house. "Feel any better now that you've literally run all over the place?"

"Now, yes. Why?"

"Ridge, just sit down and stop being a pain in the backside. I get you have ants in your pants. You always have."

"Faith, you wanted me to keep you safe. This is what you're paying me to do. If security isn't here…"

She kissed him. "Sit."

"Let me finish the check and then we can sit." He kissed her forehead like he had in high school and finished checking the house.

When he came downstairs, she was another glass of wine in. She had a glass for him with Jack and Coke in it. "Faith."

"Your Jack and coke. Plain and simple," she said.

He shook his head and sat down. It wasn't worth explaining. "What did you want to do," he asked.

"Movie. Alone. No calls. If I can't be at the beach, then I want us to relax here."

He agreed to it, knowing that she had planned something else out in her head. "What movie," he asked.

"Notebook or The Best of Me."

He took a deep breath and she looked at him. "What's wrong?"

"I know what you're doing."

"And," Faith asked.

"Why did you really send security and the housekeeper off?"

"I wanted us to have time alone." He looked at her. He knew. He'd told her before that he wasn't doing anything with everyone there. Then him saying that he wouldn't make a move in her mom and dad's house. He had no excuses left unless he concocted another one.

He handed her the remote. "Pick a movie," he said as he grabbed a faux fur throw from the other sofa and slid it over her. He was happy that he'd at least closed the curtains and shutters so nobody could see in.

"What," Faith asked noticing that he was looking around.

"Nothing. As long as you and I are safe, we're good."

When she pressed play on The Choice, she leaned into his arms and got comfortable. "Faith."

"Yes."

"Warm enough?"

She nodded. "You comfortable?"

He shook his head with a smirk. "Sort of."

When he saw her smirk, he knew a mile off what she was doing.

He took a sip of his intentionally strong drink and shook his head, watching yet another sappy movie. He knew why she'd picked it; he knew why she'd given him an overly strong drink, and he knew why she was leaning up so tight to him.

"What," Faith asked.

"I know exactly what you're doing," he teased as he took another sip of his drink. She paused the movie and turned to look at him.

"Which is?"

"It's gonna take more than three shots of Jack in a glass of Coke to get me to make a move right now."

"Meaning what," she asked.

"Meaning if you're thinking that getting rid of everyone means that you're getting some, it's not happening."

She shook her head. "And if I wanted to just curl up on the sofa and be together without anything else?"

"Then you need to quit trying to slide up closer."

Faith shook her head, went back to where she had got comfortable and flipped the movie back on. "An arm would be nice," she said. He kissed her shoulder. "What was that?"

"Live with it," he teased. They kept watching and when she moved her hair from her shoulder, giving him access again to her neck, he smirked. He knew better. "You're trying too hard," he teased as he saw her get goosebumps up and down her arms. Faith shook her head, and she slid her hand in his. He shook his head and took a gulp of his drink. When it got to the end of the movie, Faith was sniffling. He grabbed a tissue and handed it to her.

"Good movie," he said.

She shook her head and refilled her wine glass. He took it out of her hand. "You don't need more wine, Faith." "

Yeah, I do," she said taking the glass back.

"Four glasses?"

"Yeah. Four," she said as she shook her head. She put her wine on the table. When she got up, she grabbed his glass and went to make him another drink.

"Faith."

"What?"

He got up and grabbed the glass. "I don't need the triple shot," he said. Faith shook her head, made his drink with two shots, and walked back over to the sofa.

"Sit," she said determined to get comfortable.

"I know what you're doing. You think if you get me drinking then I will…"

She kissed him. "Watch the movie with me."

He shook his head, sat back down and she curled back up against him with her wine in hand. He shook his head, and he slid his arm around her like she wanted. She flipped on Safe Haven, and he shook his head.

"What?"

"Nothing," he said as she paused it and looked at him.

"Ridge."

"Every single Nicholas Sparks movie?"

She nodded. "I have other options, but you won't want to watch them."

"Then pick something else."

She flipped on another movie then turned to face him. "What," he teased.

Faith put her wine down, slid his glass from his hand and put them both onto the table. "Faith."

She kissed him. "What?"

He shook his head and his hands slid to her backside as she leaned against his chest. "What do you want from me woman?"

She kissed him and he shook his head. "That's what you want?" She nodded. "Fine. I know exactly what movie you put on. If that's what you're thinking, then you really need to stop with the wine."

She smirked. "You already said you weren't..."

He kissed her, pulling her tighter to him as he felt her legs slide around his hips.

"You have to make it through the entire movie without doing anything. Nothing," he said.

"Meaning what?"

"Did you think I didn't see that the screen said Fifty Shades?"

She smirked and he shook his head. He kissed her again to the point that she was trying to pull his shirt off. "Behave," he whispered.

"Seriously?"

He nodded. "Turn around and watch it," he said as he handed Faith her drink and took a gulp of his, noticing it was definitely stronger than the last. She sat back down, leaning against him and sliding his arm around her.

"Faith," he said almost purring in her ear until her body started bursting into goose bumps.

He knew her heart was racing. He could feel it against him. When his phone buzzed, she paused it. He grabbed his cell and answered. "Yep."

"Everything is clear, secure and safe. We put the system in at the beach house that you suggested. All good. We're getting some z's. We're staying in the two guest rooms. Hers is off limits."

"Yeah. Thank you, guys, for that. I appreciate it. If you need anything let me know."

"We were gonna order some groceries."

"Just clean up after you're done so it looks like it did when you got there."

"Already done."

"I'll get what you need sent over. I'll come by in the morning."

"Alright boss man," his buddy said as they hung up.

Chapter 4

"And," Faith asked.

"House is secure. Updated system with more security. The guys are behaving contrary to you," he teased. She shook her head and he saw her little smirk. He put his phone down and took a sip of his drink. She got comfortable and slid her hand in his. There was no point in pulling away. She was itching to do something. He watched the movie and he felt her sliding as tight to him as possible. The further they got into the movie, the faster her heart was racing. When he kissed her neck, her breath almost hitched.

"What's wrong," he whispered as she paused the movie.

"You're teasing Ridge."

"You started it," he teased.

He kissed the spot where her neck and her shoulder met. "We could just stop..."

"You're watching the end," he teased.

"Then stop taunting."

"Didn't mind in the first movie."

"Ridge."

He kissed up her neck. Her head leaned back. "Turn it back on."

"Ridge."

"Turn it back on. You wanted to watch it," he teased.

She shook her head and she saw the first scene that she loved. When she slid her hand out of his and had her hand on his thigh, he shook his head. "We could just watch the rest later," Faith said.

He shook his head. "You wanted it, you watch."

She shook her head and took another sip of her wine. He smirked. She was even more hot and bothered by the time she paused it again. "What," he teased.

"We could just watch the rest upstairs," she suggested.

"Don't think you'll make it," he joked.

"I think that you're almost as bad as I am."

"It's called restraint," he whispered as her heart started racing again.

"Then no taunting," she said.

"You're the one who is attempting to tease until you get what you want."

She turned to face him. "Ridge."

"What?"

"Are you going to stay with me?"

"When?" She looked at him. "Not sure," he joked.

"Will you?"

"Depends on whether you can get through the movie without trying to tease me into sleeping with you," he replied.

"You're not really fair."

"Why? Because I know you won't?"

"Because I think we should watch the rest upstairs."

"I've seen it. You want to watch, go ahead," he teased. She shook her head and kissed him.

That kiss deepened. She could feel it in her belly. That kiss was hot enough to make her pounce in 3.2 seconds. "Watch your movie," he said as he kissed her again and turned her to face the screen. She slid in tight to him again, and he smirked, taking another gulp of the drink.

Barefoot Bodyguard

She got up, grabbed the Jack and made him another drink, pouring it into his glass as she emptied the last of the wine into her glass. "Like I said, you didn't need to drink the entire bottle," he joked.

"Then finish your drink," Faith teased.

He shook his head, and she sat back down, sliding back to where she was. He slid her blanket up and she pulled his arm around her. "Comfy," he teased.

Faith nodded and realized there was another hour of the movie. She took a deep breath and pressed play.

When Ridge felt her getting warm, he smirked. He kissed the edge of her earlobe then down the back of her ear. "Ridge."

"Mm," he almost purred as she pressed pause.

"You're taunting me."

"I can do taunting if you want taunting," he teased.

"Ridge."

"What?"

"You aren't playing fair, and you know it."

"You're just prolonging the inevitable," he whispered.

"Quit." He grabbed the remote, pressed play and sat it beside her hand.

It got deeper into the movie, and he was getting beyond hot and bothered. The fact that she was way too close was causing an issue. When he felt her hand on his thigh again, he moved it and wrapped it around her. He had another gulp of his drink and shook his head. He was starting to get a buzz. One he hadn't planned on. They kept watching until he knew that her heart was pounding out of her chest. She was way too warm. He smirked when they got to another scene that made her even more hot and bothered. When it was finished, she pressed stop. She put her empty glass on the table and saw his glass empty.

"You awake," Faith asked.

"It's not even 10."

She slid the blanket off as he caught it and put it on the back of the sofa. "Now, what were you saying," Faith asked.

"Kinda stunned."

"Did you think that we couldn't make it through the movie," she asked as she turned to face him and slid into his lap with her legs curling around his hips.

"Surprised."

She shook her head. "And now what," Faith asked.

He kissed her with a kiss that she could feel right to the tips of her toes. Her body was almost trembling against him. His hands slid to her backside. "Are you coming with me," Faith asked.

"Not sure. We could watch the next one."

She shook her head and he smirked, pointing out that he was joking without saying a word. "You said..."

He kissed her again. He could feel her heart racing against his chest. "Tell me what you want," Ridge asked between kisses.

"You. All of you," she said as his arms tightened around her.

"Really. I didn't realize that was in the job description," he teased.

Faith shook her head with a smirk and kissed him again as she felt his hands against the back of her thighs. "You need to go to bed," he joked.

"And I need you naked." He kissed her, picked her up, flipped the tv off, grabbed his phone and walked her upstairs with her still wrapped around him.

He walked into her room and leaned her onto the bed. When she wouldn't let go, he fell into her arms. "Faith."

"What?"

"Let go."

"No," she replied. He slid her up to the pillows and tried to regain his composure. "Where are you going," Faith asked as he leaned to his side.

"Turning off the lights."

"Stay."

"You drank an entire bottle of wine. You need sleep."

She shook her head. "You told…"

He kissed her again until her legs slid tight around him. She went for the button of his jeans, and he stopped her. "Ridge."

He kissed her. "Stay here."

"No," Faith said. He kissed her again and got up, flipping the lights off on the lower level. He put the glasses in the dishwasher, got two glasses of ice water and came upstairs, putting them on the bedside table.

"Did you give them more than today off?"

"Until Tuesday."

"It's Saturday."

"I know."

He shook his head and went into his room. "Ridge."

He shook his head, grabbed something from his drawer, grabbed his charger and came into her room, plugging the charger in and sat back down on the bed. "We can wait."

"No," Faith said.

She slid closer to him. "Faith, you drank an entire bottle of wine."

"And you drank something too," Faith said.

"First off, getting me buzzing was not exactly a great idea."

She got up and walked over in front of him. "Ridge, tell me what you don't…"

He kissed her and pulled her onto his lap. "It has nothing to do with it," Ridge said.

"You don't want to..."

He shook his head and kissed her again, leaning her back onto the bed and leaning into her arms. "Like I said, it has nothing to do with you. It has to do with respecting each other. That's it," he said.

"I know you respect me. I respect you. I also want you," Faith said.

"Then take our time."

She kissed him and his arms slid around her, snuggling her tight to him. "I don't want to," she said.

"What?"

"Take our time." He devoured her lips, and she pulled his shirt off then went for the zipper of her dress.

"Faith."

She went for the button of his jeans, and he stopped her. "Not yet," he said.

"Why? What's so wrong," Faith asked.

He devoured her lips until she kicked her shoes off and tried sliding her dress off. He shook his head. "Dress down."

"Ridge."

"What?"

"I need it off." He shook his head and kissed down her neck. He knew her toes were curling. He could feel it in her legs. He slid her straps off and kissed the front of her neck.

"Take it off," Faith said. He slid it up and over her head and he kissed down her torso. When he saw her stomach almost trembling, he knew that one way or another, him staying in his own room wasn't happening.

He got to her hip and she was reaching for him. He kissed her inner thigh and saw her toes curled into knots. "Ridge."

"What?"

"No teasing."

"But that's half the fun," he joked. She reached for his hand, and he smirked.

"Ridge."

"You sure," he asked.

"Yes."

"Faith, promise me that it's not the wine saying that."

"It's not."

"Faith." She looked at him. "Are you sure?"

She nodded and he kissed up her legs.

"Take them off," she said. He took a deep breath. There was no backing out. Not at that moment. When his phone buzzed, she almost laughed.

"Don't you dare," Faith said as he smirked. He slid the almost nothing panties off and answered.

"What's up," Ridge asked.

"Just wanted to say thanks for the food."

"Most welcome. Get some rest. I'll see you tomorrow if I can get out there," Ridge said as he quietly kissed her inner thigh.

"Alright boss. See you tomorrow."

He hung up and Faith grabbed his phone, putting it on her charger as he got closer to the one spot that had been throbbing through the movie. "What," he teased.

"I know what you're doing."

He made one move that had her toes curling all over again. He taunted and she grabbed at him. He reached a hand up and she tried pulling him closer. When his other hand took over the teasing, she shook her head. "Ridge," she said almost breathless. He smirked.

"What," he asked as he kept going.

"Now," she said.

"Now what," he joked as he kissed her lower belly.

"Take the jeans off."

He smirked and the taunting got deeper until he felt her body tense around his fingers. "Come here," Faith said.

"Oh I'm not done," he teased.

"Yeah, you are. Jeans." He moved his way back down her torso and nibbled at her inner thigh, taunting her even more. "Ridge."

"You want me to stop?"

"Come here."

One nibble and her legs were shaking. "I'm working my way up there," he teased. One more nibble, one more lick and he worked his way back up her torso, pulling the bra off on his way up as his other hand kept teasing.

"You are so not playing fair," Faith said.

"You never said fair was part of it. You were the one trying to rub up against me on the sofa." She shook her head, and he kissed her as she went for the button of his jeans and undid it along with his zipper. "Faith."

"What?"

His hand moved from taunting and slid up behind her as he smirked. "Determined much?"

She smirked. "You're the one that was teasing. Off."

"What?"

"Jeans and the boxers, off," Faith said.

He grabbed the packet that he'd grabbed from his room. "No," Faith said.

"No what?"

"I…"

He kissed her and she knew that she was not getting her way. "We either use it or I'm sleeping alone," he replied. She kissed him. "I mean it."

Barefoot Bodyguard

"Fine," Faith said.

He kicked his jeans to the floor and her legs almost instinctively wrapped around him. He opened the packet, sliding it on and Faith kissed him again. "You sure," he asked. She kissed him and his hands slid into hers, almost pinning her to the bed. "Yes or no," he asked as his boxers slid to the floor. She nodded and he devoured her lips until he could feel her toes curling all over again.

In the back of his mind, he kept saying that he'd dreamt about that moment all the way through high school. Hell. Half of his college years and military time he'd dreamt of her. He'd dreamt of having sex with her until her body melded to his. Until she craved him and wanted him every minute of every day.

When he slid into her, she was trembling all over again and her hands broke away, wrapping around him. He could feel her nails digging into his back as they kept going and started slowly increasing their pace. The kiss didn't break until he was getting stronger, and her nails were digging into his back. She called his name more than once. When his body couldn't hold back anymore, her body clenched around him, and his body climaxed.

"Crap," he said. He kissed her again and she wouldn't move. Her body was still throbbing around him. He shook his head and went to roll to his side, but she wouldn't let him. He rested his head on her chest and kissed her.

"Holy crap," Faith said as her heart raced against him, and she was trying to catch her breath. When he went to move, she wouldn't let him.

"What," he asked with a smirk.

"Feels too good. Don't."

He kissed her and slid to his back.

She slid to his chest and rested her head on it, sliding her arm around his chest and her leg around his. "You okay," he asked as he pulled a blanket up.

"I waited since high school for that?"

"What?"

"I waited since high school for that."

"Faith, what are you talking about?"

"I waited. I was thinking about it and wondering…"

He kissed her again. "Less wine."

"Ridge, it has nothing to do with it. I've dated before, I've slept with other people, but never in my damn life did I imagine that we would…"

He shook his head and kissed her again. "Breathe."

Barefoot Bodyguard

She shook her head. "It was worth it," Faith said as she slid her hand to his chest, just over his heart. He smirked.

"Now you understand what I meant," he asked.

"You know there are two more movies," she teased.

"You have a couple of days. Breathe."

She kissed him again and he got up. He cleaned up as she saw his tattoo. She'd never noticed it. "What's the tattoo of," Faith asked.

"My first pup's paw print," he said as Faith smirked. And he was just as dang sentimental. He walked back into the bedroom, grabbed his clothes, and stepped out of the bedroom.

"Where are you going," Faith asked.

When he came back in, he was in fresh boxers, and she saw the other tattoo.

"What's that one?"

"The guys and I that I trained with the military. We all got them together."

He sat down on the side of the bed and Faith leaned to face him. "Come to bed," she said.

"I'm going," he teased.

"Ridge."

He kissed her. "Sleep off the wine."

"Then stay in here with me. We're completely alone. Come on." He kissed her again and she got up and slid into his lap. "Stay."

"Faith, I need actual sleep."

"Then sleep." She kissed him and he shook his head, curling up on the bed with her.

"Not gonna give in are you," he teased.

"Nope."

He pulled the sheet and blanket back up and handed her a glass of ice water. She took a few gulps and he put it back on the side table as he drank down the entire glass he'd got for himself.

"Ridge."

"What?"

"Are we still okay," Faith asked.

He kissed her forehead and snuggled her to him. "We're fine. Just remember that I'm still your security, okay?" She nodded and curled up resting her head over his heart and wrapped her leg around his as he slid his arm around her. "Get some rest okay," he asked.

Faith nodded and kissed him. "Are you okay," she asked.

He nodded and kissed her forehead again. "I'm good," he replied as his eyelids started getting heavy. They both nodded off not long later.

When Ridge woke up the next morning, she was still asleep. He went and had a quick shower, got dressed and went downstairs and made them breakfast. One day without a workout wouldn't kill him. Not after that last night. He shook his head and checked emails. He took a deep breath and made the omelets and bacon, slid her coffee on the tray and came upstairs to see her still asleep. When he saw her smirk, he knew.

"You can quit faking it. Wake up," he teased.

Faith smirked. "What did you do?"

"Breakfast. I have to run out for an hour or two. You okay?"

She nodded. He looked at her. "I'm not going anywhere. I have emails," Faith said.

"Or you can come with me."

"Where," she asked.

"Beach house to see what they're doing. I need security here though."

"They're nearby just in case," Faith said.

"Can you get them back here for an hour or two?"

"Probably," Faith said.

"Just while we're out." She nodded and he sat down with her while she ate.

"Did you eat?"

He nodded. "I wanted to let you sleep, but leaving the house without someone else here isn't gonna work."

Faith smirked. "You sleep okay," she asked.

He nodded. "I actually slept. Good sign," he teased.

"So, are we watching a movie tonight?"

"Not what you were watching last night."

She smirked. "Ridge."

"You're sleeping in her by yourself tonight." Faith smirked. "What," he asked.

"You sure that I can't talk you into it?"

"Behave yourself. Leave it at that."

"You sure you don't want to have a do-over," Faith teased.

"Eat your breakfast. I'll meet you downstairs." She kissed him and he went downstairs. He went through the info in the security room and got the notes that he needed. When his phone buzzed with a text from Faith, he smirked:

> *Security are on their way over. They're hanging until 3. Thank you for breakfast.*

He smirked and relaxed, going through a list on his laptop. He did a chore list for security to do. They had a list to do on the hour, a list to do per day and a list of things that had to be maintained. He printed out copies for the guys at the beach house and left the others for the security guys she'd hired.

When they showed, Ridge walked them into the security room. "I know that you guys are used to the old way, but something big happened at the beach house. We now have to make sure it doesn't happen here. I made up a list of stuff I usually check, if y'all are up to checking them. We can do it together."

"Sounds good," Charlie, her head of security for the house said.

"I know that you two have been here longer than me, but if we work together, we can make sure that she's safe. That's all that any of us want I think," Ridge said as the other security guy agreed.

When Faith came downstairs, he was just coming out of the security room. "You ready," Faith asked.

Ridge nodded. "We sort of talked through the security stuff. Hopefully, it'll be a little easier."

"Good. Can we take the SUV," Faith asked.

"I guess," Ridge said.

Faith grabbed the keys. "We'll be back in a couple hours. If you need anything, my cell number is on the desk," Ridge said as he walked Faith outside.

He helped her into the SUV, and they headed off. "Do you need more coffee?"

Faith smirked. "I'm good for now. Honestly, I'm kinda looking forward to being back at the beach. Hopefully there's no damage after that storm," Faith said.

"The guys cleaned it up already. I let them know that we were on the way."

"And you know these guys how?"

"Military. They decided to work for me when I started doing security and bodyguard work. They're stricter than I am," he teased.

Faith shook her head and slid her hand in hers. "I think we need to watch another movie tonight," Faith said.

Ridge shook his head. "I get what you are trying to do, but I'm there to do a job Faith."

"And? Can't do both?"

He shook his head. Getting in a fight while they were in the SUV wasn't a good move. By the time they got to the beach house, the water on the roads was gone, the beach was packed with bikinis, and they were pulling into a pristine house. They got through the gate and saw the truck for the guys. "I can't believe that you talked them into coming so fast," Faith said. They parked, Ridge got her door, and they locked up the SUV and headed inside.

When they walked in, the guys were double-checking their work. "Boss man," his buddy Leo said.

"Hey. How's everything looking," Ridge asked.

"Good. This must be the boss lady," Leo said.

"Faith, Leo. Leo, Faith."

"Hold on. You aren't the Faith that he went to high school with," Leo asked as Ridge tried to tell him to stop.

"I am actually. Introduce me to the guys," Faith asked.

Leo went and introduced her around and she did a walk around and looked at everything. She didn't even notice that anything was different. "Thank you for all of this," Faith said as they made their way downstairs.

"Most welcome. We do have a list of what we pulled. Boss man wanted us to box everything."

When they came downstairs, Ridge was in the security room and saw the two boxes of devices that they'd found. From cameras, to microphones, to pin hole cameras. All of it almost freaked him out. Showing her wasn't an option. He shook his head again, put them into a bag and put them into the safe. He wanted to go to her dad's office and hand them off to his security, but Lily would know something was up. "You okay," Faith asked poking her head into the security office.

Ridge nodded. "Just checking paperwork," Ridge said as he gave Leo the look. Leo gave him a silent nod.

"So, what did they find," Faith asked.

"Cameras and a few other things. I'm gonna get them to your dad's security and let them research it," Ridge said.

"How many," Faith asked.

"Enough. It doesn't matter," Ridge said.

"At least they're gone then," Faith said looking at Ridge to try and guess why he'd almost snapped.

"Back in a second," Ridge said as he pulled his buddy Brian aside.

"What's up," Brian asked.

"I put them in the safe. I need you to take them quietly and subtly to her dad's office to his security. I'm gonna take them out and hand them to you. Can you do that without causing a fuss," Ridge asked.

Brian nodded. "Always. Just let me know what the address is."

Ridge texted it to him, came downstairs and got the bag, handed it to Brian and went back in to see Lily heading outside.

"I got it," Ridge said as he walked outside and came up behind her.

"I know you're not gonna let me see them."

"Brian's taking them to your dad's security guys at the office. They're expecting them. It's fine," Ridge said as she slid her sandals off and went to walk along the beach. Ridge pulled his shoes and socks off and rolled up his jeans a little. "You don't want to see them."

"How many were there?"

"Faith."

"How many?"

"25."

"What?"

"Like I said."

She shook her head. "At least they're gone right?"

"And the base and all the wiring to them and the memory tower."

"How did nobody know they were there?"

"Your dad's security said it had been deactivated. Obviously, someone reactivated it."

Faith sat down on the sand and Ridge sat down beside her. "Promise me that I'm safe," she asked.

"You are. Just let me keep you that way."

She nodded and leaned her head on his shoulder. "They're good guys," Faith said.

"Always have been. They're the best. Best in their field, sharp shooters too. They're not even allowed to fist fight. They consider them a weapon with all the training they had."

"And you."

"I only fight with you. Much easier," Ridge joked.

"Thank you."

"You don't have to thank me, Faith. That's my job. That's why you and your folks hired me." She snuggled in a little closer. "Cold," he asked.

Faith shook her head. "Walk?" She shook her head. "Shell hunting?"

Faith smirked. "That we can do," she teased.

They found a few small ones to add to the collection she had on her deck. "I still can't believe you keep them all. We collected those for years when we were teenagers."

"I made a lamp with them. I put them all into this big clear ginger jar looking lamp and made a seashell lamp with it," Faith said.

"You'll have to show me." He was trying to distract her brain from overthinking all the hidden devices that his team had found within the house. It was too much for him to comprehend let alone trying to get Faith to be alright with it.

"This was the place where I felt almost invincible Ridge. Where I had the freedom to just be myself. Now, I keep thinking that I'm not as safe as I thought. Going for a walk on a public beach almost freaks me out."

"That's why I'm here Faith. Let me keep an eye out for the bad stuff. That's what I was trained to do."

"I just don't understand what would cause someone to do all of that. I saw the bag that you gave that guy. That was more than you're saying. I know you aren't telling me."

"You don't need any more stress. They're gone. There's nothing left for anyone to spy on you with unless they're on the beach. Your security system was even upgraded. You're safe. I promise you." She nodded and brushed a tear away. "Tell me what you want me to do so you're feeling better," he said as he tried to get her to at least laugh.

"Walk?"

He nodded, getting up and helped her to her feet. "Point us in the direction you want to go."

A half hour later, they made their way back up the steps to the beach house to see one of the guys on the deck keeping an eye out. "Your phone was buzzing. Didn't answer it, but you may want to check," Leo said.

Ridge nodded and they came inside. Faith went and got herself a sweet tea and he checked his email:

> *Received items. I can't believe that you found that many of them within the walls. I had cleared the house myself when she moved in. You have one heck of a team to handle all of this. I did a check and the items are registered to a former homeowner. When I did a further check, he was the one that had caused issue with Faith's parents. He had to put the house up for sale when his business tanked from what I see. If you need anything or Faith does, contact me. Let the team know that we're gonna need contracts signed and background checks, but beyond that we're good.*

Ridge took a deep breath and Lily came into the office. "What's wrong," she asked.

"Nothing. Just got the info that I needed. Everything's fine," Ridge said.

"And what did dad's security say," Faith asked as she sat down.

"They found out who the stuff was registered to and at least that's a step. They have the entire system, wires and all. This house is safer than either of us expected."

"And?"

"The guys are on staff now."

Faith nodded. "I do strangely feel better with the entire team of those guys around."

"Good. That's why they're here Faith."

"Are we heading back," she asked.

"Determined to get home?"

She smirked. "They're heading out at 3."

"It's up to you." She nodded and got up. He got up walked over to her and gave her a hug. That's what she really needed even if she didn't say it. "Home," he asked.

Faith nodded and didn't let go of him. "What?"

"Can we have a night alone?"

"Like last night," he teased as he saw the smirk come onto her face.

"Except we're getting takeout, and we need to make a stop on the way back," she said.

He shook his head. "Let's go then sunshine," he teased. She let go of him and he went and talked to the guys outside while she got whatever she needed.

"What's up," Leo asked.

"Talked to head of security. There are contracts coming. She wants you to stay and so do I. I trust you guys. Deal is, two people have to be here at all times. If she comes up here, I'm with her, but we have to keep the house safe. If y'all want to rotate between here and the main house, that works. The security she has there now isn't exactly willing to work with us. Can you guys handle that," Ridge asked.

"Sign me up," Leo said as all the guys agreed. The fact that they'd already worked so well as a team in the military told him that they could be trusted. "We're in," Calvin said.

"Good. I'll let you know the rest of the info, rooms to sleep and stuff," Ridge said. They all agreed, and he walked inside.

"Ready," Faith asked. Ridge nodded and they headed out, hopping into the SUV and making their way back up towards the main house.

When she held his hand in the SUV, he knew something was wrong that she wasn't saying. "What's wrong," he asked as he made his way up to the bridge.

"Tired," she replied.

He smirked. "That's your fault. You should've slept in. I could've handled all of this."

"I know," Faith said as he kissed her hand. "Can we stop somewhere?"

"Such as?"

"Angel Oak?"

"Tea place?" She nodded. "Whatever you want to do," he replied as he kept going then turned off and headed towards the Angel Oak and the Tea gardens. "Why here," Ridge asked as they walked into the park, looking at a historic oak that was absolutely breathtaking.

"Because it gives me perspective. This tree has stood for this long even when there were floods and massive storms. It's still standing," Faith said as he smirked, and she held his hand.

"Better?" Faith nodded. "When you want to go, we can head to the tea gardens," Ridge suggested.

"Peach tea?" He smirked. "Yep," he teased.

"I did find a really good blend. We can try it out tomorrow."

Ridge shook his head. She was alright. She was starting to feel better. Whether it was the salt air, the tree or whether it was the fact that she had Ridge beside her, she was back to her old self. "Do you want to go," Ridge asked. Faith nodded and they made their way back to the SUV, hopped in and went down to the tea garden. They walked around a bit, and she got two flavors of tea, paid for them and they headed out. "Seriously," Ridge asked.

"Tastes like peach cobbler," she joked.

He smirked and they went outside. "Are you feeling better though," Ridge asked. Faith nodded. They headed off a little while later, grabbed takeout on the way back and made their way to the house. When they showed, security was at the door.

"Any problems," Ridge asked.

"A package arrived. We scanned it and had to remove it," the security said. Ridge walked into the security office, and they showed him where they put it.

He slid on gloves and a mask and opened it, seeing photos of Faith on the bed in the beach house. There were even photos of Ridge and Faith together talking. He made a call and let the guys know to scan the ceilings. In the box was another item that looked like it was Faith's. Ridge took a deep breath, put everything into bags and put the box somewhere secure. He sent a message to her dad's security to let them know what had arrived and within a matter of minutes, he got a call.

"Hendrix," Ridge said.

"Those look like overhead photos."

"They're doing a full scan of the ceiling as well. It'll be handled."

"What I don't understand is how someone could've got into the house to steal her clothing."

"I don't know either, but it's a good thing that we changed security to my team," Ridge said.

"Just keep her safe. I'll get these to the lab and let the authorities know," her dad's security said.

"Thanks. We're at the main house tonight. If you need anything just call my cell."

"Will do." They hung up and Ridge came into the living room. "What," he asked seeing the look on her face.

"I'm getting something delivered. That alright?"

"For dinner?"

"Sort of."

He smirked. "Does it involve alcohol?"

Faith nodded. "You do realize that Jack didn't cause last night, right?"

She smirked. "Helped," she joked.

"What do you want me to make for dinner," he asked. She got up and came into the kitchen, grabbing steaks from the fridge and the fixings for a salad. "Alright. I'll grill," Ridge said.

"Good. Do you want to do outside grill or inside?"

"I think outside, and fresh air might do us some good," he teased.

"Good thing I ordered wine then," Faith joked.

They had some lunch, got the dinner and salad ready for whenever they wanted to eat and curled up on the sofa together. "You gonna tell me what the delivery was," Faith asked.

"Photos and a few other things. We don't need more creepy crap today," he said.

"Ridge."

"What?"

"I mean it."

"That's all it was. It's being handled. Promise." She turned and looked at him. "What?"

"Come with me," she said.

"Faith." She took his hand and walked him upstairs, closing the bedroom doors behind them.

"Faith, what are you doin," he asked.

"Sit."

He shook his head. She walked over to him and hugged him. "You okay?" She shook her head. He snuggled her a little tighter. "Do you feel better about the beach house?" She nodded. He looked at her. "Faith, talk."

"The only time I felt safe was last night. I slept almost 9 hours straight. I haven't slept that well in months."

"And?"

"Stay tonight with me."

He smirked. "I know what you're really up to Faith. We're getting real sleep."

"Just stay in here with me."

"Faith."

She kissed him and slid into his lap. "Please," she asked.

"You know that you're safe. What's…" She kissed him again and he couldn't help but pull her tight to him. "We can't keep doing this. I'm supposed to be your security."

She held on and wouldn't let him see her. "I don't want to be in here alone."

He shook his head, and she went to kiss him again. "I get it," he said.

"Why can't you," she asked.

"We can figure it out later. Who knows. You could end up falling asleep on the sofa," he teased.

She kissed him again. "Why can't we just date," Faith asked.

"Because you hired me to be security. I can't do that and be your…" She kissed him. He leaned her onto her back on the bed. "I can't do that and be your man at the same time."

"Then just sleep in here with me."

"Faith." She went to slide her arms around him, and he grabbed her hands, holding them away from him. "We can't keep doing this."

"Why," she asked as he felt her legs slide around him.

"You hired me to be security. To keep an eye on you and make sure the house is safe. I can't."

"Then be my bodyguard and stay in here."

He shook his head. "You're frustrating as all get out. You know that right?" She nodded with a smirk ear to ear. "I'm getting up."

"No."

He shook his head. "Faith."

"Don't leave." He kissed her until she was pawing at him and got up. He walked downstairs as she laid there trying to catch her breath.

He walked into the security room and sat down, talking his body down from pouncing on Faith. He went through the last of his emails and tried to make sense of all of it. If he was gonna date Faith, he couldn't do both. It was dang near impossible. He wanted to call someone and ask if that was even allowed. He knew there was nobody to call. He took a deep breath and called Leo.

"What's up," Leo asked.

"I need to ask you something and I need you to keep it private."

"Go for it buddy."

"Have you ever done security for someone that you ended up dating?"

"Twice. Second one is how I met the wifey. It's not like all of us didn't see it when you and Faith showed."

"Still."

"Dude, you've known her since you were kids. Did you think that we wouldn't see that both of you have a thing? I could even see it. It's fine. Just remember that the job comes first."

"Thank you."

"Second, she is kinda hot."

"Got it. Thank you."

"Welcome."

Ridge hung up with him and got up, coming into the living room.

He sat down to go through emails, and within a matter of minutes, his phone was taken from his hands, and she slid into his lap. "What," he asked.

"You can't just do that and walk away."

"Meaning what," Ridge asked as he reached and got his phone.

"You know what."

He smirked. "Why are you sitting in my lap and straddling me?"

"Because you pulled that upstairs then took off."

"Faith."

She shook her head. "Do you want this or not," she asked.

He shook his head. "I can't just…"

She kissed him and he deepened the kiss until he could feel her going for the button of his jeans. He grabbed her hand and she leaned onto his chest. Luckily, the other security had headed out and the house was secure. They were alone. She tried pulling her hands free and he wouldn't let her. "Tell me what you want," he whispered.

"You," she said.

"Why?"

"Upstairs now," Faith said.

He shook his head. "Faith, say it."

"I want you. I want us redoing last night."

"Because you're worried or…" She kissed him. "Faith, stop."

"What," she asked.

"Tell me."

"Because I wanted last night to happen the day you freaking got here."

"There are toys for that," he teased.

"Ridge."

"If that's why you hired me, why am I even here?"

"Ridge." He walked outside. Part of him had worried that was why she'd really hired him. He didn't want her to cloud why he was there. He looked at his watch and shook his head, warming the barbecue up.

His phone buzzed a minute or two later as he sat down:

Come inside. Please.

He ignored it and sat back down by the water. When he heard the swish of the sliding door behind him, then footsteps, he didn't even move. "Ridge."

"You can't have it both ways."

"I knew that you were the best one for the job. When I sat down with you, I was happy to have you with me. I felt safer. The closer we got, the more the other stuff started."

"I get it Faith, but if me being hired to do that had anything to do with you trying to get me to sleep with you..."

She kissed him. "Why can't we just try," Faith asked.

He shook his head. "You can't have both Faith. I need to be able to protect you. I can't do that when you're handing me the one thing I wanted since we were kids."

She got up, grabbing his hand. "Come," she said as she walked him back inside.

"I flipped the grill on," Ridge said as Faith shook her head.

"Doesn't matter."

"Faith." She sat down on the high-top chair and looked at him.

"What? We can do both. You know we can."

"Faith."

She looked at him. "What?"

"You sure this is what you want?"

She nodded. "Ridge, I feel safe with you. You know that."

"You also have to understand that I'm putting your safety first. Period. I need to do this the right way, so I know that nobody is gonna hurt you."

She kissed him and he shook his head. "Faith."

"I'm not gonna beg you, Ridge. I'm just not."

"Tell me that you can understand what I'm asking."

"I get it."

"If I say that you have to stay in the house, or stay somewhere, you have to do it." She nodded. "If I have to go somewhere, and can't take you with me, you have to stay with the other security guys."

"Ridge, this isn't negotiating a jail term."

"Say it."

"I get it. My dad tried making me have security before. I know what I need to do."

He kissed her and she almost felt like she was levitating. She could feel it down to the tips of her toes. That liquid lava feeling in every inch of her body was starting to bubble. "Ridge."

"What?"

"This mean you're staying in my room tonight?"

"Nope." He smirked, kissed her forehead and went to sit down.

"Oh no you don't," Faith said as she followed him and leaned into his lap.

"What," he asked.

"You can't do that and walk away."

"I was sitting."

"Does this mean that we're gonna try and date?"

"Maybe," he replied.

She gave him a look. A look that said that he needed to quit teasing and just have sex with her already.

He smirked. "Faith, it's not even 4 pm. We have lots of time."

"I hate waiting."

"Delayed gratification," he whispered as her body burst into goosebumps.

"We could wait and have the steaks after."

He shook his head. "I know better Faith remember?"

She shook her head. "Then we eat now."

He laughed. "You are so bad. You know that right," he asked.

"Yeah. I also know that we're not watching that movie."

"Yeah, you are actually. You have it saved or something right?"

"Ridge."

"Then I'm going to bed alone."

She shook her head. "Teasing is not fair."

"You have no idea the kind of teasing I can do," he teased.

Faith shook her head. "Don't you have emails or something?"

"I told them I was taking a couple days off. I went through them."

He shook his head. "Emails, then dinner and the movie."

"Ridge."

"You'll find out the rules later." She shook her head, kissed him and got up, grabbing her phone. She sat at the opposite end of the couch from him and when there was a buzz at the gate, Faith smirked.

"What did you order?"

"You'll see when it gets here," Faith teased.

Ridge got up, checked the gate and saw that they were there for the delivery. "I'll be there in a minute," Ridge said as he pulled his runners on and walked down the front lawn to the gate, grabbing the delivery, and walked back up. When he put it on the counter, he saw two bottles of wine and two bottles of single barrel Jack plus Coke and a few other things from the grocery store.

"Faith."

"What?"

"Two bottles?" She nodded.

Chapter 5

Ridge shook his head and Faith put everything away, chilling the wine and one of the two bottles of Jack. "Faith, I did mention to you that trying to get me drunk isn't a good thing right?" She nodded. He shook his head and went and got the steaks. "What else are you putting on them?"

"A spice I used to have all the time. It's called Georgia Boy." Faith smirked.

"I know it well." When he noticed the time, he walked outside and put them on low. Lily walked outside a few minutes later and handed him a drink. "Already," he asked.

Faith nodded. He kissed her and she smirked. When he took a sip, he walked inside and put more Coke in it. "What," Faith teased.

"Double shotting the drink?"

"Yep." He shook his head, kissed her and walked back outside.

When he came in, steaks in hand, he plated them both and went and sat down at the table with her. "You kinda outdid yourself," Faith said.

"Good?"

"Better than Hall's chophouse. That spice mix is amazing."

"And I added something else to it," he teased.

"I know. It's amazing."

He smirked and finished his steak, then refilled his drink and had some salad.

"Can you…"

He refilled her wine glass. "So, which movies are we watching," Ridge asked.

"We can watch Safe Haven."

He smirked and kissed her forehead. "Your choice."

"Or we can watch The Lucky one."

"We're watching that and the second movie," Ridge said.

"What did you decide you wanted to do about that?"

"You'll find out when it comes on."

He finished his food, and she had a smirk ear to ear. "What," he asked.

"Nothin," Faith said.

She finished dinner and he got up and did the dishes. He intentionally kept his drink close to him. When he turned around, Faith was sitting on the countertop. "What," he asked.

"Dessert," she teased.

"Faith."

"I got strawberries," she teased.

"I bet you did," he joked as he picked her up and set her on her feet.

Ridge took his drink and sat down on the sofa. "Now, what were you saying about the rules," Faith asked as she brought the wine bottle and the bottle of Jack and put it on the table.

"Let me make sure everything is locked up. Throw on that sappy movie you wanted." He cleaned up the barbecue, flipping the gas off and locked up the back door. He made sure the rest of the doors were locked, made sure the house was secure and grabbed something from his room, coming back downstairs.

"Are you comin or what," Faith teased.

He smirked and drew the curtains and the shutters then sat down on the sofa. She grabbed a blanket. "And," she asked.

"What?"

"The discussion we were having."

"After."

"Meaning what?"

"After this one and before part two of the other movie."

She shook her head. "Fine. Before I press…"

He kissed her. She slid into his lap, leaning her body against him. When she slid her arms around him, he broke the kiss. "What," Faith asked.

He smirked. "Watch the movie and behave," he teased.

Faith shook her head. "Fine, but I need…" He kissed her again and her body was bubbling with passion. She wanted him right then and there. She could feel it to the tips of her toes. Whether it was his strong lips, the fact that he got her turned on in less than a second, or the fact that she knew what she wanted and would have, she was almost ready to just pounce then and there.

He devoured her lips until she was almost reaching for his jeans. "Watch your movie," he teased as they came up for air.

"I swear, at some point, you're gonna..."

"What?"

"We're gonna end up on this sofa naked."

"Nope," he replied.

"Ridge."

"Turn around and watch it," he said. He kissed her shoulder and she turned, curling up tight against him and he flipped the blanket over her. When he saw that she'd intentionally put on a sundress with way too flimsy straps, he shook his head.

"What?"

"Changed into a dress that might as well be lingerie?"

She nodded and leaned her head against his shoulder.

During the movie, more than once, his phone buzzed with updates. The guys had found 3 more cameras, but they were completely disconnected. They'd scanned the ceiling in every room, every hallway and every nook and cranny of the house including in the attic. They had everything cleared and worked that night at covering the damage. He watched the movie with her, and when the part came that he knew would make her anxious, she slid her hand in his and wrapped it around her. By the time they had made it through that movie, she was two glasses into the bottle of wine. He got up and made himself another drink, intentionally putting one shot in instead of two. "Refill," Ridge asked as she got goosebumps. She nodded. He topped up her glass and handed it to her, sitting back down behind her.

"And what are your little rules," she asked.

"No touching. No taunting. You have to pause it, you're in for it."

"Ridge."

"And if you try reaching for anything other than that glass, you're sleeping alone."

"And if I don't," Faith asked.

"Then last night is gonna feel like an appetizer."

She turned to face him. "I should probably change," she teased.

"If that's what you want," he joked as he saw her get a grin ear to ear. She got up, walked upstairs and got changed into lingerie that should've been illegal. She slid his sweater overtop and unzipped it when she sat down.

"Really? And that's gonna make you not get up?"

She nodded and slid in close to him. He shook his head and kissed up her neck. "No teasing."

"Right," he teased. He kissed her shoulder.

"Ridge."

"My game. My rules," he teased.

She shook her head and pressed play. He finished his drink and got up. She paused it. "Where are you going?"

"Getting some coke from the fridge." He poured a half glass of coke and put some Jack in, putting the coke bottle beside the bottle of Jack. He sat back down, and she slid in tight to him.

"Press play," he whispered as she burst into goosebumps again. She slid her hand in his and they watched. He taunted her through the whole movie. When he could feel her heart racing again, like it had the night before, he kissed the back of her ear and down her neck.

"Ridge."

He kissed her shoulder. "Mm," he said almost purring into her ear. It got to the final big two scenes of the movie and he taunted even more.

"You aren't playing fair," she said.

"Fair? Really? You don't say," he teased as he slid his fingers through her hair and kissed the back of her neck. As soon as the movie finished, she turned the tv off, leaving them in darkness. "What," he asked.

"We made it through the movie. No more taunting."

She turned to face him and kissed him as he slid forward and pulled her legs tight around him. Fine. Taunting her was a turn-on for him too. Seeing her perfect skin through the naked lace was getting him even more turned on. Knowing that she'd done it intentionally almost had him laughing. He kissed down the front of her neck, sliding the straps right off her shoulders.

"Ridge," she said as he knew what she wanted.

"Yes," he teased.

"I thought you said we weren't on the sofa."

He smirked and his hands slid to her backside. "We aren't."

"Ridge."

"What?"

He slid her tighter to him and she kissed him. His hands slid to her inner thighs. When she tried to pull away, he pulled her closer and started taunting. "You aren't…"

He nibbled her lips and kissed her with a kiss that had her toes curling and her heart racing. "We should watch the other one…"

She kissed him and he smirked. He picked her up, wrapping the blanket around her. He handed Lily her wine, he grabbed his drink, and they walked upstairs. He leaned her onto his bed, kicking the door closed.

"Ridge…"

He kissed her again. "Can't see anything?"

"Light."

He shook his head and undid the hoodie. "Ridge."

He kissed her neck, then down her torso, sliding the lace lingerie off on his way down.

"Aah," she said as he nibbled her inner thigh and his hand started getting her even more hot and bothered. Her legs were trembling, her belly was trembling and he was still fully dressed. He kept going until he felt her legs shaking and knew her toes were curled into pretzels. He kissed her hip and Faith was almost panting.

"Still think you're gonna win," he teased.

"Ridge. Please."

He kept going, speeding up until her body was moving with the flick of his fingers. "Crap," Faith said.

"What?"

"I want you. Now," Faith said.

When he grabbed something from his drawer, he smirked and quietly flipped the buzzing on.

"What are you..."

All he had to do was put it near her inner thigh and she was almost melting. He smirked and kept going, taunting until he knew that she was past the point of stopping. He slid it to the apex of her thighs, and she pulled his shirt and pulled him to her as he leaned in and kissed her. "Ridge," she said.

"What," he asked as he kissed down her torso and nibbled at her breast. He knew that she was climaxing. He also knew that if he stopped, his jeans would be shredded on the floor. She pulled him to her, and he devoured her lips as she cried his name in his mouth.

"Now, what was that you were saying," he teased.

"Come here," she said.

He shook his head and flipped it off. She tried again to reach for him and felt his kisses down her side. "Ridge."

"Appetizer," he teased.

"I can't even move."

"Good," he teased as his hands took over the taunting all over again.

"Ridge."

"What," he asked as he kissed her inner thigh.

"You're teasing. I'm not even gonna be able to walk." All it took was the feel of his lips against the apex of her thighs and her body almost exploded. "Oh my god," Faith said.

He kept going then worked his way back up her torso. She grabbed his shirt, pulling it off and pulled at his belt. "Off," Faith said.

"You sure," he asked as he almost purred in her ear again.

"Belt off."

He pulled it off, slid it to her side, letting the leather rub against her stomach and she went for his jeans. "Faith."

"What?"

"Let go of the jeans."

"No. Off." He smirked and quietly undid the zipper as his other hand continued to tease and taunt her. He grabbed the little packet from his bedside table, and he slid it on silently. "Ridge, I mean it." He pulled her down the bed and her legs were still shaking. He grabbed the little buzz and taunted her even more.

"You sure," he asked.

"Mm," Faith said. They had sex and her body was almost vibrating with the buzzer. They kept going and when he taunted even more, he took his time. When he finally started going, she was literally panting and almost screaming his name. He kissed her and when his body gave way, she could barely move. He leaned up behind her and wrapped his arm around her torso, curling her to him and pulling her up to the pillows.

"Now, what were you saying," he asked.

"Oh my God," Faith said.

"Drink," he teased.

"I don't think I could even move."

"Good. No more taunting me. Means I can actually sleep," he teased as he kissed her shoulder.

She turned to face him, and she was still shaking. "Back in a minute," he teased.

"Ridge."

He kissed her and got up, cleaning up a little. When he came back in, she was curled up in the blankets. He put their phones on his charger, finished his drink and sat down. He laid down beside her, snuggling her to him and she curled up to him. "You good," he asked.

Faith shook her head, and he knew she had a grin ear to ear. "I don't think I could move even if I tried."

He smirked. "Really," he joked.

"I'm beginning to think that my legs can't handle dessert," Faith teased.

He kissed her neck and pulled the blankets up. "Get some sleep beautiful."

"How are you walking?"

He kissed her shoulder and got her to relax. They both nodded off a while later and just as he was about to close his eyes, his phone buzzed. He looked and saw that the police had picked up the devices. He took a deep breath and went to sleep. He needed it. Not as bad as she did, but he was still tired.

The next morning, he woke up with her curled up tight to him. He smirked, kissed her head, and went to get up. "Where are you going? It's too early," Faith said.

"Workout. Sleep. You need it," he said.

"Ridge."

He kissed her, pulled his joggers on, and walked downstairs. He got a full 2-hour workout in, came upstairs and made breakfast, inhaling his food. He finished eating, made something for Faith and came upstairs. Just as he hit the top step, she was coming out of his bedroom in his hoodie. "And now she's stealing clothes," he teased.

He walked into her room and put the tray on the table. "Did you eat?"

Ridge nodded. "Starved," he teased as he kissed her.

"What did you make?"

"Take a peek," he teased.

When she saw eggs that looked like a rose and bacon, she smirked. "Ridge."

"Eat," he teased as he went and had a shower. When he stepped out of the shower, she was sitting on the counter.

"Faith," he said as he wrapped the towel around his hips.

"So, it's raining."

"And?"

"What are you gonna do today," she asked.

"Paperwork. Check on mom and dad, eat dinner, go to bed."

"And," Faith asked.

"What?" He smirked and kissed her. "What do you have planned?"

"Watching a movie with you." He smirked. "You may need a day off," he teased.

"Probably, but tonight maybe."

He shook his head with a smirk. "Just make sure you know what you want," he teased.

Faith shook her head and slid her legs around him, pulling him closer to her.

"Yes," he asked.

"You sure," Faith asked.

"You barely managed to move after last night sexy. I don't think you can do it."

"Fine. We're relaxing today anyway."

"Groceries. Walk at waterfront park."

"Really," Faith asked.

"I'm not sitting around all day," he teased.

Faith smirked. "Alright," Faith said as he kissed her.

"You gonna sit there and taunt me or are you…" She slid her arms around his neck and kissed him.

"Faith."

"What?"

"You do know you forgot to get dressed right?"

She nodded and slid tighter to him. His body reacted just the way she wanted.

"You sure?"

She kissed him and he picked her up, walking back into his room. "What," Faith asked.

Barefoot Bodyguard

"You sure you wanna do this?"

She nodded and he shook his head. He grabbed the packet, slid it on and she kissed him. This time, there was no extreme taunting. There were no buzzing toys, no body humming. This time it was just body throbbing sex until she couldn't breathe. He kissed her again, and her body almost exploded more than once. When he finally climaxed, her legs were shaking, and her toes had turned into knots.

"You okay," he asked.

Faith smirked. "I missed this."

"What?"

"Morning sex."

He shook his head. "You're so bad," he replied.

"Can't you just move your stuff into my room?"

"I'm still your bodyguard," he replied as he got up and kissed her then went in and showered and cleaned up. Faith shook her head. He wasn't just a bodyguard. He never would be. She managed to get up, walked into her bedroom and hopped into the shower. Ridge came back into the bedroom, pulled on his jeans and a tank, grabbed his hoodie and slid his shoes on. He headed downstairs, went through the rest of his emails and saw one from the guys at the beach house:

One issue last night. We caught a photographer outside. We found out he was hired by that Zack guy. Obviously, they found out that we got rid of the cameras and the bugs. We set up a schedule for around the clock security. If there's anything else you need us to do, let me know.

Ridge smirked. At least that was a good step. Faith came downstairs barefoot in beat-up blue jeans and a t-shirt. "Hey handsome," Faith said.

"Hey yourself. How you doing," he teased.

She threw a pillow at him as he caught it mid-air. "Fine. My legs are sore."

"All you need to do is work out," he teased.

"You aren't funny."

He pulled her into his lap. "Where do you want to go," he asked.

"Somewhere relaxing."

He smirked and kissed her neck. "Walk by the water?"

She nodded. "With a Starbucks stop."

He kissed her shoulder. "Alright sexy." He picked her up, flipped her over his shoulder, handed Lily her sneakers and her phone and purse and saw his security buddy. "Heading out for an hour or two. If you need anything, let me know," Ridge said as they headed out the door. He sat her in the SUV, and they headed off. He got their coffees, and they made their way downtown. When she smirked, he knew. "Second Saturday," he asked. Faith nodded.

Downtown was full of people and blocked off to vehicles. He managed to find a parking spot and took her downtown to wander the stores. They got a few things, and she got him a few things even after his complaining and they stopped off somewhere for lunch. "Still want to go to the park," Faith asked as she sipped her sweet tea.

"Kinda up to you. All of this shopping is kind of a good workout," he teased.

Faith smirked as they finished up their food. "I was kinda thinking that we could go and talk at the park if the rain holds off."

"And what might you be all determined to discuss," Ridge asked.

"If we start dating, are you still gonna be security?"

He nodded. "That's why I said something about it. It's gonna be kinda awkward without your folks knowing."

Faith looked at him. "You have a point."

He smirked. "Maybe call them?" She nodded and made a call.

"Hey baby," her mom said.

"Is dad around?"

"We're both here," her dad said as she looked at Ridge.

"I was gonna ask a question. Remember when I told you that I was hiring Ridge?" She could hear the smile come across her mom's lips and her dads.

"Yes," her dad said.

"Well, we were kinda talking."

"If you want to date him, you don't have to ask me. You know that," her dad said.

"I just wanted to make sure you wouldn't be mad."

"Are you getting a replacement for your security?"

"No. He has his team working on the house stuff and even upgrading the security at the main house. I'm comfortable," Faith said.

"Just remember that he's security first," her dad said.

"I will."

"And tell Ridge that I said hi," her mom said as she heard her push Faith's dad.

"I will mom. Love you guys."

"Love you too," her mom said.

"And," he asked.

"Dad was annoyed. I could hear it," Faith said.

"And?"

"He's fine." Ridge shook his head and she smirked. He paid for lunch, and they headed out, with her stopping at a lingerie store.

"Faith."

"What?"

"I know what you're doing."

She smirked and he shook his head. She grabbed a few things, paid and they headed off to the truck. "What," she asked as Ridge shook his head.

"None of that is even necessary and you know it," he teased.

"I like it."

"I see that. Still don't know what you need all of it for," he teased as she slid her hand in his.

"Well see, this guy I kinda like having around sometimes needs a little eye candy. It's kinda fun to taunt him," Faith teased as they got to the truck. He helped her in and shook his head, walking around and seeing a photo of them on the side of his window. He shook his head, grabbed it with his shirt and slid some stuff out of her store bag, sliding the photo into the bag. He messaged the officer that was taking care of the case and messaged the security at her dad's office with the info.

"What's wrong," Faith asked.

"Nothin," Ridge said.

"And that's why you're clenching your jaw. Just say it."

He shook his head and his phone buzzed. He slid an AirPod in and answered. "What was the photo of," her dad's security asked.

"Faith and I. We were out downtown."

"I'll get the officers to come over and get it. Try and get a photo of it before you hand it over."

"Will do. I'll send it."

"What are you talking about," Faith asked. He hung up and got on the road to head back to the house. "Ridge."

"I found something on my window. That's why I needed the bag," he said.

"What is the picture of?"

"You and me walking on the street."

Faith looked at him with her jaw dropped. "We're heading back to the main house."

"Ridge."

"Whoever it is, is coming after you and trying to tick me off while they're doing it. I need to figure out who it is."

"Ridge."

When he saw her hand shaking, he pulled over. "Faith."

"Why?"

"I don't know. I really don't."

"Ridge, this isn't..."

He undid his seatbelt and wrapped his arms around her. "I'm getting you home safe. We're gonna figure this out. I'm gonna hunt this idiot down if I have to," Ridge said as he saw her eyes welling up. She got out of the truck, and he hopped out, running around to her side and wrapping his arms around her and holding her as tight as he could. "You alright," he asked.

Faith shook her head. "I don't understand."

"Either do I. The cops are gonna handle it, and when I find out who it is, they'll be served to the dang sharks."

She shook her head. "Tell me that we're safe."

"You're with me. You're right here. You're gonna be alright. We're safe so long as we're together. Promise you that."

When she finally calmed down, he helped her into the truck and went around his side, hopping in. "You sure you're okay," he asked.

Faith nodded and held his hand. She was almost white knuckling it. They made their way to the house, made sure the gate closed behind them then headed inside and locked up, making sure the house was secure. She walked upstairs to her bedroom, put her things away and Ridge walked into his room, taking a photo of the photo they found then sent it off to her dad's security and the guys. He remade the bed, put the photo aside and within a half hour, got a call from the guys at the beach house.

"What's up," Ridge asked.

"I'll come get it. The cops can come over here so she's feeling better."

"Just make sure there are people guarding the house."

"Three of us here. I'm coming over there to keep an eye out for you."

Ridge gave him the address and went and checked on Faith. When he saw her sitting on the bed in the fetal position, he shook his head and walked over to her. "Faith."

She shook her head. "Let me see it."

He pulled it up on his phone and showed her. "Ridge." He nodded. "Maybe we should've just hung out around here," she said.

"Faith, it's fine. We deserve to have a life. You deserve to. When we find out who this is, then we can whoop some butt. Until then, I'm keeping you safe. That's why I keep making sure the curtains and the shutters are closed at night."

She looked at him. "Ridge, promise me that we're okay?"

He nodded and kissed her.

"One slight issue."

"What?"

"We kinda need food. I'm gonna order some stuff in and I can get Leo to bring it with him." Faith nodded. "Anything you want?"

"Whatever," Faith said.

He kissed her, put a grocery order in and sent the info to Leo to pick it up on his way through. When he got a thumbs up answer, Ridge smirked. He got the grocery store to pack the order up to pickup and went back into the bedroom.

"What did you order," Faith asked.

"Seafood, fresh fruit, peaches and a little of this and that. You're good," he teased.

"We need more wine."

"Faith, there's 4 bottles downstairs. You're good." She shook her head, and he hugged her again. "Tell me what you need."

"Distraction."

He kissed her, devouring her lips and picked her up, wrapping her legs around him. "What," Faith asked.

"You asked."

She smirked and he walked downstairs to the kitchen. "What are you doing?"

"You want a distraction, you get one." He handed Faith a knife and the small bowl of peaches.

"What's this for?"

"Cobbler." He kissed her, got everything going and ready for the peaches. By the time that the food arrived along with Leo, the house smelled like cobbler.

"You made the cobbler. Damn dude. You didn't tell me it was torture treatment time," Leo joked as they started putting the food away.

When Faith sneaked a peek, Ridge smirked. "Yes, it's mom's recipe in case you're wondering. One of those things that she intentionally taught me to impress the ladies," he teased. "Are you sure that I can't just have some now," Faith asked.

"Not cooked yet," Ridge teased as he kissed Faith.

"Y'all alright," Leo asked.

"Rough afternoon," Ridge said.

"When the timer goes off, it still has to set. No sneaking a taste either," Ridge teased as he walked Leo into the office.

"So, you and boss lady?"

"I've known her since I was born. We sorta decided to date. Leave it. The photo most definitely has fingerprints. She wasn't happy with it, and either was I. Part of me thinks it might be that idiot's kid or something," Ridge said.

"I mean, that is an option. We can look it up. Do you want me to stay and keep an eye on the house?"

"If you can get the photo in the bag to the police station, I'm good. She wasn't happy and she's barely stopped shaking since we got back. Thank you for grabbing the groceries by the way."

"Welcome. If you want me to stay so you know the house is secure, I can do that. Just say the word. The wife is off on a mama weekend."

"I appreciate it. I'll let you know." Leo nodded, slid the photo and the bag into a clear bag that he had and took it off.

"Bye Miss Faith," Leo said.

"See you," Faith said as she watched the timer like a kid waiting on chocolate chip cookies.

"Faith."

"Can we just take it out and eat it already?"

"Goes with dinner. You're not taste testing," he teased.

"You are so bad," she said.

"Do you want to eat outside," he asked.

"After that? No." He shook his head and kissed her. "What did Leo ask you?"

"Why we were kissing," he teased.

Faith kissed him. "Good." Ridge shook his head.

"You're bad. Really bad."

"And you love it," she replied.

"Getting used to it. Might keep you around," he teased.

"You aren't funny." He kissed her and he heard the timer go off. He flipped the oven off and took it out of the oven as Faith watched.

"Ridge."

He turned and looked at her. "What," he asked.

"Who do you think was taking the photos?"

He wasn't about to scare her even more. "Could be anyone. Part of me thinks it may have something to do with that idiot that used to date your mom. Like his kid or something." Ridge said as he made sure that the cobbler was done.

"Seriously?"

He nodded. "Could be someone getting back at your folks, or mad at you for something with work. Just don't start worrying."

"That's why I wanted you to stay with me," Faith said.

"Just another reason why you were taunting me."

She smirked. "I'm glad that you're here. Honestly, I do feel better with you here."

"Um hmm. I bet," he teased as he kissed her. She smirked and he shook his head.

"Sexy woman, no more teasing. We still have another movie to watch." Faith shook her head and slid her legs around him as he heard a buzz at the gate.

He looked and saw a blacked-out truck. "Yep," Ridge said answering the buzzer.

"Here to see Miss Faith," the voice said.

Ridge messaged Leo to turn around asap. That someone was at the gate. "Name?"

"Open the gate."

"Either you give me your name or you're not coming in." When he went into the office and saw the security gate camera, he got a few photos of the guy and sent them to her dad's security.

"Cameron."

"She's not here."

"Yeah, she is. I saw you two leave downtown," Cameron said as Leo messaged that he was coming up the street to the gate.

"Stay here," Ridge said as he grabbed his gun from his lock box and took off outside towards the gate when he saw Leo patting the guy down. "And you are," Ridge asked.

"She knows I'm coming."

"Yeah, no she doesn't."

He called the police and within a matter of 3 minutes, they were there and put Cameron in cuffs. "What are you doing here," Ridge asked.

"Needed to talk to her about something," Cameron replied.

"Which is," the officer asked.

"Handled," Ridge asked.

The officer nodded. His partner put him in the back of the squad car and the other officer went up to the house with Ridge. "Leo," Ridge said. Leo handed him the photo and gave him a thumbs up. When they came into the house, Faith was curled up on the sofa.

"What happened," Faith asked as they walked in. Ridge put his handgun back in the lock box and came downstairs.

Chapter 6

"Are you alright," the officer asked.

"Scared crapless, but I'm okay now," Faith said.

"Do you know Cameron Fairchild," the officer asked as Ridge started clenching his jaw and Faith's hands started shaking. He slid his hand in hers.

"He was in our high school I think, but he was younger than us," Faith said.

Ridge was about to snap.

"We're gonna see if he was the one who was taking the photos. If he wasn't, he's still going to be charged with stalking."

Faith nodded and Ridge gave him the photo. "Touch," the officer asked.

"Touched with my shirt and put into the bag." The officer got everything and headed out, and Ridge went and called her dad's head of security.

"What happened," her dad's security asked.

"The officers just left. Cameron Fairchild showed at the house, demanding to get in. My team member managed to get him while I ran for the gate. Cops showed maybe 10 minutes later. They have the photo. Cameron was arrested for stalking."

"Good move. Very good. How's Miss Faith?"

"Shaky but okay. Nothing cobbler can't fix."

"Alright. Keep me posted," he said as Ridge came back into the TV room to see Faith still curled up.

He got her a shot of Jack and put it into a glass, handing it to her as he sat down beside her and curled her into his arms. "You okay," Ridge asked.

"At least we have an idea of who now," Faith said.

"Are you feeling better though," he asked.

"No."

"What did he do in high school?"

"You mean other than trying to bully me?"

"That was the idiot?"

Faith nodded.

"Well, then he's just as pissed at me."

"What are you talking about," Faith asked.

"I heard about him and went to chat with him after a game."

He remembered that moment. Towering over the 15-year-old in the locker room after his game. He'd told him to leave Faith alone. That she was off-limits, and if he touched her again or even muttered her name, he was getting buried in a locker. "He wasn't exactly happy with knowing that he couldn't talk to you. All I knew was that if someone started making you feel uncomfortable, that they were messing with me."

Faith looked at him as he saw the empty glass of Jack. "Ridge, we weren't dating in high school."

"We were friends. We always have been," Ridge said.

Faith hugged him and he wrapped his arms around her. "I wasn't letting anyone hurt you."

Faith kissed him. "Ridge."

"What?"

"Thank you."

He shook his head. "That's why I'm here Faith." Not two minutes later, her phone rang with a call from her dad.

"Hi."

"Are you alright," her dad asked.

"Yeah. Ridge got him. It's okay."

"Tell me what happened," her mom said. She put the phone on speaker. "I put you on speaker," Faith said.

"What happened," her dad asked.

"There was a buzz at the gate. I went straight to the cameras, and it was a blacked-out pickup. He didn't want to even answer my questions, but when I realized he was a little too shady, I started running for the gate. One of the guys on my team had just left and did a u-turn and came back to the house, blocking him in and called the police. We got his actual name. He'd taken a picture of us when we were out today. He left it on the SUV," Ridge said.

"But you're both alright and safe," her dad asked.

"I'm okay dad. I promise. Kinda really glad that Ridge is here."

"As long as you're alright. Do you need me to come home," her mom asked.

"No. It's fine. I promise. He's not leaving."

"Okay. I'll see you when we get back. If anything else happens, let me know," her mom said.

"We will," Ridge replied.

"Don't tell me that you made the cobbler to make her feel better," her mom teased.

"Of course."

Faith smirked. "Alright. Love you baby girl and thank you Ridge."

"Most welcome," he replied. She hung up with them and Ridge slid his arms around her, giving her a hug. "Better," he asked.

Faith shook her head. "I could be better. That kinda freaked me out," Faith said.

"At least we have the culprit. That's at least a first step. We're good," he said.

"And? I don't even know why he's doing this." Ridge had a couple ideas. Part of them were about a vendetta that Cameron's dad had against Faith's folks. There was a million and one reasons for someone to act like that, but making sure that Faith was alright was all he was concerned with. He snuggled her close until he felt her shaking subside.

"You sure you're okay," he asked.

"I will be. That scared me. I don't know what would make him do that," Faith said.

"Well, it could be just about anything. Honestly, if it's about something with your folks, that's their deal. There's no reason to come for you."

"Yeah, I thought that too until he showed up here," Faith said as he kissed the top of her head.

"Alright. Distraction. Come make dinner with me?"

Faith nodded and kissed him.

He kissed her again and grabbed the seafood from the fridge. "What are you making now?"

"Something that is meant to completely distract you. Steampots," he teased. Faith shook her head, and he filled up the pot, putting the spices into the water and then put it on the stove.

"Ridge, we don't have to go all out," she teased.

He went and got her a drink, handing one to her and they sat down while they waited on the water. He put the butter and garlic on to melt and when the water hit boiling, he put the seafood in and got it going, setting a timer.

She watched him and somehow it was comforting. He was a good guy. A really good guy. How she never realized that when they were hanging out together in high school she didn't know. She'd fallen so fast. Now, she realized deep down that she loved him. More than anything in the world, she didn't ever want to lose him. Not now. It wasn't the sex; the mind-blowing sex that she'd never felt in her entire life. It wasn't the feel of his arms around her, comforting her and giving her the sense of safety again. She was just simple and easy Faith. The girl who'd never dated the right guy until that moment. Seeing the one person that she'd always wanted in the guy that had always been there waiting.

Maybe he'd dated, maybe he hadn't. Maybe he'd thought that somehow he'd find the right one when it was meant to happen. Maybe that time was now. It had started as her needing security, and maybe she had always needed it in more ways than one.

"What's wrong," he asked as he pulled the seafood out of the pot.

"Nothing. Just thinkin."

"About what beautiful?"

"Timing." He smirked and put the seafood on the kitchen counter for them to share.

"What about timing," he asked putting a little more seasoning on the food.

Faith shook her head and kissed him. "Nothin."

"You gonna tell me what you're talking about or am I guessing?"

"Just realizing things. It's nothing. I promise."

"I know you, Faith. Whatever's running around your head, just say it."

She kissed him and they ate. Watching the smirk on her face was slowly becoming one of his favorite things. "What's with the big smile handsome?"

"Just realizing that maybe the one thing I always wanted was right in front of me," he said as he cracked the perfect crab leg and handed it to her.

The fact that they were both thinking the same thing made her smile. "What," he asked.

"I was thinking."

He took a deep breath. "About what," Faith replied as he pulled her chair closer.

"Tell me what you were thinking."

"I hadn't dated in a long time when you showed up," Faith said as he got a grin. "I honestly didn't even know if I ever wanted a relationship again. I was happy the way things were. I could go anywhere, do anything. I just kinda realized that I was wrong," she said as he kissed her hand.

"And?"

"I was just waiting for the right time."

"Faith."

"I kinda think maybe now was that time," Faith said. He looked at her in awe.

"Meaning what," Ridge asked hoping that she'd say the words. That she'd say that she was falling for him like he had been falling for her. Maybe. She looked at him.

"Meaning I think this is the right time."

He took a deep breath. "Faith."

"What?"

"What are you saying," he asked.

"I know that it's been a really crappy day, and I know that we sorta went through the ringer."

"Faith, just say it."

"I think that I might…"

Just as she was about to say it, his phone buzzed. He ignored the call. "Might what?"

"Be in love with you."

He looked at her. "Say it again," he replied.

"Ridge."

"Say it."

He looked at her. "I think that I'm..." He kissed her and pulled her into his arms.

He devoured her lips until they both started laughing. "Took us long enough right," he teased.

"That's what I was kinda thinking," Faith replied.

He kissed her again. "You sure?"

She nodded and he fed her another piece of crab. "I think we're gonna need to eat," he teased.

"And why's that?"

"Because we're watching the third one," he teased as he nibbled at her lips. They finished the seafood, cleaned up together then he picked her up and carried her to the sofa.

"You know, we could just watch it upstairs," Faith said.

"And ruin the tradition? No," he replied as he kissed her and handed her a drink.

"What am I drinking?"

"You poured one for me, I pour one for you."

She shook her head, and he kissed her. He handed her the remote, shut the shutters and curtains, made sure the house was secure and they sat down on that same sofa they'd sat on that first night that she'd made him dinner.

"Which one are we watching first," he asked.

"Longest ride."

He kissed her neck. "Go ahead," he teased.

Faith shook her head. "Before I do," she said as she turned to face him.

"What," he asked.

She kissed him and he snuggled her into his arms. "You never told me what you think," Faith said.

"Meaning?"

"How do you feel?"

"That it took way too long. I loved you when we were kids. I never really stopped Faith."

She kissed him and he snuggled her tight to him. "How," she asked.

"High school to military to security to now."

"Nobody?"

He shook his head. "Not anyone that was worth the time or effort."

"Meaning what?"

"Never anything that lasted more than a week or two. I knew what I wanted," he teased.

"What took you so dang long?"

"All it took was a phone call," he teased, snuggling her to him and devouring her lips.

"And, if I hadn't called?"

"I would've tried to find you. Honestly, I've been on that beach past your place a million times. I came down and saw your folks with my mom last time I was in town before this. I never saw you there."

Faith looked at him. "What?"

He nodded. Knowing that changed so much. The fact that they'd practically grown up as siblings had always made it seem wrong, but when she knew that he had been in love with her that long and been that close...There was no way.

Devouring her lips was the only way to make her understand. He didn't have the words. Not like Faith did. She barely managed to let go until he picked her up and walked up the steps, leaning her onto the bed. She didn't need the movie and either did he. He leaned her into the pillows and they were making out like two teenagers in heat. Her shirt slid off, then his. Her jeans, then his. Her bra and panties then his boxers. He grabbed a packet from her bedside table and slid it on.

"Ridge."

"What," he asked as he kissed down her neck.

"Promise me something."

"What beautiful?"

"Nothing changes after this."

"What do you mean nothing changes?"

"When there's no more stalker and no more stress, tell me that nothing will change with us."

He shook his head, devouring her lips. "You think that this is gonna be different? How? You can't exactly turn us off Faith."

She looked at him. "Promise?"

He shook his head. "You seriously think that all of it's because I'm here keeping you safe? That all of this is because I'm your bodyguard?"

"Ridge." He shook his head, getting up. He pulled his jeans on, grabbed his clothes and walked into his room, pulling on a hoodie. He walked back downstairs, finished cleaning up, put the extra food away and poured himself a triple shot of Jack and walked outside.

He flipped the firepit on and opened his phone, seeing a missed call from his mom. He called back. "Hey," Ridge said.

"I heard that there was a big thing today," his mom said.

"At least it's something. The cops have him in custody."

"Ridge. What's wrong?"

"Nothing. I'm fine."

His mom knew him better than he thought she did. "I'm waiting baby."

He shook his head and took a gulp of his drink. "She told me that she loved me."

"What?" He took a deep breath. "Ridge, that's good isn't it?"

"Until I realized that it was temporary."

"Ridge, I get that you're jaded after dating that idiot woman up in Charlotte. I do. Stop. This is Faith that we're talking about. Whether she admits it or not, she's been in love with you as long as you've been in love with her. I love you baby boy but breathe. You got spooked for a half-second. You're fine. She's scared that when there isn't an imminent threat, you'll vanish."

Ridge shook his head. "I don't know what to do."

"Then take a breather. If you want to fly out and meet us, say so."

"I will. Thanks mom," he said.

"And stay safe alright? Please?"

"I will. Tell Dad I said hi."

"I will baby." He hung up with his mom and finished his drink.

When he heard the swish of the door, he took a deep breath. "Ridge."

He walked inside, got himself another glass and walked back outside. "What," he asked.

"I don't think you know what I meant," Faith said.

"And?"

"I meant that when there isn't a problem anymore, we'll still be together. That's it," she said.

"You think that one idiot is why I'm here? Your dad and mom have had security for years. Your dad had security before your folks got together again. This isn't temporary. It's not for me anyway. Never has been, but obviously for you it is."

He took a long gulp of the drink. "Ridge."

He took a deep breath. "What?"

"It isn't."

Faith looked at him and he turned to face her. "Meaning?"

"I just don't want you thinking that when the threat is gone, I'm not gonna still want you around."

Ridge shook his head. "Whatever," he said as he flipped the firepit off.

"Ridge."

"If the only reason you want me here is to work, then I'm working. Period. Nothing else. You need to head inside. Not exactly safe out here."

"Ridge." He drank down the rest of his drink. He opened the door and walked her inside, putting his glass away. He locked up, flipped the alarm on and walked into the security office, going through work emails.

He could flip off emotion as easily as flipping on a light switch if he had to. When he heard the door close and saw her walking towards him, he shook his head. "What now," he asked.

"Come here," Faith asked.

"Why?"

"Because you aren't switching me off."

He shook his head and sat back in the chair. "Faith, if you want this to stay business, it will be," he said.

She walked over and sat down in his lap. "I know that you think that's the only reason. It's not. You need to know that."

He shook his head. "You need to go and watch your movie."

"Then come with me."

"No." Faith looked at him, got up, took his hand, and walked him out of the office, sitting him on the sofa. "What?"

"When you got here, I thought the feelings were because you were here and keeping me safe. When

I realized that it was more than that, I sorta worried that it was a mistake. That it might just be being thankful for you. That wasn't it Ridge. You know that. You know it was a lot more than that."

"Can you let me get up?"

"No." She was determined to make him hear her even if she had to scream it from the rooftop.

"I love you. I have for a long time Ridge. I know you felt the same. I know you still do."

"And?"

"I'm just as freaking scared as you are. I'm just as worried that if something changes, it won't be the same. I'm not willing to let it change. I don't want it to. That's all I was saying."

"And when I have to work for someone else?"

"According to my dad, you are on staff."

"Faith."

She kissed him and slid into his lap, straddling him on the sofa. "What?"

"Let me up?"

"No. Are you even hearing me?"

He picked her up and sat her on the table. "I hear you, Faith. I also know that if you think that is gonna..."

She kissed him again and slid into his lap again. "I'm not walking Ridge. Either are you. I want you and me. If that means that you're still here doing security, fine. I just want what we have going. What's wrong with that?"

"And when that isn't enough?"

Faith shook her head. "Ridge, nobody else has ever been enough. You're the only one that is. That always will be."

"Now," he said. She kissed him and shook her head.

"Ridge." He tried to push her away, but she wouldn't let him.

"What do you want me to say Faith?"

She kissed him. "That you love me. That's it."

"I always have. Not like it matters." He got up and walked upstairs.

"Ridge, stop walking away. It's not gonna change how you feel. It's not gonna change that I love you too."

He walked into his room, closed the door, and locked it behind him.

"You realize that I have the damn key for the lock right," Faith said.

When there was no answer, she walked into her bedroom and sat on the bed. She took a deep breath and sent one single text. One. One that she hoped would make him see what she meant:

> *I loved you when we were kids and didn't know that this is what it would become. I want this with us. I never want to give that up. I love you. If that's not enough, fine. I'm in my room. When you can get your head around it, come in here. Please.*

Faith took a deep breath, curled up on her bed and went through the million and one emails. Maybe a weekend off wasn't gonna work. She could go into the office and avoid being in the house with him. A lot less chance of them getting in the middle of everything. A smaller chance of her losing her mind altogether.

She went downstairs and got a drink, making herself a Jack and Coke. When she went to turn around, Ridge was coming into the kitchen. "What are you drinking," he asked as he went and got the bottle of Jack and poured himself a glass.

Barefoot Bodyguard

"Why?"

He shook his head, put the bottle away and sat down on the sofa. She sat down on the chair by the edge of the sofa. "Are you talking to me," Faith asked.

"If the only reason you're here in this moment is because you want to get laid, say so."

Faith shook her head. "So, you do this now? Really," Faith asked.

"If the only reason…"

"Ridge, you have no idea, do you? You think that us messing around was what caused all of this? I loved you like family. It got more intense when we ended up in a room together. I know that I love you, Ridge. Whether you feel the same or not, I don't even know."

"Until you…"

"Ridge."

"Until you said what you did, I didn't doubt how I felt. Now, you even saying that it's because I'm here keeping you safe?"

"That's not what I said."

"Then what did you say?"

Faith took a deep breath. "Did you even read the text?" Ridge nodded. "And?"

"I don't want it unless it's unconditional. I want what my folks had. What your folks do. You think there's a reason. There isn't Faith. I just love you, period. I wanted this. If it's not gonna work, then say so." He got up and walked upstairs.

Faith went to get up and follow him and he closed and locked the door to his room again. She walked upstairs and knocked. When he didn't answer, she went downstairs and flipped the lights off, making sure the doors were locked and came back upstairs, walking into her room. She slid into her satin nightgown and slid her lotion on. She took a deep breath and went and looked at some more emails. She shook her head and got comfy, flipping on the TV. She nodded off an hour later, flipping the tv off and went to turn the light off when she heard his door open.

"Ridge," Faith said.

He walked over towards her door. "What," he asked.

"I love you. I get that you can't hear it, and you can't see it, but I know dang well you feel it even if you won't let yourself feel it." He took a deep breath, gulped, and looked at her.

"I never said I didn't love you too Faith." He walked downstairs, got another drink, put the bottle away and went to walk upstairs. He saw Faith sitting on the steps. "What," he asked.

"Why are we fighting about this if we both love each other?"

He shook his head. "Because maybe it's not enough."

She got up and walked towards him. "It's more than enough. Can't we just start tonight over?"

He shook his head. "I'm going to bed," he said.

"Then come and sleep in my room." He shook his head and walked upstairs, walking back into his room, and sat back down. He took a deep breath and got undressed, sliding under the blanket. He flipped the light off, threw his phone on the charger and went to bed.

In the middle of the night, he felt arms wrap around him. "Faith."

"I'm not fighting about something stupid. Second, I can't sleep. I never could."

"Why are you in here at 2am?"

"Because I can't sleep in there alone after today."

He shook his head. "You realize he's in jail, right?"

"Doesn't change anything. Still can't sleep."

"Then sleep Faith." He shook his head and tried to go back to sleep, but he could feel her staring at him. He turned to face her. "What?" She kissed him. "Faith," he said as they came up for air.

"What?"

"If you're not in this because you actually want this with us, say so."

"I'm not sleeping in that bed without you." He shook his head and got up, pulled his boxers on, and walked downstairs, curling up on the sofa, and got shut eye alone.

Faith woke up the next morning, coming downstairs, fully expecting to see Ridge post workout. When she saw Leo at the counter, she shook her head. "Morning," Faith said.

"Hi. Ridge said he wanted to go for a run. That's all. I'm here until he gets back," Leo said.

"I thought you were supposed to be hanging with the wife?"

"Nope. I'm getting as much work done and research on this idiot. You okay after all of that yesterday?"

"Not exactly. I'll be fine though. Leo, I get that you're trying to be nice and all, but how pissed is he?"

"He just wanted to do a run. That's all." Faith nodded and took a deep breath, making something to eat. Just as she sat down, Ridge came back inside.

"You good," Leo asked.

"Thanks. I needed the run. Cleared my head," Ridge said as he came into the kitchen and saw Faith.

"I'm heading out. I'll see you later on if you need me," Leo said as he hung out. Ridge nodded, locked up behind him and went to head upstairs.

"Not a word," Faith asked.

"What?"

"Ridge."

"I went for a run. I needed to clear my head, but I wasn't about to leave you here after yesterday. You're fine. I'm going to wash up."

"Seriously," Faith replied.

"What?"

"I tell you that I love you and you refuse to come near me. You refuse to even be in the same bed. You sleep on the damn sofa of all places and then when I wake up you're gone? Tell me what I'm supposed to say here Ridge, because I'm about to whoop some serious butt right now."

"I don't want you saying it because I'm here and I'm helping you with the stupid idiot problem. I don't want it for any other reason than because you actually do. I don't think that's the reason Faith. I'm not gonna cloud it all with us sleeping together."

"Ridge, would you look at me?" He took a deep breath and looked at her. "Did I say it was conditional? That it was because of the situation that's going on? No. I said I loved you. I didn't want anything to change when the imminent threat is over. I don't want you to leave. Do you understand that?" He nodded and walked upstairs. "Ridge." He walked into the bathroom, washed up and when he stepped out of the hot and steamy shower, she was sitting on the counter. Still in the same way too sexy nightgown from the night prior.

"What," he asked as he wrapped the towel around his hips.

"Not even gonna say anything?"

"What do you want me to say Faith?"

"That you don't want to lose me. That you don't want to leave either. That you aren't gonna vanish the minute the threat is gone. Pick one," Faith said.

"You sure you want that answer?"

"Ridge, stop being a damn child. Say something."

"I'm not leaving. I got my clothes from the storage locker this morning. I don't want to lose what we're starting. I just want to be sure that you are in this 100% or I'm not letting myself get attached."

"Too late. You already are. I'm not going anywhere. I'm the one that told you that I loved you. I'm not taking that back Ridge."

He nodded and walked into his room. He pulled on boxers and was about to pull his jeans on when she walked in and closed the door. "Do you want this or not," she asked.

"I wouldn't have come back if..." She kissed him and slid into his lap. "What," he asked when they came up for air.

"Stop being a pain in my butt," Faith said.

"I could be if you're into that," he joked.

"No more stupid..." He kissed her until the goosebumps came up again. His hands slid up her legs and pulled them tight around his waist. When he leaned her onto the bed, somehow by some stupid chance moment, his phone buzzed.

"Don't," Faith said as he slid his phone off the counter.

"It's the police." "Officer," Ridge said.

"I wanted to let you know. The judge gave Faith a restraining order against him. They pushed to hold him, but he managed to get bail. No idea how either. He's not allowed within a thousand feet of Faith or any of the properties she owns. Nothing. We're keeping an eye on him, but I wanted to let you know. We're gonna have an unmarked car outside the house we picked him up from. Extra layer of safety," the officer said.

"Thanks. We're staying around here today anyway," Ridge said.

He hung up with him and Faith sat up. "And?"

"He's on bail. We both know who paid it."

"Now what," Faith asked.

He finished getting dressed. "We're staying here. You want to go outside, we can, but we're not staying out there long."

"Ridge."

"What?"

"Do you think we're okay here?"

Ridge nodded. "Better than anywhere else."

"Ridge."

"What?"

"Does this mean that we're okay?"

"For now," he replied. She looked at him. "Did you eat?" She nodded. He went to leave the room and Faith grabbed his hand and stood up. "What," he asked.

"Are we okay?"

"As in us or as in safety?" Faith gave him a look that spoke volumes. "Can we talk about it when you're not in a sexy something?"

"No," Faith teased.

"Get dressed. We can…" She walked over and kissed him.

"Are…" He kissed her again, picked her up and wrapped her legs around his waist, walking her into her bedroom. He leaned her onto her bed, and she felt the material slide up her legs. "Faith."

"What?"

"You're sure," he asked.

"I swear, if you ask…"

He smirked and kissed her. "Get dressed."

"Why," Faith asked as she sat up.

"Because I don't want you naked downstairs in case we need to leave."

"You do know that you could always just stay in bed with me right? We could hang out all day and just watch movies," she teased.

"Way too tempting. You need clothes."

She kissed him. "Or you get in bed with me."

He shook his head. "You have work to do, and I have emails to finish. We're having a g-rated afternoon," he teased.

"So, are we gonna do the movie tonight?"

"If you can manage to wait that long, we can talk about it," he said.

Faith kissed him. "Where did you go this morning," she asked.

"When you aren't half-naked, we can talk about it." He kissed her and walked downstairs.

He threw the box that he'd gone hunting for into his bag and hung the clothes up that he'd got from his rental. When he finished, he headed downstairs and made coffee, grabbed his laptop and sat down on the sofa. He started going through the emails, making sure that everything was running the way it should and saw a single email come in from his Dad:

> *I know you don't need me to tell you this, but please be careful. If that man is anything like his father, he's dangerous. Zack was a pain in Emerson's side, and almost had stalker tendencies with Lily. If he's coming after Faith, there's a lot to it and I'm worried about you. Also heard that you and Faith finally got over yourselves and admitted your feelings. Keep me posted.*

He smirked. His dad always did have a way with words. Ridge went through his emails, paying some bills and making sure everything else was working right. He got the guys paid and took a gulp of his coffee when she came downstairs. "My folks said hi," he said as she came and sat down beside him. He got up and grabbed her a coffee and she shook her head.

"What," he asked as she closed the laptop.

"Talk," Faith said.

"I went to check on the guys at the beach house, then went for a run on the Battery. I grabbed breakfast, got the stuff from my storage locker, and took the scenic route on the way back. That's all," he said.

"Note next time maybe?"

He nodded. "I will. What emails do you have left to work on," she asked.

"Nothing too important. Regular stuff. Why," he asked. Faith smirked. "Can we talk about all of this so the fighting doesn't start again?"

"Which part," he asked.

"I don't want you to leave. I don't want you to walk away, I don't want to lose you in my life, and I want you to be here with me. I want you in my life no matter what it takes," Faith said.

"And," he asked.

"What about you," Faith asked as she took a gulp of her coffee.

"I get it Faith. I do. All I want is you and me. However that looks, or whatever that takes, I want it. We date. See how..."

She kissed him and slid into his lap. "See what," she asked.

"See where that goes."

"You sure?"

He nodded and kissed her. "Can we just get on with the day?"

She nodded and smirked. "What do you want to do," Faith asked.

"Sit outside while we can."

She smirked. "Swim?"

He shook his head and walked her outside. "I don't want you to feel all trapped in the house. He's not coming here. That I do know. He's stupid, but he's not that stupid," Ridge said as they sat down on the chaise and had their coffees.

"You sure?"

"We have to take the time while we can. Who knows what's gonna happen next."

"This mean that we can kinda hang out for a day instead of working?"

"Since you have emails to answer you mean? We can't just hide from life Faith."

"I took the weekend off. The long weekend. A very overdue one," Faith said.

"Then check emails and get work in. I have a bunch to answer too," he said.

"And I'm taking an hour off. We deserve to have a little time to just relax," Faith said.

"I get wanting to stay in the bubble, but you do know that life exists outside of this house right?"

Faith nodded. "Just want to put it off for a few days. That's all," Faith said.

He gave her a hug. "I get it. Just don't keep putting it off, okay? You have a real life outside of our bubble here. I know it's..."

She kissed him. "I want to make up for all of that last night for a little while."

He shook his head. "Faith, you know you don't have to. What's done is done," he said.

"And," she asked.

"We can sit down and have dinner tonight. Have a do-over, but we need to get work done."

"Swim first."

He shook his head and Faith kissed him. She walked upstairs, changed into a swimsuit and he followed, changing into his swim trunks. They came downstairs and walked outside as Faith cannonballed into the pool. He shook his head, sliding in and swimming over to her as she surfaced. "Like," Faith asked as he saw her in an illegal bikini. One that should've been anyway. Strings instead of cover. He shook his head.

"And you're wearing the practically dissolvable bikini why," he asked as he pulled her legs around his hips and leaned her against the wall of the pool.

Chapter 7

"Because I was attempting to distract you. Did it work," Faith teased.

He kissed her, devouring her lips until he shook his head. "Stop taunting Faith."

"So, it's okay for you to taunt until I can't walk, but it's not for me to taunt you in the pool until you're too hot and bothered to even run for…"

He kissed her. "Still not doing this in the pool," he teased.

"Meaning what," Faith asked.

"I can taunt you until you explode 50 times over without needing anything remember," he teased as he started taunting.

"Ridge."

He kissed her and he felt her nails against his back. "Round 1?"

"Ridge." He kissed along her neck then down her shoulder as he felt her legs curling tighter. He went to undo the side and she shook her head. "Don't."

"You started it," he teased.

"Ridge."

"What?" She shook her head. He devoured her lips and untied the bikini bottoms.

"No, you aren't," Faith teased.

"Says who," he asked.

Faith shook her head, and he kissed her. "Tell me what you want."

"Upstairs."

"You sure?"

Faith nodded and he picked her up, hopped out of the pool, wrapped her in a towel and carried her upstairs, closing the bedroom door behind him. He leaned her onto the bed. "Don't move."

"Where are you going?"

He kissed her and went and grabbed something from his room. When he came back in, he slid something onto the counter and leaned into her arms.

"What..."

He devoured her lips and pulled her legs back around him. "Now, what were you saying?"

"Um."

He leaned in with another kiss that had her entire body curling around him like vine on a live oak. "That's what I thought," he teased as he smirked.

"What," Faith teased.

"You really want to make up for lost time last night?"

"Ridge."

"Yes or no?"

She smirked. "You know the answer."

He devoured her lips and taunted. Just as he was about to peel her bikini top off, her phone buzzed. "And now you know why it's so much easier after dark." She grabbed her cell, seeing her friend Lacey's name.

"Lacey," Faith said.

"Hey. Are you around," Lacey asked.

"Sort of in the middle of something. Why," Faith asked.

"Remember Jackson? Jackson Dean?"

"What about him," Faith asked.

"I'm pregnant."

Barefoot Bodyguard

"Shit. Are you alright?"

"Not really. I need a girl night. Something. Anything. Where are you," Lacey asked.

"I'm at my house. Not the beach house. Long story. If you want, come over and we can do dinner tonight or something," Faith said.

"Okay," Lacey said in between sniffles.

"I'll see you around dinner," Faith said.

"Okay," Lacey replied as they hung up.

"So, now I get another blast from the past? Really? Lacey of all damn people?"

"Meaning what," Faith asked as they both realized that the moment had passed.

"The woman talked smack behind your back every time you two got in a damn fight." Faith looked at him.

"Are you gonna stay in here with me," Faith asked.

"Unless you want her in here. She's gonna end up trying to get the guest room to herself," Ridge said as he kissed her and got up.

He walked downstairs, grabbed his laptop and started doing a background on Lacey. When he saw that she was connected with Cameron, he shook his head. Whoever Jackson was, was a lie from what he read. She'd never lived or had a lease with anyone with that name. If she was coming to the house, there was one very large difference. She could plant anything from Cameron in the house. She'd be back to worried all over again. He was determined, one way or another, to make sure that nobody planted anything in the house. He called his buddy Clay and then had to figure out how to say it.

"What's up," Clay asked.

"Are you busy tonight?"

"No, why? Asking me on a date," Clay joked.

"Do you remember Lacey?"

"Lacey as in the fakest non friend to everyone? I remember her from back in the day. Why?"

Ridge told him what was going on and Clay agreed to come as a buffer between them all. He'd keep Lacey away from doing anything. She'd be the one on the defensive instead of Ridge and Faith.

"What," Faith asked as she came downstairs and slid into his lap.

"I was gonna kinda hang with an old buddy tonight. You okay if he pops over?"

"Who," Faith asked.

"Clay Adams."

"As in the guy who was on the team with you in high school?" Ridge nodded. "Why?"

He explained to her about his suspicions. "How did I not know about her and Cameron?"

"Faith, I only knew because I did a background. I don't want her here on his behalf. That's all. He's a buffer to make sure she doesn't plant anything like there was at the beach house."

She looked at him. "Okay. I mean, I can always call and tell her that something came up," she said.

"It's up to you. I just wanted you to know before I went inviting the entire security team," he teased.

Faith kissed him and slid her legs around his waist. "Faith."

"What?"

"You feeling better then?"

"Thanks for telling me."

He kissed her and snuggled her tight to him. "It's up to you if you want her to still come. I kinda figured that if he's here, it'll at least have an extra set of eyes out to make sure she didn't plant anything."

"It's a good idea," she said.

"And what about food for dinner?"

Faith smirked. "Would it be bad to have a do-over of seafood night?"

He kissed her, sent off a message and ordered double what they'd got with the last pile of seafood. "You sure," Faith asked. He nodded, kissed her and she snuggled back into his arms. "Are we okay," Faith asked.

"Depends on what part of okay you're talking about."

"Ridge."

"If she's coming, no movie night," he teased. Faith shook her head.

"You realize that she's not coming until 6 or something right?"

He kissed her. "It's 11. Not enough time," he teased.

"Ridge."

"You have to wait. Delayed gratification. You want to have her over, we can wait. All I ask is that you don't invite her to stay."

Faith kissed him. "Ridge, I never had any intention of inviting her. Kinda have plans with this handsome, sexy guy that I know. Honestly, if I'd known the connection, I never would've told her to come."

He smirked and devoured her lips. Just as she was trying to peel his shirt off, her phone buzzed. He smirked and handed it to her when she saw Lacey's name. "What's up," Faith asked.

"Do you need me to bring anything tonight," Lacey asked.

"Nope. Ridge and I ordered seafood. We're gonna do a low country boil. He mentioned that his friend Clay is coming too," Faith said hinting that maybe she might want to rethink coming as she slid out of his lap and leaned against the edge of the kitchen counter.

"Clay who?"

"Clay Adams. You remember him," Faith said dropping a hint.

"Why," Lacey asked.

"They were planning to meet up anyway. Now, it's sorta like a reunion," Faith said as Ridge kissed up her neck.

"Oh."

"I mean, you're still welcome to come."

Ridge kissed back down the nape of her neck. "Maybe another…"

"Lacey."

"Fine. I'll be there," Lacey said. She put the phone on speaker and Ridge cleared his throat.

"Everyone's getting frisked before them come in. We sorta have to after a security issue at the house," Ridge said.

"Whatever. Did you think that I'd do that to Faith?"

"I mean, we sorta have to after Cameron decided to try and break the gate down," Ridge said.

"I'll see you at dinner," Lacey said as she hung up and Ridge kissed down Faith's spine.

"Ridge."

He smirked. "What?"

"I know what you're up to."

"You have no idea," he said. Faith went to turn and look at him and his arms slid around her waist.

"Don't," he said.

"What," she teased. He kissed down her back as it arched. She leaned forward and he slid her shirt right off.

"Ridge."

"What?"

"What are you doin," she asked.

"Taunting you. Weren't you trying to make up for that interruption or what," he teased as he kissed the base of her back.

"Depends on what you're planning."

"Kick them off."

"Ridge."

"Do it," he whispered as she got goosebumps all over.

"You sure," she asked.

He kissed her side. "We can't..."

He stood her up and sat her on the high-top chair. He peeled her jeans off, slid off the barely nothing panties and kissed her.

"Here," Faith asked. He kissed her, devouring her lips until she was practically fumbling with the button of his jeans. He had a plan. One that would get her so hot and bothered, that she'd kick Lacey out in less than 3 seconds. He teased, taunted, teased some more until her toes were almost in knots and he was still fully clothed. When her body was almost humming, Ridge got a grin ear to ear. "I swear, you're doing this intentionally," she said.

"I am." He kissed her as his fingers took over the taunting until she gave him that look. The one that said if he didn't stop, they'd end up having sex on the floor or on the dang counter.

He smirked and she shook her head. "Ridge."

"What?"

"Stop taunting."

"Nope."

He smirked and Faith finally went for the button of his jeans. He playfully smacked her hand. "Hands off," he teased.

"Ridge."

"Delayed…"

"Not fair. Not even a little bit," Faith said as her body tightened around his fingers.

"What were you saying," he teased.

"So grounded."

"You sure about that," he teased as he kissed her. When he felt her legs shaking around him, he smirked.

"I know that smirk. What are you up to," Faith asked. He kissed her and went to completely step away when she grabbed the front belt loops of his jeans. "Don't you dare," she said.

"What," he teased.

Faith shook her head. "Off," she said.

He shook his head, and she undid the button of his jeans. "Faith."

"Mine," she replied.

"Nope," he teased.

He went to do his jeans back up and she stopped him. "Ridge."

"Not until tonight," he teased. Faith shook her head and knew there was no point in trying to even walk. She pulled her legs around him and pulled him to her, undoing his zipper. "Faith."

"What," she said.

"You need to behave," he said.

She shook her head and kissed him, pulling her legs tight around him and pulling him to her. "Faith, we aren't."

She nodded and he shook his head. "Not until tonight," he teased.

"Ridge, I swear…"

He kissed her and taunted her again until she was almost screaming his name from him teasing her into orgasm. "Ridge." He picked her up and carried her up the steps, walking into her bedroom and leaning her onto the bed.

"Faith."

"What," she asked as he smirked.

"You good?"

"No."

"Power nap?"

"Ridge, I swear, if you don't get into..." He kissed her, nibbling her lips until she was hot and bothered again. She wanted to rip his jeans off and not let go for a second. Just as she went to make a move, his phone buzzed. Faith smirked, shook her head and he got up, walking out of the bedroom and down to the security office.

"Yep," Ridge said as he walked in and closed the door.

"We got the fingerprints back from the cameras and the hidden microphones. It's Cameron and his dad. Every one of them has both their fingerprints on them. The cops got the info, but I wanted to let you know. How much security do you have on the beach house," her dad's head of security asked. "3 rotating. I'm at the main house with Faith. I can get extra here. She gave them the weekend off."

"I want two of you at the house. When does her other security come back?"

"Tomorrow I believe."

"Fine. I want you with Faith 100% of the time. Two doing security and rotating doing the outside of the main house. I know that you and Faith are now a couple, which will make it easier to keep her safe. Just keep her out of the line of fire."

"I will."

"Your check was deposited to your account. I have the rest of the team on contract and direct deposit. If you need to add someone, tell me."

"Will do," Ridge said as he hung up.

He sent an email off to the team with the updates and when he came out of the office, his phone buzzed:

Get your butt back up here.

He smirked and walked upstairs. When he leaned onto the door frame of her bedroom, she looked at him. "Come here," Faith said.

"Why," he teased almost smirking.

"I'm kicking your butt," Faith said.

"Go for it sexy. I'm going to go grab the seafood and get it ready."

Faith shook her head. "Ridge, I swear."

"What," he teased still not coming near her.

"Come here. Please?"

He shook his head, walked over, kissed her and picked out a sundress for her to wear that night out of her closet. "You are so not playing fair," Faith said.

"You didn't want to wait until tonight remember?" When she tried to get up, she managed to catch the pocket of his jeans and pulled him towards her. "Faith."

"Off. Now."

"Nope." He kissed her again and went into his room. He grabbed his black jeans, black shirt and was about to grab a hoodie when he felt arms slide around him and undo his jeans.

"What you up to over there," he said realizing that with one touch, she'd turned him on. All it took was the feel of her skin against his in any form. She peeled his shirt off. "Faith, you realize that I need to get changed right," he asked.

She walked around him and leaned into his arms. "What," Faith asked as he pulled her tight to him.

"You sure you want to do this," he teased.

"You taunted."

"I think I need to add it to my resume," he joked.

"Taunting me?"

"Torture," he teased.

"I want you. No more stupid…" He kissed her. Those three words were the only ones that he wanted, needed and craved to hear. He picked her up, sitting her on the counter and she wrapped her legs tight around him. When he went to try and back away, she stopped him.

"Faith."

"No. Now," she said.

"Faith." She kissed him and slid his jeans down, pulling him to her.

"We need…" She kissed him and they started having sex. He felt too good. Way too good. Hotter, warmer and she felt like he was almost melting into her.

He shook his head, nibbling and devouring her lips. They were doing the one thing he promised he wouldn't until he knew that they'd be together for life. Going without anything wasn't his idea of a smart move, but the fact that she didn't want to meant more than just the chance that she could end up pregnant. If she ever was, he wasn't leaving her side. He wasn't walking out on her anyway, and never would, but the two of them having a kid? The sex just got hotter to the point that his body couldn't give in, and refused to give in until he knew that she couldn't take anymore. The sex got hotter. It got more intense. He wanted more. A lot more.

"Faith." She kissed him and he picked her up, laying her on his bed and kept taunting. He teased as his body tensed. "Not yet," he said silently to himself. Her body throbbed around him and his gave in and exploded into her like a bomb going off in the midst of a war. He leaned onto the bed on top of her.

"Oh my lord," Faith said. He didn't want to move. She felt too warm. Like her body was memorizing him. Like her body curved to fit him.

"You are so bad," Ridge said.

"You're the one that spent an entire hour taunting me until I could barely move," she replied.

"Faith."

"What?"

"Kinda forgot something."

"I don't care Ridge."

"You're okay with that risk?" She nodded and kissed him, devouring his lips until her toes were curling all over again. He hadn't moved.

"Faith."

She looked at him. "What," she asked as he looked at her.

"We didn't use anything."

"Doesn't matter."

"Yeah it does love. Trust me, it definitely does."

"Ridge, it's fine."

"No, it isn't. We're using something. Period."

She shook her head. "I love you. I don't need it. We don't."

He looked at her. "What?"

"If we do, fine. We don't, doesn't matter."

"This is how you're thinking?"

She nodded. He shook his head and kissed her then got up. "Where are you going?" He walked out of the bedroom and went and got showered.

He shook his head, closed the door and flipped the shower on. "You idiot," he said to himself. He showered, got dried off and slid the towel around his hips. He went to walk out and took a deep breath. He went into his room, and she was sitting on his bed, wrapped up in his blanket.

"What's wrong," Ridge asked as he grabbed boxers and pulled them on.

"Why are you mad," Faith asked.

"You realize that we can't just mess around without using anything right?"

"Ridge."

"We need to. I get that you don't care, but I do."

Faith shook her head. "Why is it so dang important? It's not like I can even get pregnant. I'm on birth control."

"Which is what," he asked.

"Shot." He shook his head.

"And when's the last time you went?"

"Over two months ago. I go every 3."

He shook his head. "Fine. At least I know," he said. She got up and walked over to him. "What?"

"I meant what I said," Faith replied.

"Meaning what?"

"I love you. I want you and me. If we get…"

He shook his head. "Don't."

"Then tell me what's going on."

He kissed her and slid into his jeans. "You might want to go get dressed," he said.

"Why?"

"Because it's almost 4."

"Then tell me why you're worried."

"Faith, I get that we've known each other forever and that you love me and I love you and all of that, but..."

"Hold on. You just said..."

"Faith, I'm not..."

She kissed him. "You just said that you love me."

"I don't know that I'm ready for kids alright?"

"Multiple, no. One?"

"Faith, go get dressed."

"No."

"Fine. Be naked."

He pulled his shirt on, put the cologne on that he knew she loved and went and hung up his towel. He needed to stay away from her. One breath and they would be at it again. One breeze in the right direction and they would be christening every damn surface in the house until one of them collapsed from exhaustion. He walked downstairs, got the seafood delivery and pulled the pot out, heating up the water and throwing in the spices. He set the table and poured himself a double Jack and coke. When he got a text that Clay was there, he grabbed the phone, buzzed Clay through the gate and went and got him a drink.

Ridge opened the door and gave Clay a guy hug. "So, what's the situation," Clay asked as Ridge told him.

"We sort of confronted her about it. She's getting frisked and her purse checked when she gets here. I don't trust her, and I never have." Clay nodded.

"Gotcha."

Clay flipped on some music, Ridge handed him a drink and they sat down at the counter. When Faith walked downstairs in a backless sundress, Ridge shook his head. "Hey Clay," Faith said as he got up and gave her a hug.

"Long time no see," Clay said.

"How have you been," Faith asked as she made herself a Jack and Coke. Ridge took it out of her hand and handed Faith a wine glass.

"I'm good." She took her drink back and looked at him, like she was upset.

She went and talked to Clay and Ridge made sure he had everything ready. He slid some of the seafood in, looking at his watch. He almost hoped that Lacey would stay away. When there was a buzz at the gate, Ridge shook his head and handed the phone to Faith. "Hey Lacey. Come on in," Faith said. She hung up, put the phone onto the charger and sat back down. When Lacey made it to the door, Ridge opened it, saw her and she walked in. He patted her down, grabbed something from the office and did a anti-stalking treatment on her and her purse. When there was a buzz, he took a deep breath.

"Cell phone," she said. He nodded and kept a close eye. He walked her in and went to grab her a drink.

"Wine, soda or Jack and Coke," Ridge asked.

"Water if that's okay," she said as Faith gave her a hug.

He got Lacey an ice water and went and slid the rest of the seafood in, melting the butter and putting the fresh garlic in it. When Clay got up and came into the kitchen, he saw Ridge clenching his jaw and deafeningly quiet. "What," Clay asked.

Ridge shook his head and slid the lid on the seafood. "It's fine."

"Dude, you're gonna grind your teeth into nubs at the rate you're going. What's wrong?"

Ridge shook his head. "Disagreement."

Clay shook his head. "I still don't like Lacey," Clay said.

"Either do I. Honestly, I partially wish she'd bailed."

"What's going on with you and Faith," Clay said quietly.

"Long story. Sorta surprised me," Ridge said.

"How's the food comin," Faith asked as she came over to them.

"It's good. Half hour and it's ready," Ridge said as Faith looked at him.

"Gimme a sec," Ridge asked as he took Faith's hand and walked her into the security office.

"What," she asked as he closed the door.

"Faith."

"You walked away Ridge. You could've just asked me if we needed to."

"I have protection. I don't want to risk it."

"Ridge."

He kissed her. "I don't wanna fight about it. I just want us to be safe. You okay with it?"

She nodded. "Just know that I have it covered."

Ridge nodded and kissed her. "By the way, if she has something, it's in her phone. Not impressed."

Faith shook her head. "Breathe. Clay was practically hitting on her," Faith teased.

"Yeah, that's playing nice. He doesn't like her either."

"Ridge."

"Like I said. Buffer."

"And?"

He backed her up to the door so her back was flat against it. "Not the dress I was thinking," he teased.

"Really? Well, there's a surprise for you."

"Which would be," he asked. When she got that look, he shook his head. "You didn't."

She linked their fingers and his hand slid to her inner thigh. "Still think you can end up being able to stand," he whispered. Faith nodded and his hand slid up her legs to the uncovered apex of her thighs. "So bad," he whispered.

"All yours if you stop being a butthead," Faith said.

Barefoot Bodyguard

One last kiss and they stepped out of the office. "You two alright," Clay asked.

Ridge nodded as Faith slid her hand in his. They went into the kitchen, and he checked on the food. He barely managed two words to Lacey. He knew how awkward she felt. He could see it. Like someone had tried to talk her into doing something she wasn't comfortable with.

"Food's almost ready. Anyone need a top-up," Ridge asked.

Faith smirked. He shook his head, made her another drink that was intentionally strong, and handed it to her.

They all chatted somewhat, and Ridge got the food put out, handed everyone butter and napkins and they ate. It was a relaxing meal, but he was still on edge. When Faith's hand slid to his jeans, he looked at her. He shook his head with a smirk, and they finished up the food.

When they all finished, he put the leftovers into the fridge. He'd always loved leftover seafood. He got everything cleaned up and Faith came up behind him. "What," he teased.

Faith smirked. "Thank you."

He kissed her and she smirked. "What," he teased.

"Counter."

"You just wait," he whispered as he walked her hand in hand back into the tv room.

When everyone started getting ready to go, he was itching to kick Lacey out. When Lacey and Clay both headed out, Ridge locked the door behind them, did a full sweep of anywhere and everywhere that Lacey had been and found something in the chair. He picked it out and showed it to Faith. It was the chair that Lacey had been sitting in during dinner. She couldn't deny it. He deactivated the bug and put it into the safe in the security office and came into the kitchen to see Faith grabbing another drink for each of them.

"You sure that you really want to go there," Ridge asked.

Faith nodded. He kissed her with a kiss that gave both of them goosebumps. He picked her up, wrapping her legs around his hips. "Promise me something," she said.

"What?"

"You get mad, we talk. No walking off." He kissed her with a deep kiss that had her toes curling and her body warming up.

"Now, about this dress. You should've just come down here naked," he said.

"Then neither of us would've even made it to dinner."

"Good point." He smirked and walked back up the stairs.

"Where are..." He leaned her against the door frame of her bedroom.

"You sure you want to start? You're just gonna end up mad tomorrow."

"And why's that?"

"Security and housekeeper are back."

She smirked. "And?" He shook his head and slid the hem of her dress up her legs.

"You sure you are gonna be able to make it out of bed," he teased.

"Probably not, but I'm completely good with it so long as you're still in bed with me," Faith said.

He kissed her again until her legs almost instinctively started trembling. "You sure," he asked. She kissed him and he shook his head. "Faith."

"What?"

"You sure that you don't want to..."

She kissed him, nibbling at his lips. He smirked when they came up for air.

"What?"

"I don't think you're gonna need the cardio tomorrow."

"And why is that," Faith asked.

"Didn't even need a movie," he teased.

He kissed her then got up. "Where are you going?"

"Getting the drinks and locking up." He kissed her, walked downstairs, locked up and closed the shutters and curtains, made sure the alarm was on and the motion detector was on, then grabbed the drinks and walked upstairs. He put them on the bedside table, put the phones on the charger and smirked.

"Now, where were we," he asked.

Faith was on her stomach with her head on the pillow. "Come here," she said.

He slid onto the bed, sliding in close to her as his arms slid around her. "Yes sexy."

"You were right," she said.

He smirked. "I just don't like her. I never have. That's all it was. Clay even got a bad feeling about her."

"Thank you for putting up with it."

"Babe, it's your house. No matter how I feel about her, she's your friend."

"And if something else comes up like that again, promise that you say no right off the bat."

He nodded and untied the single little bow holding her dress up. "Ridge."

"Mm," he purred into her ear as every inch of her body jumped to attention.

"Um."

"What," he asked as he kissed down the back of her neck again.

"I love you."

"Love you back," he teased as he slid the satiny fabric from her shoulder, revealing that she literally had nothing on under the dress.

"You were basically walking around naked intentionally. Nice. I mean, if it's us, go for it, but you had people over."

"Oh, I know handsome. I was taunting you intentionally."

"It worked. Now about this dress."

"What?"

He kissed down her back and his arms slid around her hips. "Ridge."

"What?"

"What are you doing," she asked as he started teasing again.

"Starting over from this afternoon," he teased as his fingers teased and taunted until her body was throbbing for him. "What," he teased as she tried to slide in closer to him. He taunted and taunted until her body was going into overdrive and her heart was pounding so loud, she could hear the swoosh of her blood in her ears.

"What," she asked noticing the taunting getting worse.

He kept going and he was still fully dressed. "Ridge."

"Mm," he said as he kept going.

"I want you."

"I know," he teased.

"No more teasing."

"Because you give up," he joked.

"Because I need…"

He kissed her. "Need what," he teased.

"Ridge."

When he pulled her on top of him, her heart was racing, and her legs were getting shaky. "What do you want," he asked as he kissed the edge of her ear.

"Jeans off."

He smirked and kept going. "What do you want Faith? Say it," he said. She went to grab the button of his jeans and he held her hands. "Say it."

"I want you. I want…"

He kissed her neck and she turned to face him. "Faith."

She undid the button of his jeans. "Tell me baby. Just say it." When she undid the zipper of his jeans, he smirked. "Say it or I'm going to bed."

"You aren't leaving this room."

"Well?" He kissed her. When he felt her hand slide down his boxers, he shook his head.

"So, now you're gonna attempt to tease me are you," he teased.

"Only fair," she joked.

She was at one heck of a disadvantage. A large one. One heck of a major disadvantage. When he pinned her hands to the bed, she was back to being the one being taunted. "Ridge."

"What?"

"Jeans off." He smirked and nibbled her lips.

"Alright." He kicked his jeans off then pulled his shirt off, pinning her hands back down to the pillow. He linked their fingers, and he kissed down her torso.

"Ridge."

He looked up. "Yes sexy."

"Boxers off."

He smirked. "You sure?" She nodded.

He had to admit, his jeans were getting uncomfortable around her. He was too turned on. When he slid the boxers off, Faith was looking him up and down like she was in shock. "What," he asked.

"Nothin," Faith said as he slid her legs around him, briefly letting go of her hands.

"Now, tell me what you want."

She went to try and move closer, but he wouldn't let her. "Say it."

"I need you. I..."

He kissed her again. "Say it," he replied.

"I want you to...Shit Ridge" He kissed her. When she muttered the words that he'd never heard pass her lips, he smirked.

"You swear," he teased.

"Usually under my breath," she joked. He kissed her again, taunting her into a frenzy again and when his body connected to hers, it was like someone had plugged her in and turned her libido on high. They kept going. More than once, her body had almost clamped on him as she climaxed over and over. When his body gave in, he could barely move.

"Ridge."

"Sexy."

"I think maybe I might need a drink," she teased.

"Good thing I brought it up."

When she grabbed his, and he saw it, she drank three gulps and put it down. "That was not mine."

"Nope," he teased as he kissed her neck. She shook her head, and he went to move when her legs tightened around him. "Don't move."

He smirked and kissed her. "At the rate you're going, we're gonna be unconscious all day and night tomorrow."

She smirked. "I don't really need to get up," she joked.

"I do babe. I promise you." She kissed him and he shook his head. "I'm getting up." She shook her head.

He smirked and managed to get up. "Ridge."

"I'll be right back," he said.

He kissed her and went into his room. Faith shook her head and when he came back in, he slid onto the bed and right into her arms, pulling the blankets over him. "What were you doin," Faith asked.

"Taunting 2.0," he joked.

Faith kissed him. Just as she went to curl into his arms, her phone went off.

"Don't care," she replied. He kissed down her neck and his phone went off. He shook his head, put the toys down that he'd got from his drawer and reached over her to grab his cell.

"It's your dad," Ridge said. He answered putting it on speaker.

"Sir," Ridge said.

"Faith alright," he asked.

"I'm fine dad. What's wrong?"

"You didn't hear about the storm," her dad asked.

"Rain," Ridge asked.

"Flood."

"We're at the house. No issue at all."

"Good. Baby, you alright?"

"Yes. I'm happy," Faith said. "Good. Keep me posted. Did you get an update about the stuff they found at the beach house," her dad asked.

"Sent you over the information. Both of the people we suspected."

"Thank you for taking care of what I couldn't," her dad said.

"Most welcome. Enjoy your vacation. We're good," Ridge said.

"I will. Love you baby girl," her dad said.

"Love you too. Give mom and aunt Addy a hug for me."

"Funny," her dad said as they all hung up.

He smirked and kissed her. "Maybe we should go get some sleep," Ridge said.

"Depends on what you were planning," Faith teased.

"You need rest love."

"Like I said, depends on what you were planning before that call." He shook his head and kissed her. "Ridge."

"You're sleeping. We have lots of time sexy."

She slid into his arms. "Tell me."

He kissed her. "Stay here." He took the things that he'd brought into the room and took them back to the guest room, hiding them into his bag. He grabbed his joggers, put them on the chair in her room and when he went to slide into bed with her, she was out cold. He smirked. He washed up and slid into bed beside her. He slid his arms around her and snuggled her tight to his chest.

"I love you," he said quietly as he kissed her shoulder.

"I love you too," he heard Faith say while she slept. He went to nod off and her fingers linked with his.

He looked at her, curled up to him. His body craved her every second of the day. Every inch of him wanted her at every slight breeze. He was hot and bothered so many times. She'd made him a freaking mess and a horn dog all in one. He loved the scent of her hair, the feel of her skin against his. Everything about her was becoming an addiction. Her little movements when they curled up watching a movie. When he knew that she was getting hot and bothered and could just tease and taunt her. All of it had him past hot and bothered and falling head over heels in a matter of a week. He had his grandmother's engagement ring burning a hole in his bag. Calling his name. Calling him to put it on the finger it was always meant to be on. Instead, he had her in his arms. He had his angel in his arms saying I love you like it wasn't a big thing. It took one weekend. One. He worried that it was just because neither of them had dated in way too long. When he realized that it was love and not just a fling, he'd never thought twice. Now, he just had to figure out if they were really gonna make it.

Chapter 8

Ridge woke up the next morning and was about to go get a workout in when Faith woke up. "Where are you going," she asked.

"Sleep babe. I'm gonna go get a workout in." He kissed her and she pulled him into her arms. "Faith."

"I'm gonna come with you."

He kissed her. "Sleep."

She shook her head and he smirked. "Alright then sexy get up. We're doing a workout." He kissed her again and she got up. He smirked, grabbed her hand and she slid into her workout clothes. He walked downstairs, flipped off the motion detectors and walked downstairs into the gym. He flipped the lights on, went and grabbed two reusable water bottles and put everything together for the protein smoothies after the workout.

He flipped the music on and warmed up on the treadmill, running full speed for a half hour. When he spotted her on the steps, he smirked.

"What are you smiling at," he teased.

"Watching my sexy man running," Faith teased as she stretched out and did her yoga out of his sight line. When he finished on the treadmill, he went to start doing weights.

"Ridge."

"Sexy."

"Can we go down to the beach house?"

He took a deep breath. "Your people are coming back. Kinda want to be here when they get here."

"They're not coming until 6."

He shook his head. "Then we're staying today. That okay?" Faith smirked. "And you're actually doing work this time instead of walking around in a naked dress with nothing on under it."

"I like that dress," she teased as she hopped onto the treadmill with a smirk.

"I'm sure you do. That dress is not happening outside of the house. Agreed," he asked.

"Nope." He shook his head.

They did a workout, taunting each other the entire time. From weights to machines to stretches and more weights. When they finished, she was watching him with a smoothie in hand and the other made for him. She handed him the other smoothie and he sat down with her. "You good," he asked.

Faith smirked. "Yep."

"You nodded off," he teased.

"I know. I guess you were right. After all of that yesterday, I was kind of exhausted."

He kissed her. "Come on sexy. I'll make you breakfast."

They walked up to the kitchen, and she went and put the pan on to make omelets. "You're cooking," he asked. Faith nodded. He kissed her and went to make coffee.

"No," Faith said. He smirked. "Alright then." He smirked, chopped up the fruit, put a little on each plate and made the bacon, plating it as she plated the omelets.

They sat down to eat, and Faith smirked. "What are you all smiley about," Ridge asked.

"Well, I was kinda thinking. What if we just hung out? I can get some work stuff done, then we can watch a movie or something."

"I know what you're thinking Faith. We both have to actually get work done."

"What would you think if we went for a drive later then?"

He kissed her. "We can go out for dinner if you want," he said.

Faith looked at him. "Okay," she said.

"An actual date." She nodded and he kissed her. "Whatever makes you happy beautiful." She smirked.

By the time they finished breakfast, they were back to taunting each other. He put the dishes away then Faith taunted him. "What you up to there sexy," he asked as her arms slid around his torso, feeling his ab muscles.

"Thinking," Faith said.

"I bet," he teased.

When Faith went for the drawstring of his joggers, he grabbed her hand. "Do not start that. I swear, we are gonna be upstairs instead of working. No taunting."

She shook her head, kissing his shoulder. "Faith." He turned to face her. "If you start, you do know that you're gonna be working from bed right," he teased.

"And? I can write emails anywhere."

He shook his head, picked her up, wrapping her legs around his hips and made his way upstairs and walked into his bedroom. "What are...."

"You seriously think that I forgot about this," he teased. Faith smirked and he shook his head, leaning her onto the bed and kicking the door closed, leaving them in complete darkness.

"Ridge." She felt her shorts sliding off, then her sports bra.

"What," he whispered as her body burst into goosebumps.

"You're taunting."

"And you started it," he joked.

Faith shook her head and she heard a buzz. "Ridge."

"Yes sexy," he said as she felt him kiss up her inner thigh.

"I know what you're doing," she said.

"Really. Huh. Go figure," he said as she felt him against the apex of her thighs and felt the heat of his lips against her.

"Ridge."

"Mm." When he slid her legs over his shoulders, he could feel her legs almost shaking. He smirked and that buzz was working up her leg.

"Ridge."

"Faith." When she felt the warm buzz against her, she reached for him.

"What," he teased as she felt his lips kissing up her torso.

"Come here."

He kissed her breast, nibbling. When the buzzing made her toes curl almost into knots, she was about to lose it. He kissed her, devouring her lips and deepening the kiss to the point that her legs were wrapped tight around him. "Faith."

"What," she asked as her body tensed and her nails dug into his arm.

"I love you." She got a grin ear to ear and kissed him as he deepened the kiss and had her entire body throbbing and her toes curling into pretzels.

"So, about that whole thing about you taunting me," he joked.

"Fine. I give in."

"Oh, I know. I'm just getting started," he teased.

Faith shook her head and he could see every movement. Her being in the dark meant that she had no idea what he was up to. When the buzz started again, she shook her head as her body almost tensed the moment it was near her skin. "Ridge."

"Sexy," he said as he kissed her.

Her arms slid around his neck. "No more..." He kissed her with a kiss that gave her goosebumps and made her heart almost leap from her chest. "What are you trying to do," Faith asked as her body tensed.

"Taunt you until you can't move. Kinda part of my plan," he teased.

"And then what," Faith asked.

"Remind you that I'm never ever leaving your side."

"Someday."

"What," he said as he turned the speed up on the buzzing.

"Someday I'm gonna get you back for this," she said as her toes turned into double knots.

He kissed her, then kissed his way down her torso, still taunting her. "Ridge."

"What?"

"I need you now."

"Oh, I know sexy. I'm not done yet," he teased.

He could feel the smile that he knew she had ear to ear and leaned her to her side. "What," Faith asked. He smirked and slid his joggers to the floor as he leaned his body onto the bed behind her. "Ridge."

"Umm hmm," he almost purred into her ear. He felt her back arch against him and slid his arm around her torso, sliding the buzzing away from her. He threw it into his bag and she went to turn to face him when his fingers took over. Her hand slid over his and held his hand steady.

"I can't," Faith said.

"Yes or no," he asked.

"Yes. A million times yes." He pulled her tight against him and they had sex. Her body was already humming and he kept taunting until her body tensed around him. He kept going until he had her pinned onto the bed with their fingers linked, hers almost turning into a fist and listening to her almost screaming his name. "Ridge."

"Baby."

"I can't," she said as she was almost panting. He exploded into her and she dug her nails into his fingers.

"Oh...my..." He kissed her, muffling her from making more noise. "Ridge." Her body shuddered around him and he leaned to his back, bringing her with him.

"Faith," he said as she leaned her head onto his chest.

"What," she said as he felt her face smile.

"You good?"

"I don't think I can move," she said.

He kissed her forehead. "You sure," he teased.

"I can't move."

"Good," he teased. He flipped a light on and they curled up on the bed.

"Ridge."

"Yes."

"I don't think you can leave the house."

He smirked. "And why is that sexy?"

"Because I don't think that I can live without you."

"It's been a week."

"It's been a lot longer than that."

"Since we met up again." He kissed her forehead. "You're talking crazy."

"No, I'm not," Faith said.

He shook his head, snuggling her to him. "Wait until you're at least rested. Right now, your mind and your heart are of in la la land," he teased.

"Ridge." He shook his head, feeling her heart racing against his chest. Feeling her breathing start to calm back down. "And what would be so wrong with us together?"

"What are you saying," he asked.

"I'm saying we waited years for this. Years. We've known each other since we were little kids. What's so wrong with us being together now?"

"We are. All I'm saying is that we need to slow down. I love you, and I always have, but if you want more than just dating, you need to tell me."

"Why? So, you can walk out and never come back?"

He shook his head. "You have no idea," he said. Faith looked up at him. "What," he asked.

"Say whatever it is," Faith said. He shook his head and slid her up closer to him. "Look at me." She shook her head and wouldn't do it. He slid one finger to her chin, lifting her gaze so she was staring into his eyes.

"Faith."

"What?" He looked into her eyes, falling into the endless pools of emerald green. Her eyes almost glowed when she was crying.

"Look at me." She stared up at him and gulped.

"Do I look like I want to vanish from your life?"

"Ridge."

"Do I? Do I look like the man who'd walk away and never want to see you again?"

"No, but that doesn't..." He knew she was worried. He knew the fear she had because he'd seen it in himself every time he'd tried to get the guts to contact her.

"That doesn't what?"

"It doesn't mean that you won't."

He kissed her. "I crave you. I crave your skin, your body, your hands, your lips. I crave every inch of you. A breeze passes me by around you and I want to kiss you and carry you to wherever we can be alone enough that I can get another feel or another…"

She kissed him. "Ridge."

"I'm not leaving you. I'm not going away, I'm not leaving town, I'm not leaving the country and I'm not leaving this damn bed until you understand that."

"Meaning what," Faith asked.

"Speak. If you want us to be a damn us, say it. I already know what I want. I never said anything different," he said.

Faith looked up at him. "Ridge, I love you. You know that."

"And?" He kissed her. "Whatever you're gonna say, just say it Faith."

"I love you. I don't want to mess all of this up. That's all."

He took a deep breath. "You won't."

"Ridge, please."

"What? Nothing is gonna change unless you tell me to walk out the door. There's nothing tying me here except your security. I love you Faith. Just tell me what you want."

She looked at him. "Ridge."

"Say the words. For once, just say the dang words."

"I want you here. I want you to stay. I want us to be together. Us. You and me," Faith said.

"About freaking time," he said.

He kissed her and she slid into his lap. "I don't want to ever lose you."

He smirked. "Literally took all of this. You exploding. You losing every inhibition you've ever freaking had. It took you getting…"

"Us."

"It took your toes curling into quadruple knots for you to just say it."

"I wanted to say it before this."

"Then why didn't you?" She shook her head and he lifted her gaze back to meet his.

"Because I didn't want…"

He kissed her, pulling her legs around his waist. "Faith, you are beautiful. You're amazing. You're inspiring You're the love of my dang life. All I want is you. What else do you need me to say?"

"Ridge, do you really want this," she asked. He devoured her lips. Just as he was about to say something else, his phone went off, then hers. She looked at her phone and answered.

"Hello," Faith said.

"Miss Faith, it's Agrid. I was in a car accident. I wanted to let you know."

"Are you alright?"

"I'm in the hospital. I can't come back to the house tonight."

"Alright. We'll figure something out. Keep me posted. I'll come to the hospital if I need to."

"Thank you. I'll send you the information."

Faith hung up with her and Ridge went to get up. Faith stopped him.

"What do you mean there was an accident," Ridge said as he got up and pulled his joggers on.

He walked downstairs to the security office and his phone rang with a call from her dad's security. "There was an accident. The security that Faith originally had for her house were injured.

Obviously, something else is going on, but we need you to step up. Can you add to your team," her dad's security asked.

"I have two other guys who were in our platoon that I added to the security team for outside jobs. I can definitely get them here," Ridge said.

"I want two posted at the house at all times. Just keep her safe. Something seems really off."

"Her friend Lacey showed last night and attempted to plant something here too. We got it before anything was noticed. It's in the safe in the office."

"Good. I'll come over tomorrow and pick it up. Just please keep her safe."

"I will." Ridge hung up with him, called Clay and Kellen and got them to come down and take over the security for the house. When they replied back that they were packing and on the way, Ridge leaned back in the chair. When he felt his chair being pulled back, he shook his head.

"Faith."

"What?"

"Work."

"Oh, I know," she teased as she slid into his lap in nothing but his t-shirt.

"Clay and Kellen are coming."

"Why," Faith asked.

"Both of your security are out. They're taking over."

She shook her head. "And if I said that I had all the security I wanted?"

"Then you'd have to get used to them being here. Your dad's orders."

She shook his head. "I want to get back to our conversation," she said undoing the drawstring of his joggers.

"Faith."

"What?"

"We're not doing this in here." She shoved the door closed. He shook his head and she sat down on the desk, sliding his laptop closed and out of her way. "Not in here." She nodded and he shook his head, picking her up, wrapping her legs around him and walked up the steps to her bedroom, leaning her onto her bed.

"Stay here," he said.

"Why?"

"Faith." Just as he said it, her phone rang. She grabbed it and ended up in a meeting. He shook his head, went and got showered and stared at his bag. There was no way in hell that he was proposing now. Not after that. Not when she'd finally opened her mouth and spit it out. She'd finally said what he needed her to. His hands slid to either side of the shower head as he leaned against the wall, letting the water hit him in the face to knock him out of the idiotic thoughts running through his head. When the water wasn't doing enough, he shook his head, finishing his shower, and stepped out. He wrapped a towel around his waist and freshened up. He shaved, put his cologne on that she loved, and went to slide into dress pants when he heard footsteps. He smirked and turned.

"I have to go into the office."

"Then we go."

She looked at him and slid in close. "You smell too good," she teased.

"And you, my love, are completely and utterly under-dressed to go to the office."

"You're wearing that?"

"Was considering pants," he joked.

His short hair was even hotter when he was clean-shaven. "Ridge."

"I'm not leaving your side. The other two guys are on their way over here anyway."

"Other two?"

"Clay and Kellen."

Faith shook her head. "I don't really have a choice in that do I?" He shook his head, kissed her with a minty toothpaste kiss and she went and showered alone for the first time in days.

He slid a dress shirt on, slid on his dress pants and grabbed his wallet, earpiece and phone. He sent off an email to the team about Kellen and Clay and the earpieces. Within 5 minutes, he had a reply from them all.

Faith stepped out of the shower, wrapped herself in a warm fluffy towel and towel-dried her hair. She freshened up and went into her closet, grabbing a dress and a pair of heels. Enough to get Ridge's undivided attention if she wanted it. She did her hair and makeup, slid her jewelry on and grabbed her cell, putting it in her purse as she made her way downstairs. Just as she did, Kellen and Clay were coming in.

"Oh," Faith said as she looked up.

"Just gonna show them the office, then we're out of here," Ridge said. He showed them to their room, grabbed something from his bag and brought them down to the security office. He handed off the info they needed and gave them the full layout of the house to keep everything secure.

"So, you and the lady are together," Kellen asked.

Ridge nodded. "I'm going to the office downtown with her. Are you guys good for a few hours?"

Clay nodded. "All handled. See you tonight," Clay said as Ridge walked towards Faith.

He handed Faith her laptop, grabbed his and they headed off in her SUV. "Ridge."

"What?"

"I like the suit."

"Thanks," he teased still all business.

"Question. Is there a reason we have to add more security?"

"Yes."

"That's all you're gonna give me?" He nodded. "Are you seriously carrying a gun?"

He nodded. "Part of the uniform."

"Ridge."

"Yes."

"Since I get to be boss for a while, what are you gonna do?"

"Keep you safe."

"Does that include you and I on my sofa?"

"No."

She shook her head. "Ridge."

"I'm there to work Faith. It's not a game."

"I know, but still."

"Didn't have enough this morning?"

"Nope," she teased as he saw her leg almost tremble.

"Faith."

"Fine. Legs are shaky. That's all."

She tried to reach over the center console to at least hold his hand, but he shook his head. "I know what you're doing."

Barefoot Bodyguard

"No you don't. I was trying to hold your hand."

"My hand isn't where you're reaching Faith."

She smirked. "And?"

"You're like a damn rabbit right now."

She put her hand out and he slid his hand in hers as she linked their fingers. He kissed each one, holding her hand to his face as he drove. "I have no idea why you were single. I mean really," Faith said.

He smirked. "Dress," he teased.

"Yep. Why," Faith asked.

"Are you at least wearing…"

"Why don't you find out for yourself," she whispered as they got stuck in traffic.

"Because we're behaving Faith." She shook her head and went to slide his hand to her inner thigh. "Faith."

When she slid his hand under her dress, he knew. At least she'd finally understood that she had to wear something under the dress.

"I swear, you are so totally not the woman I knew way back when."

"And it's all your fault," she teased.

They pulled into the office, parked and he got her door for her, locking up the SUV and grabbing their things. "Ridge, promise me something," Faith said as they walked into the elevator.

"What?"

"Promise me that you will stay with me."

He shook his head. "Concentrate on work. We can talk about the rest later."

She nodded and slid her hand in his. "Office. Work."

"Mine," Faith teased.

He shook his head, handed Faith her bag and as soon as the elevator door opened, they headed inside. He walked Faith to her office and was stunned.

It was wrap around glass, 5 chairs that were way too comfortable looking, a massive sofa, marble table and an all-glass desk. It's like she was on display for the damn world in that room. Luckily, her door was solid and bulletproof. Nobody could see through it, and there were no windows facing the rest of the office. She had a private bathroom, but other than that it was like a protective bubble. She sat down at her desk and went into work mode, plugging in her laptop and going through papers. When there was a knock at her office door, Ridge got up.

"Miss Faith," the secretary said.

"Kelly, my bodyguard Ridge. Ridge, Kelly," Faith said as she handed Faith her latte and the paperwork she needed for her meeting.

"Thank you," Faith said.

"Most welcome. Ridge, did you want a coffee?"

"Please," he said.

"Same as mine," Faith replied.

"I'll get it," Kelly said.

"Faith."

"You don't have to come to the meeting. My dad's security is guarding the office."

"Still," Ridge said.

"I know. It's fine. I promise you."

He shook his head and Kelly came in with a latte for him. "I appreciate it," Ridge said.

Kelly headed out and Faith got up. She walked over to the door, locked it and kissed him. "I'm doing the meeting, finishing the paperwork and we can go home."

"Faith."

She kissed him again. When he picked her up, she smirked. He walked into the small powder room and closed the door. "What," Faith asked.

His hands slid up her legs as he sat her down on the edge of the counter. "What time is the meeting?"

"45 minutes. Why," Faith asked.

He smirked. His hand slid up to the apex of her thighs, and her legs almost twitched. "You were saying," he teased.

"I didn't mean now," Faith replied.

When she felt his fingers, she shook her head. "Don't start that."

"The thing you wanted to start while I was driving?"

She nodded. She took a swift inhale when she felt his fingers start the teasing. "Still," he teased.

"You are not playing fair."

"Not a fan of fair." She grabbed for his dress pants and he stopped her, brushing her hand away. Her body clamped down on his fingers as he kept going. One way or another, he was gonna taunt her into giving in and putting her in a mood for the meeting. She'd be quivering and smirking the whole way through and he knew it. "Damn," Faith said.

When he smirked and kissed the front of her neck, he knew. "Fine. I give in. I can't do…"

He kissed her. "Good."

His hands slid away from her and she shook her head. "I may need someone to carry me to the meeting."

When he licked his fingers, she almost climaxed. "Ridge."

He smirked and kissed her. "Go get to your meeting," he teased. Faith shook her head.

"Remind me that I get to pay you back for that," she joked. He kissed her, brushed her lipstick from his lips and went into her office. He grabbed his laptop and went through emails.

Faith made her way out of the bathroom and shook her head. She took her seat, with a smirk ear to ear and he unlocked her office door. When her assistant came in 10 minutes later to let her know the meeting was starting early, she smirked. She grabbed her coffee, laptop and her papers and went into the meeting room. They got the negotiations done for it when she got a message on her laptop:

> *When we're home, you're gonna regret that dress.*

She replied back:

> *Was sorta hoping backseat of SUV. I'm not done with you.*

He smirked from her office as he sat down with her dad's security to go through the updates. When he was done, he looked and saw another message:

> *I have to come back in tomorrow. You're gonna have to stop being so tempting. You even smell good. Not fair.*

He smirked and replied:

> *And here I thought you liked the professional look. Still crave you.*

He went through more emails and got a reply:

> *Oh I do. I also like the naked look. The one from this morning. Getting me turned on mid-meeting isn't playing fair.*

He smirked:

Barefoot Bodyguard

So, if I told you I wanted to bend you over your desk and take full advantage until you couldn't walk anymore?

He took a photo of his hand on her desk and sent it to her.

When he heard footsteps 3 minutes later, and the clicking of high heels down the hallway getting closer and closer, he smirked. She came into the office and he locked the door behind her. "You are not playing fair."

"Never have."

She put her laptop down and he came up behind her. "What," she asked.

"Bend over."

"Ridge."

"You asked." She bent over and within a matter of a few minutes, they were having sex with her bent over that desk. When her legs started trembling, he could feel her body almost reaching it's climax and pulled away.

"Ridge."

"Shh."

"What are you doing," she asked.

"You started it," he whispered.

"Get..."

He kissed her. "You have work."

"I don't care."

"We can finish at home."

"No. Now," Faith said.

He kissed her and she pulled him to her as they finished what they'd started.

"Holy crap," she said as her body crashed around him.

"You have no idea what I have planned," Ridge teased.

"Meaning what," Faith asked.

He nibbled up her neck and she smirked. "What time is the next meeting," he asked.

"20 minutes," she replied.

He kissed her and sat her back on the desk. "What," she asked.

"Stay."

"Why," Faith asked as she felt the teasing start all over again.

"Ridge."

"As soon as it's done, we're heading back."

She nodded as one flick of his finger had her toes curling in her heels. "I swear," Faith said.

He smirked, kissed her, and kept going until her body tensed. "Not fair at all," she replied.

When he pulled away, she shook her head. "Ridge."

"What?"

"At some point, you know payback is coming right?"

"You asked," he replied. She shook her head and he kissed her again. When there was a knock at her office door, he smirked and went and unlocked the door with beyond shaky legs.

"Miss Faith, we're ready for you for the next meeting." Faith shook her head, got up and he slid his hand in hers.

"No more teasing."

He nodded and went back to emails. He got everything up to date, including an update from everyone on the houses. When she came back in an hour later, he was on the phone with his mom. "We're just getting ready to head out. I promise you that we're fine."

"Ridge, if you're thinking about giving her grandma's ring, tell me. I want to be there to cheer you two on. I had no idea that you two were that close."

"Well, it sorta happened. I wasn't expecting it either."

"I'm glad that you finally found m glad that you finally found your one. I thought your dad and I were lucky. I can't believe that you're planning it."

"I'll talk to you later mom. Let me know how the trip is going."

"I will and good luck."

He hung up with his mom as he heard the click of her office door.

"And how's mom," Faith asked as she walked over and sat down in his lap.

"Good. She said to give you a big hug for her. How was your meeting?"

"Long. Contracts were both signed and done. All good."

"You ready to head back?"

"Dinner," Faith said.

"At home."

She shook her head. "Out. We're all dressed up."

"Where," he asked. Faith smirked and within 2 minutes, she had a reservation for the two of them way in the back of Hall's Chop house.

They got there, went out to their table and he ordered them each a glass of wine. When the waitress headed off, he slid her closer to him in the booth. "What," Faith asked. He slid his hand in hers. The waitress came back with their wine and poured them each a glass. He ordered them each dinner and Faith looked at him. "I know something's going on in that mind of yours. What's wrong," Faith asked. He kissed her and slid his fingers to entwine hers. "Ridge." He kissed her again.

"I need to do something. No interrupting."

"What are you doing," Faith asked.

"Woman, shush."

She smirked. He took a deep breath. "I have known you my entire life, and I've loved you my entire life. Up until recently, I had no idea how much I loved you. We've fought, we've screamed and we made up for a lifetime of mistakes. I don't want to waste any more time."

"Ridge."

"Your mom already gave me her blessing and so did your dad. I married you when we were 6 according to your mom, but this time it's forever."

"What are you saying?"

He gulped and tried to breathe. "I don't want life without you either. I never have. I just want you and I. Will you marry me," Ridge asked as he looked into Faith's eyes.

She looked at him with her mouth open. "Ridge."

"Yes or no," he asked.

"Holy crap. Don't you think it's too soon?"

"Yes or no Faith? The question isn't that hard. Either is the answer."

"You sure you want to do this?"

He looked at her. "I'm waiting."

She looked at him, seeing the tears welling in his eyes. When she nodded, he looked up at her.

"What?"

"Yes," she said.

"Faith."

"A billion times yes."

He kissed her, devouring her lips. When she felt a ring slide onto her finger, she smirked. One look and she was in awe of it.

"Ridge."

"What," he asked.

"It's beautiful."

"Grandma's. She gave it to mom in her will."

"How long have you had it?"

"Remember the other day when I went to the storage locker?"

She nodded. "It was at mom and dad's. I went to go get it."

"You lied," she teased.

"White lie. Worth it to see the look on your face."

She kissed him. "Mine," she said as they broke the kiss.

"Forever," he replied.

He smirked and she shook her head. "Ridge, seriously though."

He kissed her. "Discuss it when we're home."

"But..."

He devoured her lips and she managed to almost melt into his arms. "But nothing." He kissed her and the waitress came with their dinner, and a bottle of champagne from the owner.

By the time they were heading out, they had the champagne in a to go bag and were heading back in the SUV. When they got most of the way home, Faith shook her head. "I can't believe that you did that at the dang restaurant."

"It was either that, or when we were in bed. Kinda thought you'd prefer it to be at the restaurant."

Faith looked at the ring. The sparkle, but not too much, and the history that made the ring that much more special. "You know that you didn't need to do this right," Faith asked.

Barefoot Bodyguard

"The rubies are from my grandmother's ring. The stone was one I picked, and the smaller stones total the years we've known each other."

He kissed her at the light. "It's beautiful."

"And one of a kind, just like you."

Faith smirked and slid her hand into his. "Still, are you sure this is what you want," she asked.

"I never would've done it if I didn't."

She looked at him. "It's been a week."

"Nobody said it'd be tomorrow."

"So, we're waiting?" Ridge nodded. "You sure?"

He smirked. "Faith, I want you to tell your mom and dad in person. I want us to tell them together."

She got a grin ear to ear. "I like how you think," Faith joked. He got to the gate, put in the code and made his way up to the house, watching the gate close behind them. When they walked inside, Clay was at the door.

"And," Ridge asked.

"We have a small problem. I found something else in the house."

"Which house," Faith asked.

"This one."

"What," Ridge asked as he went into the security office. Clay showed him the three devices that they'd found and deactivated.

"Where were they?"

"The two guest rooms that you said were ours. There was one in her bedroom, but it was on the balcony not inside," Kellen said.

Ridge shook his head. "Did we check the ceilings and artwork?"

Kellen nodded. "And?"

"Nothing else. Double checked."

"Rescan the main bedroom, bathroom, and closets. Let me know if you find anything." Kellen and Clay went up to double check everything and Faith looked at Ridge.

"What's wrong?"

"Something is in this house. They're handling it."

Chapter 9

She looked at him. "Ridge."

"I know."

"If there is..."

He kissed her. "Come," he said as he walked her into her office. He scanned it, cleared everything in the office and sat her on her oversized desk.

"What," she asked. He kissed her, pulled the shutters closed and the curtain and locked the office door. "What," Faith asked as he slid into her arms.

One kiss. One kiss that was intense, deep, and toe-curling kiss and she was at his mercy. He slid the heels off her feet. "Ridge," Faith said.

"What?"

"Not..." He kissed her again and picked her up, sitting on the sofa so she was in his lap straddling him.

"Tell me what you want," Ridge said.

"Bedroom."

He shook his head. "Not until it's cleared."

"Your..."

He kissed her. "Now you know why that happened this morning," he teased.

Faith shook her head and he smirked. She slid the too sexy lace panties off and kissed him. "Faith."

"What?"

"I love you."

She kissed him and went to reach for the button of his dress pants when he stopped her. "Ridge."

He devoured her lips again and there was a knock at the door. He'd always had super sensitive hearing, and that moment was no different.

"Yep," Ridge said.

"Clear. Nothing else," Kellen said.

"Thanks," Ridge said. Faith went to undo his dress pants again when he stopped her. He picked her up, walked upstairs and kicked the bedroom door closed. He leaned her onto the bed, made sure the curtains and shutters were closed and the patio door was locked and walked back over to her as she undid his dress pants. "Faith."

"What?"

"Getting carried away?"

Barefoot Bodyguard

She shook her head. "Mine."

"I bet," he teased as he kissed her and leaned into her arms. She smirked and pulled at his dress pants.

"Off."

"You sure?"

"Why," Faith asked as she felt the zipper of her skirt sliding undone. One look and she knew what he was thinking.

"Off." He slid them off and slid her to the pillows.

"Now, what else did you want," he teased.

She undid his shirt and his tie, sliding it off. "You," she said.

"And?" She smirked as she slid the skirt off. He kissed up her leg and she shook her head.

"Ridge, come here."

He leaned into her arms, kissing her neck then her ear until he felt her legs curling around his. "Tell me what you want."

"All of you."

He shook his head. "Faith."

She looked at him. "I'm yours. Tell me what you want. Say it," he said.

Faith kissed him and he slid her shirt right off. "I love you," she said.

"Love you too sexy," he replied.

He slid into her arms, snuggling her tight to him as they kissed and snuggled. One kiss led to two, they led to a deeper kiss that had her toes curling, then he made love to his fiancée for the first time. The one that he had always wanted. The one that he'd always dreamed of, and the one he intended on never ever letting go of. When they managed to come up for air an hour or two later, his phone went off. "Taking bets," he teased.

"I say your mom," Faith teased as he grabbed his phone and saw the call display, putting it on speakerphone.

"Hey mom," Ridge said.

"Hey. How is everything going," his mom asked.

"Are they there with you," he teased.

"Yes," Faith's mom said.

"Well, we have a little news."

"Which would be," her dad asked.

"Ridge and I are engaged," Faith said.

"What," her dad said as Ridge heard the disdain in his voice.

"It's not like we don't know each other. We've known each other our entire lives," Faith said.

"Baby, that's wonderful. Tell me all about how he did it," her mom said as Faith heard the sound of her mom smacking her dad's arm. They talked and the more they talked, the more Ridge was second-guessing taking that step. He kissed Faith's shoulder and got up, walking into his room, and grabbing his joggers.

"Where did Ridge go," his mom asked.

"He had to check something downstairs. It's fine," Faith said. Faith talked to her folks and Ridge went downstairs to the security office.

"You okay," Kellen asked.

"Was. Long story."

"Congrats by the way. Nice ring," Clay said.

"Thanks. Did y'all find anything at all," Ridge asked.

"We have it handled. It's fine. Go be with the fiancée."

Ridge shook his head. "Emails," Ridge asked.

"Nothing. It's fine. Breathe," Kellen said. Ridge went and grabbed himself a double Jack and coke and sat down on the sofa.

He kicked himself in a million ways between the moment he sat down and the moment that he felt Faith's gaze from the steps. He finished his drink, got up and made a second one, adding in more Jack and sat back down. "You do realize it's a lot easier to just bring the bottle right," Faith asked as she walked over and took the bottle from the counter. She put it down on the table in front of him and sat down on the sofa beside him.

"What's wrong," she asked as she handed him back his cell phone.

"Nothing."

She shook her head. "Ridge, don't say it's nothing. Say it."

"Your dad's pissed."

"He is stunned. That's it," Faith said.

"He's mad. Really mad."

"Ridge."

He shook his head. "He's mad. I get it."

"He's not mad."

"Faith, I know that tone. It's the same one I heard when I told him about Cameron."

Faith shook her head and sat down in Ridge's lap, straddling him, and leaning him against the back of the sofa. "I'm telling you now, he's just irritated that he didn't know you were doing it." Ridge shook his head and finished the drink. "What's really going on?" He shook his head.

"I got too far ahead of myself."

Faith shook her head. "Look at me. Ridge, we can do whatever we want to. Stop. Neither of them get a say. If you wanted to do it, you had the right to do whatever you wanted. We're engaged. There's nothing wrong with that. There's nothing wrong with us being together."

He kissed her. "Up."

"No. What's wrong?" He shook his head and got up, sliding her to the sofa.

She shook her head and called her dad. "Baby."

"I need you to answer something. Were you mad when we told you?"

"Surprised and wondering why I didn't know anything about it. Can I speak with Ridge?"

"No. He thinks that you're mad."

"Faith, I love you, but I need to talk to him." She got up and saw Ridge pouring a glass of Jack. The special reserve extra strong Jack. She handed Ridge the phone and he shook his head. She put it to his head and kissed him.

"Ridge," her dad said.

"Sir."

"All I was trying to say was that I was surprised. I didn't know that's what you were planning. I know how you feel about her, but I honestly didn't know you were even thinking that."

"It's fine. We're waiting a while anyway."

"Ridge."

"Sir."

"Do you love her?"

"More than I even knew."

"And are you sure that you want her in your life?"

"Always have. If you don't..."

"Ridge, I didn't say that. I know you'd never hurt her because you know I'd come after you guns blazing."

"Yes sir."

"Is she..."

"No. I just realized that I wanted more than just us dating. We've known each other since she was two-days old. I think that's a long time," Ridge said as he guzzled down half the glass.

"Just slow down with the rest of the wedding stuff. Let us help you two plan it out. Deal?"

"Yes sir."

"Ridge, we're family. We've been family since you were a baby. Stop with the sir."

"Alright," he said.

"Now, can you get my daughter out of la la land and put her back on the phone."

"Not a problem," Ridge said as he handed Faith back her phone.

He finished his drink and walked back into the security office. "You good," Kellen asked.

"I guess. Did we double check all the other bedrooms?"

"We checked yours and the other three guest rooms. There was nothing else there. You're fine.

Both of y'all are safe. We're gonna start scanning outside in the morning. The rain came in and it'd be a better idea to not be in the rain," Clay said.

"Just make sure that everything is secure. If the gate doesn't look right, see if you can fix it. I don't want to be worried all night," Ridge said. Kellen nodded and motioned for Ridge to look behind him.

"Are you coming to bed or what," Faith asked. He nodded and got up.

"See y'all in the mornin," Kellen said.

Ridge nodded and Faith took his hand. "Come here," Faith said as she walked him into her office.

She sat down on the desk and he closed the door. "Breathe. I told you that he wasn't."

Ridge slid his arms around her and wrapped her legs around him. "Faith, I get that you want to interject, but let it sit. I had asked him a long time ago for his permission. I asked him when I was at the office. He didn't think it'd be now. Hell, I didn't think that I'd do it so soon."

Faith kissed him again. "Doesn't mean they aren't happy for us."

Ridge shook his head. "Babe, I can handle it. I didn't need you to call him."

"I know. Just stop. Ridge, I love you. I wouldn't have said yes if I didn't."

He kissed her. That one kiss turned into two, then turned into that kiss making her toes curl. "Ridge…"

He pulled her legs around him and went to get up. "No," Faith said.

"Here?"

She nodded as she undid the drawstring of his joggers. "Faith."

She smirked. "What," she asked as she went to make a move.

"Don't you dare," he teased.

"So, you're allowed to taunt me until I can barely move, but I don't get to taunt you?"

He kissed her and picked her up, leaning her onto the sofa. "Why," Faith asked.

"Why what?"

"Why can't…"

He kissed her again. "Because I said so," he replied. He went to start taunting again and she stopped him.

"Tell me why," Faith asked.

He shook his head. "Fine. Forget it."

"Ridge."

He shook his head and got up. "Where are you going?"

"Sleep."

He walked upstairs and Faith followed him. When he went to walk into the guest room, she grabbed his hand. "What?"

"Please?"

He shook his head. "Faith." She pulled his hand and walked him into the main bedroom, closing the door behind them.

"Are you seriously that mad?" He shook his head, kicked his joggers off and slid into bed. He was mad. Really mad. How in the world her dad was allowed to snap at him, he didn't know. He got the attitude. If her dad was that irritated, fine, He could accept it, but Faith trying to push something else wasn't happening.

He flipped the light on and threw his phone onto the charging pad. "Are you that mad," Faith asked.

"I'm not talking about it. Just get some sleep," Ridge said. Faith looked at him. She shook her head and slid in close to him. "Faith."

"Then roll over." He shook his head, took a deep breath, and rolled over to face him.

"What," he asked.

Faith kissed him. "I love you."

"I know," Ridge said.

"And?"

"Get some rest baby. I love you too."

Faith shook her head. "All because he was cranky and short with you?"

"We're not talking about it tonight."

She nodded and snuggled in close. He closed his eyes, or at least tried to, and the thoughts were running through his head. Her dad objecting to the wedding and saying he wasn't good enough. Faith realizing that he didn't have money like his folks. Her changing her mind and walking away from him. All of it was on loop in his mind all night. He went to wake up and saw it was 4am. When he looked to his side, Faith wasn't there. He looked and she wasn't in the bedroom either. He got up and walked into his room. No sign of her. He pulled on boxers and his joggers, slid a hoodie on and walked downstairs to see Faith on the sofa with a hot cocoa.

"What are you doing down here at 4am?"

"Couldn't sleep. You okay," Faith asked.

"I couldn't sleep either. I saw that you were gone and came looking for you," he said mid-yawn.

"Are you really that upset with how dad was?"

He nodded. "I can't Faith. I always kinda felt like I wasn't good enough. Your dad's intimidating as all get out," Ridge said.

"He's known you since you were little. He's protective. I promise you that."

He shook his head. "He's still mad," Ridge replied.

Faith shook her head. "Ridge, look at me. He's not. My mom said he was stunned. That's it. Even your mom said that."

"Doesn't change anything Faith. If he doesn't want us..."

"Don't even say that."

"If he doesn't, I'm not gonna force him..."

Faith shook her head, slid into his lap, and kissed him. "If he is gonna be a pain in the backside, I'll tell him that he's not invited. Stop worrying about him." His hands slid to her backside as she leaned into his arms.

"Ridge, I want to marry you. If I didn't, I wouldn't have said yes. It's between us. Not us and our parents. We were fine. We were good before they called."

"I know. I just don't want drama. I really don't."

She kissed him. "I love you even if you don't think that's…"

He kissed her. "It's more than enough. All I'm saying is that I'm frustrated. That's it."

She shook her head. "I love you Ridge. Breathe."

He kissed her and Faith slid her arms around him, curling into his lap. "I'm not letting go," he said.

"Good. I'd have to kick your butt myself."

Ridge shook his head. "Babe, I know you're trying to make me feel better, but honestly, I need a workout. Either I go for…"

She kissed him. "Not leaving without me again."

He took a deep breath. "I can go around here."

She shook her head. "Come workout downstairs with me."

"You sure?"

Faith nodded. He kissed her. "Then go get dressed. I'll meet you down there." She kissed him and got up, heading upstairs.

Ridge walked down to the gym and turned the music on quietly, letting the guys know they were in the gym, and started his warmup. By the time she came downstairs, he was a mile and a half in on a run that he needed. Faith walked down the steps and saw him, watching the man who she was going to marry on the treadmill. Sweat, the perfect body, the hot man was all hers. He was almost too sexy. Way too sexy. "Stop staring," Ridge said as he smirked and slowed down, finishing his run.

"Can't help it. All sexy over there," Faith teased. He shook his head, hopped off and kissed her as a single bead of sweat slid down his face and landed on her chest as he leaned over to kiss her.

"Feeling any better?"

He shook his head. "Getting there though." He kissed her again and went and started on weights.

"I need to ask you something."

"Go for it," Ridge said.

"Remember when we were kids and my dad said that you were already family?" Ridge nodded.

"Why would you be worried about anything he says then?"

"Because technically, I'm not family. Honorary family. Your dad always scared me."

Faith shook her head. "Ridge, whether you know it or not, he does like you."

"Not right now he doesn't," Ridge said as he added on more weight. She knew he was doing it to get the worry out of his system, but he was really going hard on the weights. She did her yoga, then started on her weights that seemed like she was lifting feathers compared to him.

By the time they were both done, he was covered in sweat and she was tired just watching him. She went to go make breakfast when he picked her up and carried her into the kitchen putting her on the counter. "I can cook," Faith said.

He handed her the fruit, kissed her, and made the omelets and bacon. She flipped on the espresso maker and made herself a latte. "Do you want one," she asked.

He kissed her. "Sure." She made one for him and sat down on the high-top chair at the counter. He plated the omelets, handed her the plates as she put the fruit on and they sat down and ate together.

Ridge put the extra bacon aside and when the guys woke up, they followed the scent of bacon. Ridge made them eggs, plated them for the guys and handed them each a plate. "Thank you," Kellen said.

"Most welcome. Enjoy," Ridge said.

"Now, what were you saying," he asked as Faith looked at him.

"Do you always do a workout like that when you're mad?"

"Normally I do kickboxing, but now that we're working out at home. I just do what I need to."

"Ridge, I love you, but you're soaked."

"I do it so I'm strong enough to fend off anyone who comes after you or anyone else. That's why. It's kind of ingrained into my system now."

"Ridge."

"What?"

"Were you really that upset?"

He nodded. "Worse. I get that you think that it's nothing. That it's just me worrying. I don't want to end up in world war three with your dad because I proposed. I just want us to be together. We can run off somewhere and do it when we're ready if that's what you want."

"We're waiting a while. Until you and dad can look each other in the eye so you aren't worried that he hates you."

"Faith."

She kissed him. "I don't want you worried. Promise me."

"When do they come home?"

"Monday next week I think unless they decide to stay longer," Faith said.

"When they're back, I'll talk to him. That work?"

Faith nodded and he kissed her, getting up to do the dishes. "So, what did you want to do today," Faith asked.

"You have emails to get done. I have some work to finish."

"And then what?"

"Up to you."

"I have to go back into the office. Are you coming with me," Faith asked.

"Funny," he teased. He kissed her and they finished cleaning up, heading upstairs to get ready.

He went to head into his shower and Faith took his hand. "What?"

"Come with me."

He shook his head. "I guess that means you're good being late."

"Excessively," she almost mewed in reply. He shook his head, picked her up and walked into her bathroom, locking the door behind them. He sat her on the counter, slowly sliding every bit of clothing off of her. His skin still glistened from his workout and it just got her more and more turned on. When he started taunting again, she went to look down and he was nibbling, licking, and kissing his way up her inner thigh.

"Ridge."

"What sexy," he teased as he kissed her hip. She motioned for him to come closer and he kissed up her torso, letting his hands take over the teasing.

"Ridge," she said as her legs started to tremble.

"What," he asked as he nibbled at her breast. When he felt her arms wrap around his neck, he smirked. "What can I do for you," he teased as he kissed and licked up her neck then leaned in to devour her lips.

"Shower," she said. He kicked his joggers off, slid his sneakers and socks off and picked her up, carrying her into the shower and flipping the hot water on.

He leaned her up against the cool tile on the wall as the hot water flowed between them. "Now, what was it that you wanted," he teased.

She kissed him and he smirked. "Say it."

She kissed him again. "I want my fiancée," she whispered as they came up for air.

He smirked. "I bet you do," he teased.

They had sex in the shower. She called his name more than once. When he felt her nails on his back, he kept going until his body gave in. Her body tensed around him and throbbed until her body climaxed. "Mine," she said.

"You're stuck with me beautiful," he said as he slid her under the water. He kissed up her neck and Faith shook her head. He tried to slide her to her feet and she shook her head.

"What," he asked.

"I love that you read my mind," Faith teased.

He kissed her and slid her to her feet, grabbing her shampoo. He washed her hair for her as she smirked and leaned against him. "What's wrong," he asked.

"My legs are like jelly," Faith teased. He rinsed her hair out, then slid the conditioner in as she turned to face him.

"Had to go and get all tall and stuff," Faith tased.

"Meaning what?"

"You were shorter than me. I liked it. Now it's like climbing a mountain to kiss you."

"Heels," he teased.

"Oh, I know sexy." She kissed him and he rinsed her hair out. "You sure you want me of all people?"

"Always have, and always will," he replied as he washed his hair. She kissed him again and grabbed the sea sponge, washing his back for him. When she started heading to his front, he stopped her.

"What," Faith asked.

"I know what you're up to," he said.

"I'm not doing anything," she said.

"Faith."

"I can be late." He shook his head and just as she was about to take advantage of the privacy, her phone went off.

"Faith, go get the phone."

"Kinda in the middle of something."

"Faith." She shook her head, got up and went and grabbed her phone, grabbing a warm towel and wrapping it around her as she answered.

"Yes," Faith said.

"Good morning Miss Cartwright. I just wanted to confirm what time you'd be coming into the office," her assistant asked.

"Most likely around 10:30. Anything important," Faith asked as she heard the water turn off.

"Emails and about 30 messages. Is Mr. Ridge coming with you," her assistant asked.

"He will be when I come in. He's coming today too," Faith said.

"Alright. I'll get your coffees ready."

"Thank you. I have a couple things to do then I'll head in."

"Yes ma'am," her assistant said as they hung up. When Faith felt arms around her torso, she smirked.

"Still want to head in now," he asked.

"We have time," Faith teased.

"Really."

She nodded as he kissed her shoulder. He slid her hair to one side and kissed across her shoulder and up the nape of her neck. "Ridge."

"Yes sexy," he said as he kissed the edge of her ear as she burst into goosebumps. She smirked and he shook his head. "What," he asked.

She turned to face him and he picked her up and sat her on the counter. "I love you," she said.

"Good. I love you back." He leaned in and kissed her, devouring her lips until she undid her towel and went to slide his off. "Nope."

"Ridge."

"Hands off." She shook her head and he devoured her lips. He picked her up, pulled her legs around him and walked her into the bedroom, leaning her onto the bed.

"Tell me what you want," he asked.

"Towel off."

He smirked. "And?"

"I want…" He kissed down her neck as she pulled his towel off.

"Faith."

"Now, where were we before the phone rang," Faith teased.

"Turn over."

She shook her head. He kissed her and slid her to her stomach on the bed. "Why," Faith asked. He kissed up her spine and her stomach started trembling. He teased until she was almost begging. "Ridge."

He leaned into her and they had sex again. This time, it was hotter, more intense. Her body was almost shaking under him as he took her from behind. When she tried to sit up at least, her back was against his chest and he started taunting again until she couldn't hold back. When her body started throbbing again, he sped up until she was shaking in his arms. "Holy crap," Faith said as his body climaxed. When he nibbled her neck again, it was like he was just taunting even more.

"Ridge."

"Yes gorgeous," he teased.

"Yeah, we're not gonna make it into the office," she teased.

He leaned against her as they curled up together on the bed. "Faith."

"What?"

He slid the blanket up and kept her tight against him. "You sure you're good," he asked. Faith nodded and linked their fingers as he kissed her shoulder.

"Honestly, I don't think that either of us are leaving this room."

"Good. We still do have to," he teased.

Faith shook her head and he kissed her neck again. "I know. I just want to stay in this spot," Faith teased.

He kissed her shoulder. "And that's not just because you can't move," he teased. Faith smirked and snuggled in tighter to him. "You start something, I swear," he teased.

"Mine."

"Always."

He kissed her neck then up to her ear. "Ridge."

"Yes gorgeous."

"Do we really have to get up?" He nodded.

"You have work my beautiful fiancée. You have a ring to show off too." She smirked and turned to face him.

"I can hear everyone gushing from here."

He kissed her, devouring her lips. "Good. Now, before you try to taunt me, get up."

"No," Faith teased.

He kissed her. "I guess I'll just go to your office on my own," he teased.

Faith knew that she had to get up. She wanted to stay in the love bubble a while longer. She needed to. The meeting she had to be at the office for was a negotiation that was gonna take hours to finish. One that her dad had warned her would be grueling. "What," he asked.

"Fine. I'm getting up." She kissed him and they both got out of bed. He went and cleaned up a little, shaved and got dressed into yet another suit that had Faith drooling. She slid into her dress and when she saw him shaking his head at her closet door, she got a grin ear to ear. "Too much," Faith asked as she looked at him with her wearing nothing but the sexy lace lingerie.

"Big meeting?"

She nodded. "Skirt and top is probably a better plan," he said.

She smirked. "We'll see."

"And by the way, I like the lingerie."

"Good," she teased as she kissed him again. He smirked, kissed the back of her neck, and went and finished getting dressed, putting her favorite cologne on again.

He went downstairs and talked to the guys, letting them know where he was headed. "She doing okay?"

Ridge nodded. "She's showing the ring off to her office. Everything going as planned," Ridge asked.

"What do you mean ring," Kellen asked.

"We got engaged. We've kinda known each other since we were babies," Ridge joked.

"Congrats," Kellen said.

"Thanks. Can we do another scan of everything to make sure that there's nothing?"

They nodded. "I get it. I did a scan of the tv room last night and we found something in the freaking fireplace of all places. Camera and bug," Kellen said.

Ridge shook his head. "And?"

"Hacked and erased. We sent it to the police last night."

"Anything else?"

Kellen shook his head. "Y'all are good. Go. Anything else you need us for?"

"Just keep a close eye on the gate. We aren't expecting anyone." Kellen nodded. Ridge grabbed his laptop, sliding it into his bag and saw Faith walking downstairs.

"Damn," Ridge said.

"You like," Faith asked.

"You look gorgeous. I mean wow," Ridge replied as he took her hand and helped her down the last steps.

"You ready to head out?"

He nodded and kissed her cheek, grabbing her purse and laptop for her. She slid her phone in her purse and they headed off. He opened her door for him and they headed back downtown. "Ridge."

"Yes beautiful."

"I'm kinda dreading that meeting. If I message you 111 it means get me out of there okay?"

He nodded. "What's the problem?"

"One of my dad's former authors is causing a massive problem. He's determined to triple what he was getting as royalty, but he won't even go do the book tour. He mouthed off at fans when we tried to do a q and a."

"Why don't you tell him that if he decides to continue the attitude, he's not getting another contract for another book? Your mom has been writing forever. She'd never do half of that stuff," Ridge said.

"I know. It's because mom is a professional. She's not about to irritate my dad when she says no to a book tour," he joked.

"Dad would go with her. He has every time."

"Exactly."

"Good point," Faith said as he linked their fingers and got them iced lattes on their way into the office.

"So, when this meeting is done, what else do you have to do?"

"Emails and hopefully we can get out of there early."

"Good. I was thinking we could maybe go out to the beach."

"Overnight?"

"Could if you want to."

Faith smirked. "I like it," she replied. He kissed her when they stopped at the light and he held onto her hand the rest of the way into the city.

When they got to the office, he could see her tensing up. "Faith, it's a meeting. You have the upper hand. You're the one that can cancel his contract completely. Breathe baby. You'll be fine." She nodded and they headed up to her office. She was almost clamping down on his hand. "Faith."

"Yep."

"I love you. I love the amazing woman you are, the powerful woman you know you are, and the woman you're worried you'll never be. All of it is the woman I know. You're the rock whether you know it or not. You got this baby. Nobody gets to trample on you."

When she relaxed a little, he looked over and tears were welling up. "Faith."

He grabbed tissues from his pocket and handed it to her as she dried them. "How did you know that's what I needed?"

"Because I remember the girl stomping her feet when she couldn't get her way. Finding a way to always get what she wanted. Talking people into letting her have her way and demanding respect. You can do anything you want to. You're amazing at things you don't even know that you know how to do. Trust me." Faith shook her head as the elevator door opened. He smirked and they made their way into her office.

"You realize that you have to quit making me cry before work right," she teased.

"Happy tears," he joked.

Faith nodded as she put her purse and laptop down and gave him a hug. "What," Ridge asked.

"Thank you."

"For what? Telling you the truth?"

"Saying what I needed to hear. What I didn't know that I needed to hear." He kissed her and her assistant came in.

"Miss Faith, good morning. I got your iced lattes. I left your paperwork on the desk and here are your messages."

"Thank you," Faith said.

"Oh, and by the way, Faith has some news," Ridge teased.

"Miss Faith."

"Ridge and I are engaged," Faith said as her assistant was awestruck.

"What?"

Faith showed her the ring and she smiled. "Congratulations to the two of you. This is beautiful news."

"Thank you," Faith said.

"I managed to push the meeting so you have a little time to relax. It'll be starting in 30 minutes."

"Thank you," Faith said as her assistant headed out. Ridge closed the door and she smirked. "Had to didn't you," she teased.

"Yep. As a matter of fact, I did," Ridge teased as he kissed her. She went and grabbed the messages and paperwork and sat down on the sofa with Ridge before she headed into her meeting.

"You ready for all of this," he asked.

"Not really. He really doesn't have much choice. We do have the control in this. He doesn't want to hand the book over, fine. He has to pay back the advance," Faith said.

He kissed her. "Much better," he teased.

Faith shook her head. "Still, if it starts getting hairy, I may need you in there."

"Faith, you've been doing this job how long?"

"7 years."

"And you're worried why? Your dad wouldn't have given you the job if he didn't trust that you knew what you were doing and are amazing at it." She gave him a hug.

The fact that he had all the faith in her was enough. It was more than enough. It was what she needed. Somehow, he always knew what to say. He knew what she needed. Maybe it was because they had known each other for so long, maybe it was that he'd known her through everything in their lives, good or bad. Maybe it was just that he'd seen her do things that she'd forgotten that she'd survived. What he'd said was filled with their history and the lessons they'd learned side by side as kids. Now, that same man was going to keep making memories with her, but as her husband. She was still a little stunned at that. She was getting used to waking up to that face. She was used to being at his side and loved him like she'd never loved anything else. That was her man. Her handsome, sexy, hot and beautiful man inside and out. Drooling over him every morning was just a bonus. She felt safe, secure, comfortable, and strong when he was there. One look and he made her the amazing woman she knew she could be. Now, she was even more in love with him.

"What," Ridge asked.

"Nothin. Just thinking about this amazing man I know."

He kissed her and snuggled her to him. "Babe, walk into it with your head up. That's how you should walk into everything."

She kissed him again and went through the last of her paperwork. When her assistant knocked, Faith knew. "Go and kick butt."

Faith smirked. "I love you."

"Love you back beautiful."

Faith grabbed her papers, laptop, and phone, and walked into the meeting, sitting at the head of the table. One way or another, this was ending the way she wanted. When the author walked in and saw Faith and two more of the executive at the head of the table, he was thrown off. "Mr. Mitchell, have a seat," Faith said as she took charge. By the time the meeting was over, they were 3.5 hours in and he had cowered to what she wanted.

"You can't ask for more royalty of the books. This is a per-book basis. You've barely helped us promote it and you won't even send us the last 6 chapters by deadline. I understand it takes time, but you were on a deadline. You're six months overdue. You need to finish, do the edits, and get prepared for a book tour. We have to in order to promote it. We'll send you the dates. You want to bring your wife, fine. We can accommodate, but you need to get us the manuscript."

"Understood," he said as he signed off on what Faith had requested and agreed to it.

She walked back into her office and saw white and purple roses in a vase on her desk. "What's this," Faith asked.

"No idea. Must've been an admirer," he teased. She saw the note attached:

> *To the woman who can do it all, even when she doesn't know she can. I love you – R*

"Ridge."

"What?" She shook her head and walked over and kissed him. "You're in a good mood. Must mean that you made it through the meeting."

"You were right."

"Mark the day down. I was right about something," Ridge joked.

"Funny. I did what you suggested. It worked."

"Took a while."

"Got all the details ironed out. I think dad will be proud," Faith teased.

"I know he will be beautiful."

"How'd you do with your emails?"

"Mom called."

"And how's my favorite auntie?"

"Funny," he joked. "She wanted to know if we were waiting for the wedding or if we were gonna do it on a beach somewhere."

"Did you tell her we were waiting?"

"I said we hadn't figured that out yet since we just got engaged last night."

Faith smirked. "What," he asked.

Sue Langford

"What did you want to do?"

Barefoot Bodyguard

Chapter 10

The entire time they talked through the plans, neither of them wanted to rush into anything. They'd known each other for a lifetime, and there was no reason to rush that either of them knew of. "We could just plan something for next year," Ridge said.

"Or we do something in November."

He smirked. "You sure," he asked.

Faith nodded. She knew what she wanted. She'd always known.

When her mom and dad got married, it was at the church that they'd always had family weddings or events at. When she'd gone to church on Sundays as a kid, and even as a teenager, they'd gone there and with Ridge in tow. "I know exactly what you're thinking. You know I do," Ridge said.

"Why don't we see when he has time?"

"Fall, summer or winter?"

"Winterish."

He smirked. "And where would you want to do the reception?" Faith looked at him. "Name it fiancée."

"You know where."

"All the way down here?"

Faith nodded. He knew she wanted it at Charleston place. The same hotel where her mom and dad had their reception. She remembered seeing photos of its opulence and beauty. "I'll see what the availability is."

Faith nodded and he sent off two emails. That was all it took.

"So, what now beautiful?"

"Up to you. I got this done a lot faster than I thought," Faith said.

"Calls?"

She went through the messages, and most of them had somewhat been handled. "I can finish them at home," Faith said.

"Beach?" Faith nodded with a smirk. "Good," he teased. He messaged the guys that they were heading to the beach house and headed down to the SUV. He helped her in then hopped in on his side and they headed off.

When they pulled into the beach house, the guys were doing their hourly check. "Hey y'all," Faith said as they came inside.

Ridge put the laptops in her office and saw her slide her heels off and almost instantly walk outside to the sand. He shook his head, changed into his swim shorts, and headed outside, towels in hand. He put them on the step and walked out and met her on the sand. "Hey beautiful," he said.

"Hey yourself. Hold on. Where did that come from?"

"Left one or two out here in case we came down to the beach."

Faith smirked. "Fine. I'm going inside to get my swimsuit."

He smirked and followed her inside. "Which one," he teased.

"You'll see when I come outside."

He shook his head, walked back inside with her, and went to talk to the guys. "Anything," Ridge asked.

"Nope. We put in the cameras outside like you suggested. We added in a buzz at the gate as you probably saw and upgraded the system in the house. She's good," Leo said.

"Just make sure he's gone. Long gone," Ridge said.

Leo nodded and Faith came down a few minutes later in a red bikini. "Faith."

"What?"

Ridge shook his head. "You sure you want to do that?"

He saw the strings. He also saw how tempting it was gonna be to not undo them.

"I'm sure," Faith said as she grabbed a beach blanket and walked outside with him.

"I swear, you are asking for it," Ridge teased.

Faith kissed him. "Did you tell the guys," she asked. He shook his head and watched her walk into the kitchen.

"Tell us what," Leo asked.

"He proposed," Faith replied from the kitchen.

"To who," Leo teased.

Faith flashed the ring and Leo almost laughed. "So, you finally did it. You've been talking about that since we were in..."

"Shh. Give away my dang secrets why don't you," Ridge said.

"Were in where," Faith asked as she walked into the sitting area.

"Since we were deployed. When we got back, all he wanted…"

"Leo, seriously," Ridge said intentionally interrupting him.

"All he wanted was to find you." Ridge shook his head and walked outside. Faith smirked.

"And?"

"We ended up getting bogged down with work when we came back, but he was always looking."

Faith shook her head. "Thank you," she teased as she walked outside and saw him walking along the shoreline.

"Were you gonna tell me," Faith asked.

"No."

"Ridge."

He shook his head. "Come walk with me."

"Only if you tell me."

"It's not a fun happy story. Leave it." She stood in front of him. "What?"

"I'm happy that we did bump into each other again. I missed you."

"Missed you too," he replied.

Faith's arms slid around him and he kissed her. "Now. Come get in the water."

"Nope."

"Faith, we didn't come out here for the view."

She smirked. He shook his head, picked her up and carried her into the water. "Ridge."

"What?"

"I love you."

"Love you back fiancée." He walked out into the waves and the warm salty water and they were up to their necks as Lily slid tight to Ridge.

"What," he asked.

"Deployed?" He nodded, determined not to talk about it at all. He never wanted to talk about it. "Then what?"

"Lost a few friends. I'd told the guys about you and they asked why we never dated."

"Why didn't we," Faith asked as he wanted more than anything to just slide under the water and swim until he forgot all the bad memories.

"Because you decided it was more fun to date the random idiot guys. The ones who had all the clout and the money and the lifestyle that you had. I'm not a billionaire Faith. I have money, but it's family money. You even know that."

She kissed him. "I love you because you aren't like any of the idiots. You're so much better. Way better."

"Now you're sucking up." She smirked and he slid under the water, trying to swim through the waves. When she caught up to him, he smirked.

"What," he teased. She kissed him and dunked him under the water. The two of them frolicked in the waves like little kids having a water fight.

When she went to head in, he pulled her feet back towards him and slid her legs around his hips. "What," Faith asked.

"I need to ask you something, and I need the truth."

Faith kissed him and smirked. "Ask away handsome."

"Really and truly, did you and Holden…"

"We never slept together if that's what you were gonna ask."

"Not really it."

"What then?"

"Did you two ever try…" He whispered the question, not wanting to have anyone else hear it.

"Never. He tried to get me in bed more times than I could count. He never got that far."

"You do realize he told everyone that you two did, right?"

She looked at Ridge. "And now you know why I didn't want him anywhere near me."

"Then why did you come to the bar that night?"

Faith thought about it and smirked. "Boredom. Partially because I just needed to get out for a while. Honestly, I was really happy when you showed up."

"He called and asked about us."

"And?"

"I told him. I mean, do you want to tell people or keep it between us," Ridge asked.

"You mean since you told the guys and we told our folks?" He smirked.

"Since everyone is gonna start asking."

"Can we just keep it to ourselves? My office knows, the security guys know and our families know. Do we really need to declare it to the world?"

"So, that's a no?"

"Ridge, we can tell whoever we want to." He nodded. She could see those were completely the words he didn't want to hear. Whatever his reason, she knew it had completely ruined the mood. "Ridge." He shook his head and swam back in, walking out of the water and grabbing a towel. Faith shook her head and made her way in, walking straight over to him. "Ridge."

"What?"

"Talk to me."

"No. It's fine. You coming in?" She looked at him. "I'll get Leo to hang outside with you."

"Ridge." He walked up the steps to the beach house, walked in and got Leo to hang outside with Faith. He needed space.

He went and had a hot shower, got dressed and sat down at the counter, getting emails done. He should've waited to propose. It was too much, too fast. Way too fast. He was convinced that the only reason she had for being with him was that she'd hired him to protect her. She'd got caught up in the emotions of it all and so had he. "I'm going for a drive. Can you two keep an eye," Ridge asked.

"You sure you're alright? I haven't seen you this antsy since we were first deployed."

"I'm fine," Ridge said as he grabbed his wallet and the keys and went out.

He drove down to the mall and walked through the stores, just for the sake of walking then stopped off and got groceries and a few things he knew he might need. When his phone buzzed with a call from Faith, he ignored it. He went and bought a bottle of Jack Single Barrel and slid it into the grocery bag, heading back to the beach house. When he got back, Faith was yelling at the guys.

"I get he went out, but where did he..."

"Where did I what," Ridge asked as he put the grocery bags on the counter and put the food away. He put the Jack into his bag from his room and when he went to turn, Faith was at the door with her hands on her sexy hips. The sexy hips that he'd had tangled around him the night prior. The hips that he'd kissed on his way down her torso to taunt her into curling the sexy toes.

Barefoot Bodyguard

"Where did you go," Faith asked.

"Out."

When she went to grab his hands, he pulled away. "Come," she asked. He shook his head and sat down, going through more emails until she was about to lose it.

"We're going to the house," Faith said.

"Why?"

"Because we are. Either you talk to me or we leave."

"Do whatever you want Faith."

She looked at him and slapped his laptop shut. She took his hand and walked him up the steps to her bedroom and closed the door behind them. "Talk."

"About what?"

She looked at him like steam was about to shoot out her ears. "What happened? I come inside and you're gone. Just tell me where you went."

"Market, walk, got a bottle of Jack and came back."

"Ridge."

"What?"

"One minute, everything's fine and we're splashing around, then you vanish. What's wrong?"

He shook his head. "Nothing."

"You're full of it. Say it."

"It doesn't matter Faith. No matter what I say nothing is gonna change how you feel. I'm not playing the game. Do what you want to do. Say what you want. All I'm here to do is keep you safe. That's it."

She looked at him and he was cold. No emotion, no frustration, no irritation even. "So, that's it? You're gonna sit there and pretend like nothing is wrong?"

He nodded. He went to head downstairs and she shook her head and walked towards him. "Ridge."

"What?"

"If you want to tell everyone, then we say it. If you want to keep it to ourselves, we can. Whatever." He nodded and went to leave the room when she stopped him. "Where are you going?"

"Home."

He left the room and walked downstairs. Faith followed him and grabbed her things. "What," Ridge asked.

Barefoot Bodyguard

"You go, I go."

"The guys can…"

"No."

"Faith, just hang out here tonight. I'll come over in the morning."

Faith shook her head and walked out the front door, walking to the SUV and put her things in.

"I'll be back over tomorrow to check on everyone. If you need anything let me know," Ridge said as he walked out to the garage and slid into the driver's seat. Before he could start the SUV, Faith took the keys and slid into his lap. She pushed the seat all the way back and went for the belt of his jeans.

"Faith."

"What?"

"Stop."

"Then tell me what switch got flipped."

"Faith, move."

She shook her head. "Say it." He picked her up and sat her back in her seat, doing his belt back up, and opened the garage door, pulling the seat back up, heading to the house.

Sue Langford

It was too quiet. Way too quiet. There was music on, but Faith couldn't get him to say a single thing. Even when she put on music that she knew would annoy the crap out of him, nothing happened. When they headed down the main road to head to the house, she tried to hold his hand and he pulled away. "Seriously," Faith asked.

"You want me to drive you to the damn house, I'm driving you to the damn house. What do you want from me," Ridge asked.

"Tell me what got you all peeved."

He shook his head. "I shouldn't have done it."

"Which part," Faith asked.

"All of it."

She looked at him. "What are you saying?"

"I shouldn't have been there, I shouldn't have slept with you and I damn well should've kept the damn ring in my pocket."

Faith looked at him. "Tell me what's going on Ridge. Don't tell me that you're taking it back."

He said nothing. Not one single word. They got back to the house, made it through the gate and pulled up to the house. He parked the SUV and went to undo his seatbelt when he saw her put the ring into the cup holder. She got out and walked into the house, closing the door behind her. He shook his head and grabbed the ring, grabbing his things and locking up behind him, heading into the house. When he walked inside, Kellen shook his head. "What," Ridge asked.

Kellen walked him into the office.

"Say what you're gonna say," Ridge said.

"She came inside in tears. What the hell dude?"

"She pushed. She asked what was going on in my head and I told her. I didn't expect her to take it seriously."

"You have two options. Go and talk to her or go into the main bedroom and make it up to her."

Ridge shook his head and walked into his bedroom, seeing that his things had been moved. When he looked, her housekeeper was back. He shook his head and walked into her bedroom, hearing her in tears. He shook his head again and saw her look up. "Faith."

"Just go."

"You asked what was going on in my head. That's what was. I doubt myself every dang morning. Every night. That's all it was."

"You don't want to be with me then don't Ridge."

Ridge shook his head. "Tell me what you want Faith. You want to be engaged, then we stay engaged. You want to break it off, I'll leave. Say what the hell you want."

"Do you love me? Really love me," Faith asked.

"I never stopped."

"That's not an answer."

He shook his head and sat down in the chair. "Faith."

"Do you?" He nodded. "Ridge, if you don't want to get married then say so."

"You don't want me Faith. You want what you think that I still am."

"I want the man who I never ever cringed being near and crave every day. That's who I want. I don't care about your past, I don't care about money. All I care about is whether you love me. Whether we are gonna be a couple or not. Whether we're gonna actually get married."

He shook his head. "I don't have money outside of family money. Not like you."

"And if I didn't work for my dad's company, I wouldn't have any of it either." He shook his head. "Tell me what happened," Faith asked.

"Meaning what?"

"When you were deployed." When he almost cringed, Faith got up and sat down on the foot stool and slid her hand in his. "I don't want to talk about it," Ridge said as he tried to pull away. She wouldn't let him.

"Ridge."

"Faith, I get that you think that you can handle it, but you can't." She linked their fingers and tried again.

"Please."

"Three of my friends in my platoon got shot and killed on a routine search. That's why the rest of us are so close. It was just traumatizing. That's it."

"Ridge."

"I couldn't protect them. I couldn't do anything to keep them safe. That's why I went into being a bodyguard. At least I could keep my clients safe."

Faith looked at him. "Why are you so worried that you're not enough then," Faith asked.

"Because I'm a bodyguard. I'm not a billionaire. I'm a simple guy Faith. I barely even have furniture of my own in my condo. I was never even there long enough to enjoy it. I come here and you have everything you could ever freaking want. How do I even fit into that?"

She stood up and slid into his lap, sliding her heels off. "You're the one thing that my life was missing. That's been missing since we went our own ways after high school. I missed you then. I missed you until you walked into my house and my jaw hit the floor."

He shook his head. "Up."

"No. If I have to sit on you so you listen, I will."

Ridge shook his head. "Faith."

She kissed him. "I don't say I love you unless I mean it Ridge. If you are worried about us getting married, fine. Say that. Tell me what you want."

He shook his head and got up, picking her up and sitting her on the bed. He went into the closet and saw all of his clothes clean and hung up. He shook his head and Faith came up behind him, sliding her arms around him.

"I guess she's out of the hospital?"

Faith nodded. He went to leave the room and she wouldn't let him. "Faith."

"Why are you so determined to push me away?"

He looked at her. "I'm going downstairs."

She shook her head. "Talk."

"Faith, I need space." She shook her head again and kissed him. If he kissed her back, she hadn't lost him completely.

The kiss went from simple, to deep and toe-curling in a matter of minutes. When he stopped and pushed her back, she shook her head. "Ridge."

"Not right now."

He walked out of the closet, grabbing his jeans and a hoodie, grabbed boxers and walked off. "Where are you going?"

"Downstairs." He went and changed in his room, noticing that the sheets had changed and his things had been moved into Faith's room. Everything including his bag. He got changed and walked downstairs, walking into the security room. He slid his laptop on the desk and sat down to go through emails.

He saw 4 emails asking where he'd gone that were all from Faith. When he saw one from her dad, he took a deep breath and opened it:

> *Pay deposited. I apologize for my reaction to the engagement. I couldn't believe that the kid that played on the floor of our house with Faith as a baby was now marrying her. I give you my blessing, even though you don't actually need it. If you need anything at all please let me know. I can take care of the dress or whatever you both need.*

He shook his head and went through the rest of the emails. There were no bugs in the main house or beach house. The security was at a higher level than her mom and dad's house. She was safe whether he was there or not, and he didn't even feel comfortable near her. He thought that maybe when he proposed, she'd be excited about telling people. That she'd be bragging about her amazing fiancée. Instead, she was keeping it quiet. She wasn't telling anyone that knew either of them short of her folks. He was her big bad secret. The exact thing he didn't want to be. If he was gonna be a secret, there was no point in her even wearing the ring. It didn't mean a damn thing.

He shook his head and put it into the safe. He changed the code and got up, walking into the living room. He wandered into the kitchen and got himself a glass of Jack. A shot or two wasn't enough. Hell. He needed the entire bottle.

He walked outside, sitting down on the chaise on the back patio. He needed time to breathe. When he heard the sliding door open and close, he shook his head. Faith came over and took his hand. "What," he asked.

"Come with me for a minute."

"Faith, let me sit."

"Come with me."

He shook his head and got up, following her with his drink in hand. "What?"

She walked him over to the edge of the pool. "Ridge."

"Faith, I'm not in the swimming mood."

"I didn't say you were," Faith said as she sat down and slid her feet into the pool. He shook his head, putting his drink down and rolled up the hem of his jeans. He sat down and slid his feet in as Faith slid closer to him. He took another gulp of his drink and Faith looked at him.

"Whatever you're gonna say, just spit it out."

"I love you."

"And?"

"I never said I didn't want us to get married."

He shook his head. "Faith, leave it."

"No." He went to get up and she stopped him. "I don't have a giant group of friends Ridge. I never did. I have us, I have my friend Sandy and that's it. I told my folks and yours. We told the guys. We told the office. Tell me what you want me to do. Who you want me to tell. There's nobody to scream it to."

He took a deep breath before he said something he was gonna regret. "You don't want to get married."

"Yeah I do. I want that for you and me. We have time to do it. If you want to do it this summer, we do it. We want to do it in the winter, fine. I just want you and me."

"Faith."

She leaned over and kissed him, tasting the whiskey on his lips and in his kiss. He shook his head. "What happens when you change your mind," he asked.

"You mean what happens when you change your mind."

He shook his head. "Meaning?"

Barefoot Bodyguard

"I'm not changing my mind Ridge. Not today, not tomorrow. Why did you have to just assume that I didn't want to be together?" She kissed him again and got up.

"Where are you going now," he asked. Faith slid his glass back a little and sat down in Ridge's lap. "What are you doing?"

"I love you. I get that you're irritated and frustrated and disappointed, but I'm not going anywhere. I want us to get married. I want kids with you. I always will."

"Meaning," he asked.

"Put the ring back on my finger where it belongs."

He shook his head. "Why?"

He finished his drink and got up as she shook her head. "Ridge."

He walked into the house, refilling his glass. "Where is it," Faith asked.

"Away." She walked into the security office and went to open the safe when the code didn't work.

"Open it." Ridge shook his head. "What's the code?"

"Does it matter?"

She put in her birthday and the door opened. She saw the ring and slid it back on her finger. "Much better," Faith said. He took a gulp of his drink. He walked into the kitchen and saw her housekeeper making grilled salmon.

"Did you need me to do anything," Ridge asked.

"Nope. You two relax," her housekeeper said as Ridge walked back outside to the chaise.

He sat down and took another gulp of his drink when Faith came outside. "What," he asked.

She leaned over and kissed him. "Move over," she said as she sat down with him.

"Faith."

"What got you all mad?"

"I don't want to talk about when I was deployed. Ever. I did things I never wanted to do, and never should've had to. The only positive thing I had to hold onto was knowing that you were safe, and you aren't. That's all I wanted when I was gone. Those cameras in the beach house and even here, were here long before you even noticed. I don't understand how your security didn't even know they were there. They suck at security. They shouldn't have been hired."

Faith looked at him. "Ridge."

Barefoot Bodyguard

"What?"

"I'm safe now. I have the best security I could ever have, and a fiancée who loves me. Can't ask for more than that."

Ridge shook his head. "One that couldn't keep you safe from someone planting them here."

She slid on top of him. "That's my fiancée you're insulting," she said as he shook his head.

"I don't want to regret anything. If you aren't ready for us to be engaged, then we put the entire thing aside. If you don't..."

She leaned into his arms and kissed him. "Never happening," she said.

He shook his head. "Faith."

"What?"

"I know what you're doing."

"No, you don't." He nodded. "Nope."

"I also know that look. What are you planning then," he asked.

Faith kissed him again. "We're having that movie night after all. Just you and me."

"Now?"

She nodded. "I told the guys and Mrs. Carter. Alone. No interruptions."

Ridge shook his head. "And if I said I wasn't in the mood?"

She smirked and slid into his arms, leaning her body against his. "I can get you in the mood," she joked.

He shook his head. "You really need…"

She kissed him as that one kiss turned into 2, two turned into 4, 4 turned into making out until he was getting turned on. He got up, picked her up and walked to the one spot that no camera would see and nobody could spot, pinning her against the wall.

"What," Faith asked.

"Don't start."

"Why?"

"Faith." She slid her hand down his torso and went to undo his jeans. He shook his head, stopping her.

"Behave for once." She shook her head and devoured his lips until her toes were curling. He picked her up, wrapping her legs around his hips and went to pull off her panties when he noticed there weren't any there. "You need to behave."

Faith shook her head and undid his jeans. "Mine. Heart and soul," Faith said. He shook his head, crashing his mouth to hers as he devoured her lips. They had sex against that very private, very out of sight wall. It wasn't making love. It was sex. Hot, carnal, don't ever stop, sex that made her forget where they were, forget that there were people nearby and forget everything else in the world. They kept going until her body was throbbing around him then he kept going, teasing and taunting her body until he finally found his release along with her. When they came up for air, he was still throbbing and so was she.

"I love you," Faith said.

"You better hope so," he joked as he slid her to her feet. He shook his head and tucked himself back into his jeans. "Taunting is not gonna work," he teased.

She smirked. "Okay," Faith replied as she kissed him again.

They walked back over to the chaise, he grabbed his drink, and she walked him inside and up to the bedroom. "I still don't understand how all of my things got moved," Ridge said.

"I told her today that we were engaged. I figured you'd be okay with having your things in with mine."

"So long as you aren't stealing my hoodies, fine." She smirked and locked the bedroom door.

"I'll consider it," Faith joked. She shook her head and kissed him then walked into the bathroom to clean up. He shook his head, and his phone went off.

"Yep."

"Sir, we just got a package at the gate. Did you want to come down and check it out?"

"On my way," Ridge said. He walked into the bathroom and kissed her, devouring her lips until she was pawing at him.

"Going downstairs."

Faith shook her head. "Work." One more kiss and he headed downstairs, walking into the security office to look at the camera footage.

"It was dropped off by an unmarked vehicle. Wasn't postal, wasn't courier." Ridge nodded, grabbed his gloves and pocketknife, grabbed evidence bags from the drawer and headed down to the gate to see what it said, sliding a mask on to protect himself in case it had something in it. When he saw that it had his name on it, he shook his head, not touching it at all. He opened the side of the package with his knife, opened the top and saw photos inside with a note:

Barefoot Bodyguard

You really think that you can protect her? Funny. Did you think I wouldn't notice?

He looked at the photos and there were more than one there of them at the beach, then two photos of them on the sofa at the house. He wasn't impressed. He called the officer that was taking care of the case and let him know what it said, taking a photo of each of the pictures that were in it. He sent it all to her dad's security and shook his head. He walked into the house, and he emailed the photos to the guys, determining the angle of where the photo was taken from. When he almost instantly realized that the one of them on the sofa was with the camera that they'd disposed of, he was happy, but something was still off. The guys went and did a full scan of the house and made sure they were clear.

Faith sent him a text and asked him to come back upstairs. "When the police come, give them the package. It's on the steps." The guys nodded and Ridge came upstairs, throwing out the mask and gloves. "Hey," Ridge said.

"Where did you go?"

"Work stuff. What did you need me for," he asked.

She motioned for him to come closer. "Faith." She kissed him and went for the button of his jeans again. "Faith."

"What?"

"You are just insatiable today." She nodded and kissed him. He brushed her hand away.

"Ridge."

"Woman, I swear." She kissed him and walked him backwards to the bed and sat him down, sliding into his lap.

"Faith, I get it, but we're not doing this. I'm waiting on the police detective."

"Why?"

"Package showed with a threat and photos."

When she stilled, he gave her a hug. "Ridge."

"It's being handled. Nobody touched anything in it. It got dropped off by an unmarked vehicle. Not impressed."

"We're okay right," she asked.

He nodded. "Just breathe. I can handle the cop stuff."

She kissed him again. "And," she asked.

"You need to behave."

She shook her head. "After dinner, we're watching the movie."

"Fine," he said. She smirked and slid out of his lap, and they went downstairs to the scent of grilled salmon, white rice, and grilled asparagus. She missed that meal. Her favorite with all the spices she loved too.

Ridge filled up his glass with Jack, got Faith a glass of wine and sat down with her. "Thank you handsome," Faith said.

"Most welcome. This looks amazing. Thank you," Ridge said.

"Most welcome. Enjoy," her housekeeper said.

They had their dinner and relaxed. For once, there was no stress. The guys were handling the police situation, and they'd managed to find a way through the drama with the ring. He was getting a little buzz and Faith refilled her glass, bringing it over to the sofa table and putting it down. "Faith."

She went and got his bottle of Jack and put it beside her wine. He shook his head and they got up after finishing dinner and went and cleaned up the dishes. "You two shoo. I'll take care of these," the housekeeper said.

"How are you feeling," Faith asked.

"Much better than I was," she replied as Faith and Ridge went and sat down.

"Are y'all up for dessert," she asked.

Faith smirked. "I appreciate the offer, but I'm stuffed. That was fantastic," Ridge said.

"Alright. I'm turning in. If you two need anything, let me know."

"Thank you," Faith said. She nodded and left them on their own.

He went and grabbed another glass, putting Faith's wine into the fridge, and poured her a glass of Jack. "Had to," Faith asked.

"It's only fair," he replied. She flipped on a calm, relaxing movie and he made sure the curtains and shutters were closed, made sure the doors were secure and sat back down.

"What," Faith asked.

"Just making sure," he said as he sat down on the sofa behind her.

"Remember the rules?"

Faith smirked. "The question is can you make it through it," Faith teased.

"So, you didn't know that I actually have a way to up the ante," he teased.

Faith turned and looked at him. "Meaning what?"

"No fifty tonight."

"Ridge."

"My turn," he joked.

When the movie came on, she shook her head. "What," Ridge asked.

"You're seriously doing that?"

"You have no idea what I have planned," he whispered as he slid the blanket over her.

"You're not seriously expecting…"

"You started the challenge," he teased as he smirked. He'd found the one movie that was more tempting than anything else.

"I still can't believe that you'd think that this would be worse."

"Have you watched it?" Faith shook her head.

He smirked and pressed play. They made it through the first 10 minutes and he saw her jaw hit the floor. "Ridge."

"Like I said. You want to attempt to win this round, you can't…"

"Pause."

He smirked, pressed pause and she turned to face him. "What," he teased.

She shook her head. "Seriously?"

He got a grin ear to ear. "What," he asked.

Faith shook her head. "This is what…"

He kissed her. "Watch the movie."

She kissed him and he shook his head. "Behave. No funny business."

She shook her head and he kissed her forehead. She shook her head again with a smirk and turned back around as she slid in closer to him. "Faith."

"What?"

"Don't start." She shook her head and he turned it back on, handing her glass of Jack to her. They got another half hour in and she was getting in closer to him. He couldn't help the smile ear to ear. 365 days was his new weapon. He had a list of movies just as hot, but this was one she couldn't possibly have seen. By the end of the movie, she was about ready to pounce.

"What," he asked as she turned to face him.

"First, I need another drink. Second, where on earth did you find that movie?"

He smirked, kissed her and she slid into his lap, straddling him. "What," he teased.

"Had to right?" He nodded and kissed her. "Yeah, I don't know if we can even…"

He kissed her, devouring her lips. "You were saying?"

She went for the belt of his jeans and he stopped her. "Not down here." She kissed him and he shook his head.

"What," Faith said.

He kissed her and linked their fingers. "You want to give up already? There's two more," he teased.

Faith kissed him. "On one condition."

"Which would be?"

"No shirt." He smirked and shook his head.

"Rules stand sexy." She shook her head and finished her drink as they both topped up their glasses and watched the second movie.

Chapter 11

She barely managed to make it through the first half of the second movie before she grabbed the remote and turned it off. "Giving up," he whispered.

She topped up their drinks, handed him a glass and took hers, got up and walked upstairs. He flipped the TV and the lights off and followed her as she walked into the bedroom. He locked the bedroom door, put the glasses on the side table and picked her up, wrapping her legs around his hips.

"I knew you wouldn't make it," he teased as he leaned her up against the door of the bedroom. Faith slid her shirt off and went to pull his off when her phone buzzed. "Not answering it. Don't ask," Faith teased as Ridge kissed her.

She pulled his shirt off and her phone went off a second time. He walked over to the bed, pinning her onto it. "Don't move."

"Ridge."

He looked at her phone. "Who's Craig?"

"Ridge."

"Who is he?" Faith shook her head and he called a third time. He handed the phone to her and walked back into the guest bedroom, finding the one thing that her housekeeper hadn't touched. He slid them into the bedside table drawer on the other side of the bed.

"Craig."

"And how's my girl," Craig said.

"Haven't been your girl for years. What do you want," Faith asked as Ridge finished his drink and went downstairs to get a refill, bringing the bottle back upstairs with him.

"I was gonna see what you were up to tomorrow. Going out for a boat ride. Wanted some company."

"Craig, I'm engaged. You can stop trying to hit on me."

"Not married yet. Come out with me."

"No."

"Faith, bring the guy. He gets a fish before me, I back off."

"And this is why you called three damn times in a row?"

"Miss you. Is that not allowed?"

"Surprised you remembered my name." Ridge shook his head and walked back downstairs. He let the guys know that they were turning in, checked emails and came back upstairs to see Faith just hanging up.

He shook his head and sat down on the opposite side of the bed. The mood was gone. Long gone. "Ridge."

"I'm not goin fishing with some loser idiot that you used to date, so don't ask."

She looked at him. "I wasn't suggesting it."

He kicked his jeans off, put them in his closet and sat back down on the opposite side of the bed. He shook his head, getting up and got ready for bed. When Faith walked in behind him and slid her arms around his torso, he shook his head. "You mad," she asked. He finished brushing his teeth and slid her arms out from around him. "Seriously?" He walked back into the bedroom and flipped his phone onto the charger.

He slid into bed and Faith shook her head. She got changed for bed, flipped the lights off and intentionally slid into bed on his slide, sliding right into his arms. "Faith."

"What," she asked.

He shook his head and rolled her to her side, pinning her onto the bed. "And," he asked.

Barefoot Bodyguard

"Do you want to do dinner with..."

"No."

"Ridge."

"No. I don't want to sit across the table from an idiotic old boyfriend who never made it past date two."

She went to kiss him and he pulled back. "What?"

"You finishing telling me what you two were talking about?"

"He asked a bunch of stupid idiot questions, then asked who I was engaged to. He remembers you."

"I bet he does. I whooped his butt in high school."

"He invited you to come on the boat."

"Rather jump into a volcano." Faith shook her head.

"You letting me sleep?" Faith shook her head.

"You started this."

"Kinda ruined the mood Faith."

"Then we talk."

He shook his head and flipped his light back on. "Babe, I get that you're all determined and everything, but I'm seriously not..."

She kissed him. "Bad timing." He nodded. She slid her legs around him. "Ridge," she almost mewed.

"Yes beautiful," he said. She kissed him again and he shook his head.

"Not gonna work," he teased.

"What isn't," she teased as she went to make a move.

He shook his head. "I know what you're about to do."

"Really," Faith asked as she kissed down his torso.

"Faith."

"What?"

"I know what you're doing."

"I bet," she teased as he shook his head and pulled her back up into his arms.

"Why," Faith asked.

"Because I don't want you doing it."

She went to mount a retort and he kissed her, leaning her onto the bed. "Ridge."

"Not happening Faith. The mood was already ruined."

She kissed him and slid her legs around him. "Nope."

Ridge shook his head. "Faith."

"What," she asked as she smirked.

"Determined right?" She nodded. "I think he intentionally called to irritate the crap out of me. Almost like a dare."

He kissed her. "And I think you need sleep love. We can figure things out tomorrow."

She shook her head and went for the boxers, daring to try and pull them off. "Faith."

She kissed him and went to slide them down. "They're staying on."

"Ridge."

He kissed her. "Just for tonight, they're staying on."

He kissed her and leaned over onto his back as she leaned onto his shoulder. "You're seriously saying no to that?"

He nodded and kissed her. "I'm not having this conversation."

Ridge shook his head and flipped the light off. "And if you woke up and..."

He kissed her. "Stop."

"Why," Faith asked.

"I'm not talking about it. I get that you think that it's not that big of a thing, but it is to me."

"Ridge."

He shook his head. "Did you hear what I said?"

"I heard you. I just..." He shook his head and got up, walking into his closet, then walked downstairs. Faith sat there with her mouth open in shock.

He walked into the security office and saw the guys. "I thought you were turning in," Kellen said.

"Everything good?"

"Doing another round to check exterior. Just finished inside. What's up?"

"I'm sleeping down here."

"You do know there's still a guest room up there right?"

"I'm not playing with her anymore," Ridge said.

"Meaning," Leo asked as he walked in.

Ridge shook his head and walked into the living room, grabbed the blanket, and threw it on the sofa then went and got a glass and poured a full glass of Jack, sitting down on the sofa. He took a deep breath and leaned back. Kellen came in a few minutes later. "What's going on," he asked.

"Kellen, I get that you want to fix it like you always do, but please just stop."

He shook his head. "What's wrong?"

Ridge shook his head, taking a gulp of the Jack. "She is determined. She's also being a royal…"

"Pain in your backside," Faith asked as she walked downstairs. Kellen motioned that he was in the office and he left Faith and Ridge alone.

"Are you gonna tell me why?"

He shook his head. "Faith."

"Say it Ridge."

"Because I don't…"

"The real reason."

"Because the last time someone did, I ended up in the damn hospital. End of discussion."

Faith looked at him. "What?"

He glared at her and shook his head taking another gulp of his drink. "That's the real reason?"

"Second, I have more respect than that for you. Just don't."

She slid onto his lap, taking the glass away from him and put it down. "What," he asked as she straddled him. She kissed him and leaned into his arms as he leaned backwards onto the sofa. "Faith."

She kissed him again and he shook his head. "Go to bed."

"Not without you."

He shook his head and kissed her, devouring her lips until he felt the goosebumps coming up on her skin. When she went for the drawstring of his joggers, he shook his head and he felt her hand on him.

"Now," she said quietly. He shook his head.

When he slid the hem of her robe up, he saw she was completely naked underneath. "Not here."

Barefoot Bodyguard

She kissed him again and slid in closer. "Faith."

Her hand started taunting faster until there was no stopping. There was no way to stop. It wasn't romance, it wasn't passion and it wasn't making love, but it was her getting her man. That's all she wanted. They had sex on the sofa. Hot, body throbbing sex. Then he pinned her onto the sofa and kept going until her nails were almost scraping down his back. When her body was almost trembling in his arms, he shook his head. "Had to go and walk down here half-naked."

She kissed him. "No more vanishing to the sofa."

He kissed her. "I just need some time to cool off."

She kissed him. "And now what," she asked. He shook his head, sitting up. He got up, pulled his joggers up and picked her up, walking her upstairs. He leaned her onto the bed and leaned into her arms.

"You good," he asked. Faith nodded and they curled up on the bed together. "What if…"

He kissed her, got up and cleaned up a bit. When he heard the shower turn on, he shook his head. He kicked his joggers off along with his boxers and turned to see her robe on the floor and her stepping into the warm water. "Faith."

She motioned for him to come closer. He shook his head, locked the bathroom door, and threw two towels onto the warmer. "Ridge."

When he stepped into the stream of hot water, Faith kissed him. "Had to," he teased. Faith nodded and slid her arms around him. "What," he asked.

"I love you. If you're that uncomfortable about it, fine. I just want you. That's it."

"Good."

She smirked. "This mean you're not mad anymore?"

"This means I'm not playing around with that." She kissed him and he picked her up, wrapping her legs around his waist.

"Ridge."

"Faith."

"What are you up to?"

"Eye to eye," he teased.

When she went to kiss him again, he pinned her against the wall. "I know that mind of yours Faith. I also know that you're gonna push that button regardless of what I say."

"I'm not gonna..."

"Faith, I'm asking you. Don't." When she went to try and kiss him, he pulled away. "Promise me."

"Ridge."

"Say it."

"Fine." He went to put her down and she pulled him back to her, kissing him. "What," he asked. She kissed him and he leaned her against the wall, pinning her there with his body.

His muscles held her there. She could feel every single inch of him against her and wanted more than anything to do something. Anything. She wanted to feel him inside her again, but it was like he was slowly torturing her. "Ridge."

"You want..." She kissed him and tried to get one arm free but he wouldn't let her. "I want."

He smirked. "You sure?" She nodded and looked in his eyes. "Bed?"

She shook her head and he slid into her with her body instantly throbbing around him. It was hotter this time, with her having no control whatsoever. They kept going and going until her body couldn't take anymore. When he pulled away, she almost yelled at him. "What," she asked.

He smirked and slid her to her feet. "Ridge." He shook his head, and she backed him to the bench, sliding into his lap and kept going.

"Faith." She kissed him and within a matter of seconds, she felt his hands teasing her. The sex was even more intense.

When her body exploded in his arms, he continued to taunt her. "Turn around," he said. She kissed him and he turned her so she faced the water as it got even more intense. He taunted her in ways she had forgotten weren't just in romance novels or erotica books. When her body was trembling, he went one step further. "What," Faith asked as he ramped up his teasing. At that moment, he could care less what was going on with him. He just wanted her past hot and turned on until she was begging him to carry her to bed. When his body finally gave in and he found his release, she was almost trembling in his arms. "You okay," he asked. Faith nodded and kissed him as she leaned against him. "Still want something?"

"May need a small power nap." He smirked and sat for a minute, catching his breath, and waiting for the blood to go back to the rest of his body.

She managed to get up, flipped the hot water off and Ridge grabbed her hand, pulling her to him. "Yes fiancée."

He kissed her, devouring her lips. "I love you."

"I know. Am I allowed to ask something without you getting mad?"

"Faith."

"What happened?"

"Broken and teeth marks."

Faith shook her head. "Okay. I won't say anything else."

"Good." She kissed him again, helped him up and they stepped out of the shower. She handed him a warm towel and wrapped the other around her torso. When she went to walk into the bedroom, he picked her up and carried her to the bed, leaning her onto it. "What," she asked seeing the look on his face.

"Two minutes." He went and pulled boxers on and walked downstairs.

"You good," Kellen asked noticing him walk into the living room.

"Just grabbing my drink."

"You sure you're good?"

Ridge nodded, patted him on the back and walked upstairs to the bedroom. "Just make sure everything is secure." Kellen nodded and Ridge went back upstairs into the main bedroom, locking the door behind him.

When he saw her curled up in bed in his t-shirt, he shook his head. "What are you wearing," he asked as he took a gulp of his drink and slid into bed on his side. "My shirt?" She nodded. He shook his head, took the last gulp of his drink, and slid to his side.

"If you don't want me wearing it..." He shook his head and kissed her neck, sliding his arms around her and sliding her tight against his chest.

"What," Faith asked with a smirk ear to ear.

"Intentionally trying to taunt me?"

"Nope. My shirt," she teased as his hand slid over her hip and to her lower belly.

"Really?" He nodded and nibbled the edge of her ear, kissing and licking until the goosebumps came back.

"Off." She shook her head and his hand ventured south to taunt her even more. "Faith." When her heart started racing again and he felt her hand slide to his arm, almost digging her nails in. "Faith."

"Damn," she said as he intensified the taunting.

When her hand slid to the waistband of his boxers, he shook his head. "Faith."

"Mine."

"Nope," he teased as he got even worse.

"Ridge."

"Mine," he whispered.

He kissed the nape of her neck until she was about ready to explode. When he pulled away, Faith shook her head and went to turn around. "Nope," he said.

"Ridge."

"Did you think that stealing my shirt was a good idea?"

She nodded with a grin ear to ear. "Kinda looks good on me," she joked.

"Always, but right now, no," he teased. Just as he was about to take full advantage of her, his phone buzzed. He shook his head, noticing the time. She went to turn around and he stopped her, pulling her tight against him.

"Ridge."

"Fiancée," he whispered as the goosebumps got goosebumps.

"No more teasing," Faith said.

"Tell me what you want," he whispered as he kissed down the back of her neck. She reached behind her and went for the waistband of his boxers. "Words Faith. Say it," he teased.

"I want them off."

"I know. What else did you want?" She knew what he wanted her to say. "Ridge." When he nibbled at her neck, she almost curled her body to him. "Please."

"Say it," he said as his boxers slid off and she slid in even tighter to him. He slid in tight to her. "Say it Faith."

"I want you. Now," she said. He ramped up the teasing and taunting until she leaned in tight to him. "Ridge."

"What," he asked as he almost purred into her ear. One move and they were having sex again, but this time it was even hotter. It wasn't just intense. It was mind-blowing, hot and passion all rolled into the hottest sex that he'd ever had. It went from her body aching for him to her facing him and the two of them lip locked. It got more and more intense until she said one single thing that pushed him over the edge.

"Ridge," Faith said.

"Baby," he whispered in reply.

"I love you." All it took was those words to make him feel like he was crumbling into her arms. His body gave way and she was tangled so tightly around him that she could barely breathe. "Ridge," she said as he kissed her, devouring her lips until her toes curled back into knots.

"What," he teased as both their hearts raced.

"I don't think that I can even move," she replied as he leaned to his back, pulling her with him.

"Better," he teased. Faith smirked and kissed him as he slid his shirt off of her. "Mine."

"I love you, Ridge."

"I love you back sexy fiancée." She curled into his arms and within what felt like minutes, she was asleep with her head on his chest and he was nodding off. His phone buzzed again, and he gently grabbed it. 4 missed calls and two texts:

> *Missing you. Come over tonight. Please? – Melody*

So now you're ignoring me? You sure you don't miss me? – M

He didn't miss his old life one little bit. He deleted the messages and blocked the phone number and future messages, checking the missed calls. There was one from his dad and one from Leo:

> *House is clear. Caught someone trying to put a camera onto the back porch. Cops have him. He said he was paid by that same guy.*

Ridge shook his head and forwarded the info to Kellen and to her dad's security. There was no reason to wake her and tell her. Not at that moment. He put his phone back on the charger and went to close his eyes when he could feel her smirk. "Go to sleep Faith."

She kissed his heart. "I am," she teased. He kissed the top of her head and within a half hour, they were both unconscious.

The next morning, she woke up just as Ridge was sliding out of bed. "And where are you headed," Faith asked watching his perfectly sexy body walking into his closet.

"Workout. Are you coming," he teased.

"I don't know that I can even walk down the steps."

Barefoot Bodyguard

He smirked, pulled boxers and joggers on and walked over, leaning over and kissing her. "You sure you don't want to sleep in," she teased.

He kissed her again, devouring her lips and stood back up. "I'm doing a workout. I'll be back up in a bit. Sleep babe." She nodded and smirked.

"Party pooper."

"If I don't work out right now, you're not gonna be able to walk for a month. I think you'd rather be able to function."

She smirked. "I do have to go in. Tell me you're coming with me."

"Depends. A bunch of meetings?"

"Two, then a call and a bunch of paperwork. Are you gonna come with me?"

"Yeah I will. Go back to sleep. I'm right here in the house if you need me. Just don't get all hot and bothered if you see me on the treadmill," he teased as he kissed her again and headed downstairs. He grabbed his water, slid in his AirPods Pro and flipped his music on, running out all the stress and drama.

He ran the treadmill until all the thoughts from the night prior were cleared from his mind. The flashbacks to the woman who literally put him in the hospital. He'd never had pain like that in his life. Her making the first move should've been the tip-off. He had almost bled out after that. Broken was an understatement. She'd pulled a knife then bit him in the one place that was most painful. The only time he'd ever let anyone in his condo. He'd been in the hospital for a few days, had a scar that thankfully healed so nobody could see it, and had completely turned him off anyone ever going down on him again. When women assumed that's what he wanted, he'd thought about how it would show that a man had no respect for a woman if they let them do it. How if it were Faith, he'd expect the guy to have more respect for her than to expect that. He was a good guy, and she was way too good of a woman. He couldn't stop her from doing it, but he was gonna put up a fight if she tried to do it without telling him.

He shook his head, stepped off the treadmill and started weights. When she came downstairs, he was almost finished, and drenched in sweat. He barely even noticed she was there, peeling his shirt off and throwing it at the stairs. He finished the weights, stretched his muscles out and when he looked at Faith, she had a grin ear to ear. "What's with the smile," he asked.

"You do realize that you're soaked right?"

"It's called actually working out and not just doing yoga and light weights."

She smirked. "I've done big workouts."

"I know. I just needed an extra-long one. I had to work through stuff."

"You said that before Ridge. Tell me what's going on."

"Just crappy memories. Stuff I needed to figure out."

Faith shook her head. "You're not gonna tell me?"

"Faith."

"Remember when you told me that I needed to tell you the truth?"

He nodded. "Then start talking."

"Faith, I told you already."

"Obviously there's more to it."

"Leave it at bite marks and someone pulling a knife on me. I had to get stitches and had them in places I never want to have stitches," Ridge said.

"You do know you could've just told me the entire story right?"

"Faith, I love you, but no."

"Ridge."

He shook his head. "I'm not talking about it. It's done and over. Long over. Leave it Faith." She looked at him. "What?"

"That the real reason?"

Ridge nodded. "Faith, you know that we were always like family. Guys push that on people when they have no dang respect for them. I respect you more than that."

"You weren't trying to make me do it Ridge. You have to tell me when stuff like this bubbles up."

He nodded and Faith smirked. "Now come on. Eat before you're confined to the sofa."

He walked towards Faith and she smirked. "What?"

"Nothin," he teased as he kissed her.

They walked up the steps and the breakfast was just being plated. "Thank you," Ridge said.

"Most welcome. I even managed fresh croissants for y'all."

"Thank you," Faith said.

"I missed this." Ridge saw the eggs benedict and was stunned. It wasn't even 7am yet and she'd gone this far? He was thankful that she was back, but he did kind of miss making out in the morning as Faith sat on the kitchen counter with her legs around him.

"I'm gonna get going on laundry. Did you need me to press anything," her housekeeper asked.

"Thank you. I think I'm good," Faith said.

Ridge's hand slid to Faith's thigh. The housekeeper headed upstairs and went into the bedroom. When she emerged 10 minutes later, she had laundry and bedsheets in hand. Faith smirked and kissed him. "This mean that everything's good now," she asked.

"Just remember what I said."

"If I voluntarily wanted…"

"Faith."

"If."

"Not having the discussion." He finished breakfast, made a protein shake and cleaned up the dishes, putting them away before the housekeeper could come in and shoo him out.

"You sure that you're ready to go," Ridge teased as they headed upstairs.

"My meetings don't start until 11. We have a little time," Faith said as Ridge smirked.

"I swear, you are turning into an addict," he joked.

"Around you, yes." They made it to the top step and he picked her up and walked into the bedroom, seeing the pristine blankets, pillows, and fresh bedsheets. When Faith almost giggled, he shook his head and walked into the bathroom, closing, and locking the door.

"What," Faith asked. He kissed her and sat her on the bathroom counter. She knew there was a reason that she loved the high counters.

He peeled her robe off, then the t-shirt. "Now, what were you saying about…"

"11am."

He shook his head and Faith went for the drawstring of his joggers. "Now," he asked. When he saw that smirk on her face, he shook his head. "Didn't have enough last night?"

"That's why we had one heck of a power nap," she teased.

He shook his head. "You do realize that the more you play like you aren't…"

She kissed him and slid her legs around him, pulling him closer. "Mine," she teased.

"Faith."

"What?"

"Are you gonna behave today?"

"Me? No. Never," she teased as she undid the bow of his drawstring.

"Faith."

"You started it." He shook his head and turned the hot water on. He put the towels on the warmer and when he went to turn around, she was pulling his joggers off.

"Shower," Faith said. He smirked and kissed her.

"Go. I'll be there in a minute."

She kissed him and went and got into the shower. "Breathe. Nothing is gonna happen, and nothing is going wrong. It's over," he said silently to himself as he freshened up. He kicked his clothes off, throwing them into the laundry and went and stepped into the shower behind her.

He slid his arm around her as she stood under the hot water and inhaled the scent of her shampoo. She reached for the conditioner and he kissed up her neck. "About time," she teased. She ran the conditioner through her hair and went to turn to face him. "What," he joked. She smirked and slid his hand down her torso as their fingers linked.

"I know what you're doing."

"And?"

He walked back two steps and sat down on the bench, pulling her onto his lap. "What," Faith teased. He turned her to face him and her legs slid around him.

"Getting a little carried away," he teased.

"Taunting my fiancée. It's kinda fun," Faith said.

He shook his head. "Breathe." She did and kissed him. "I love you Faith."

"I love you too handsome." When he felt her hand on him, he shook his head.

"Determined much?"

He kissed her and deepened the kiss until she got goosebumps and her body started almost trembling. The sex wasn't passion. Now, it was carnal need. From the bench to the wall, she was almost curled around him and molding her body to his. He felt too good. The sex felt too good. All he knew at that moment was that all of those ideas about what he'd love to do were gonna start happening. She could read his damn mind and it was almost getting him even more hot and bothered just thinking about it.

When they managed to climax and almost explode, he walked her back under the stream of hot water and rinsed her hair out with her still glued around him. He leaned her back against the wall and kissed her. "We need to get ready fiancée. Are you gonna let me get ready or are you just gonna distract me into staying naked?"

"Staying naked is kind of a bonus, but I get it. I still…"

He kissed her and taunted her even more. "Ridge," Faith said as her nails almost dug into his back.

"What," he teased.

"Crap." He muffled her moans with his kiss and kept going until she almost exploded all over again.

"Oh my goodness," she said as he slid her to her feet and sat her on the bench.

"Legs still shaking," Ridge asked as he washed up.

"Not fair."

"You started it beautiful." He finished washing up and she walked towards him. He flipped the water off, stepped out and wrapped a towel around his hips, then wrapped her in the other.

"Now, what were you saying?"

She shook her head and slid her arms around him as he hugged her. "I love you. I'm thinking you might've been right about the shaky legs."

"You did start it," Ridge teased.

Faith smirked and kissed him. "True," she joked. She sat up on the counter and freshened up and he kissed her. When she saw him pull out his razor, she shook her head.

"Really," he asked.

"Do you have to?"

He nodded and kissed her, rubbing his stubble against her. "Fine," she said giggling.

"Shorter not off." She nodded and kissed him. He grabbed his electric razor, raised up the blade so it wasn't as short and shaved as she watched. When he felt his towel loosen, he shook his head, putting the razor down.

"Faith."

"What?"

"Go get dressed."

She smirked. "No."

He shook his head again and kissed her, finished his trim, and tightened the towel back up. "Woman, cut it out." She kissed him and he stepped out of the bathroom, leaving her to do her hair, makeup and freshening up for the day.

He got dressed, grabbed his phone and laptop, and sat down on the sofa when he heard her coming down the steps. He looked and she was definitely up to something. "Faith."

"What?"

"You have a meeting don't you?"

"What about it," she asked as she smirked.

"Maybe clothes?"

"Funny," Faith said.

He shook his head and got up. "You're wearing a skirt like that to the office?"

She kissed him and smirked. "I just pulled it up to come down the steps."

"Not funny Faith." She kissed him, slid the skirt down and smirked. "Behave yourself," he said.

"Never," Faith teased.

He shook his head and walked her out to the SUV, helped her in and they made their way downtown. "Like the skirt," she asked.

"You need to stop with the short skirts fiancée."

She smirked. "I pulled it the rest of the way down," she teased.

He shook his head. "Are you actually gonna do work today, or are you gonna intentionally taunt me?"

"Both."

"Faith." She kissed his cheek at the light. "Woman."

"What?" He shook his head and flipped the radio on intentionally as she flipped the XM radio onto The Highway.

"This one is brand new from Nashville's favorite songwriter Mia Kent. Barefoot bliss by Samantha Clay. Our new number one," the DJ said. Faith got a smirk ear to ear and he shook his head.

"What?"

"We could run off and get married on a beach somewhere," Faith said.

"And I still think that we're waiting. A long wait."

Barefoot Bodyguard

"Why," Faith asked.

"Because there's no reason to rush into anything. We have all the dang time in the world," Ridge said.

"And if I said I wanted to have it sooner?"

"For us or for your folks?"

"Both."

He shook his head. "Can we not discuss this while I'm driving?"

She slid her hand in his and he shook his head as they hit morning traffic. "What," Faith asked.

"You really want to do the wedding now? Not to sound like an idiot, but we've literally been together a few weeks. I thought proposing was too much too soon. Running off and getting hitched that fast is insane."

She looked at him. "And why is that," Faith asked.

"Because it is. I love you, but you can't really think…"

She kissed him. "I'm just saying that we can go off and get married whenever. We don't have to wait if we don't want to."

"Are you determined to do this now," he asked.

"I don't want us to wait."

"Faith."

"I think we could at least book something."

"You're getting way too far ahead of yourself. You realize that right," Ridge said as they pulled into the parking for the office.

"Yep," she teased.

He parked the SUV and she slid her seatbelt off. "What," he asked seeing the look on her face. She smirked. "Faith." She kissed him. "Come here," he said.

She slid into his lap as he pushed the seat back as far as it would go. "You sure that you want to…" She kissed him, slid her skirt up and went for the zipper of his dress pants. "Faith." She kissed him and he shook his head. "Here?" She nodded with a smirk and when she slid in tighter, he knew he was gonna be in so much damn trouble.

They had sex in the SUV, got up and headed upstairs to her office and finished what they were doing on her sofa. She couldn't help herself, and there was no telling Faith no. When they managed to catch their breaths, his phone buzzed.

Barefoot Bodyguard

"You know that you're gonna get me in trouble," he teased.

"Never," Faith teased. She kissed him again, got up and they both cleaned up a bit while Ridge checked his messages. When there was one from her dad asking him to come up to his office, he shook his head.

"Right. Sure, I'm not in trouble," Ridge said as he showed her the text.

"I have an hour. I'm coming with you."

"Faith, this is business."

"And I'm coming with you like it or not handsome."

He freshened up and they headed up to her dad's office. He hadn't been in there since he was a kid, and the room seemed even bigger.

"Sir," Ridge said as he came in.

"When did you guys get back," Faith asked as she went and gave her dad a hug.

"Last night. I need to speak to Ridge alone," her dad said.

"Anything you need to say, just say it. I'm not leaving," Faith said.

Sue Langford

Chapter 12

"Dad, just say it. I'm not leaving this room."

"I saw that all of the cameras and microphones were removed from both houses. The police said that they're putting a case together to arrest him for installing them in the first place. Thank you for taking care of it. Now about the two of you," her dad said as Faith's hand linked fingers with Ridge's.

"Sir."

"Are you taking good care of my daughter," he asked.

Faith looked at him. "Dad, I know what you're trying to say, and don't bother saying it. You know better," Faith replied.

"Are you planning out the wedding," her dad asked.

"I told Faith that we needed to wait until all of the stalker stuff is long gone. I don't want anything getting ruined."

Her dad nodded. "Faith, you have…"

"Dad, if you're intending on attacking…"

"Faith, it's fine. I'll be down there in a couple. Promise," Ridge said as Faith shook her head, gave Ridge a hug and headed out.

"You were going to say," Ridge asked as her dad closed the door.

"Is she safe?"

Ridge nodded. "There's 3 staff with each house. She's safe. They're doing regular checks in and out."

"I understand the relationship between you two, but I need to know what the rush was with the proposal." Ridge knew it was coming. He didn't like that he had to explain himself, but he knew.

"We've known each other since we were kids. We've been like family since then thanks to my folks. Honestly, I know that it's soon. I also told her we were waiting a while. Long engagement. I knew that I loved her. I always have. I just couldn't wait anymore. I second-guessed myself too. Honestly, I don't think I can do this without her anymore. She's part of my life again. I'm not letting go of that."

Her dad nodded. "At least we know it's not for the money. I was almost worried that you'd say that she had a pregnancy scare."

Barefoot Bodyguard

"I promise you that she hasn't. I've made sure of that."

"Her mom was a little concerned and so was I. What else is going on with the dating situation," her dad asked.

"You have an amazing, beautiful, and brilliant daughter. She has been my entire life. I've had a crush on her since we were little. You knew that," Ridge said.

"Just make sure that the safety situation is resolved. If you need more staff, say so."

Ridge nodded. "Is there anything else you need me to do?"

"No. Just keep a close eye out for Zack. His son is the least of the worries, but he's the one behind the rest of it. He put those cameras in when Faith's mom and I had first met up again. I knew they were there. I just figured they'd be gone when the house was sold. I think he left them intentionally when he knew that Faith would be buying it." Ridge shook his head.

"It's been handled now. Is there anything else that you need me to do while I'm there," Ridge asked.

"Just keep her safe. If you think something seems a little off, get her out of there. If you have to go somewhere else, bring her to our house. Both of you are more than safe there."

"I appreciate the offer. I think that we have the security figured out. I have two guys rotating at each location. Wherever I am with Faith, I'm extra security." Her dad was impressed. "I told Faith that her safety came first and always would. You and I both know that she's determined and stubborn as a mule, but she understands it. After Cameron showed at the gate, she realized just how seriously I was taking it."

Her dad sat down, giving him the feeling that the grilling was over, or he was about to get down to actual business. "I need to ask something. I went through the resume you had for the security position. I didn't know you were in the military."

"I was. I made it to active duty then ended up coming home. As soon as I finished the one tour, I left. I couldn't do it. They allowed me to leave and I got the guys together that I knew I could trust. That's why we formed the group of security guys. Now, we're all still family but we're keeping Faith safe."

"Thank you for taking care of her. Really and truly, I don't know what her mom and I and her brothers would do without her here. All I want is to be able to actually sleep without worrying about her."

"I understand completely. She'll be fine. I promise." Her dad nodded, shook Ridge's hand and Ridge headed back to Faith's office.

"And," Faith said as he came in. She closed the door and sat down beside him.

"No raised voices or anything. It's fine. It's security stuff."

"And?"

"He wanted to make sure you weren't pregnant."

Faith shook her head. "So, he's okay with all the stuff we've done?"

"I doubt that if he knew what we'd been doing, he'd be happy with it, but the g-rated version he's good with."

"Not funny," Faith said.

"Did you want me to tell him what you were doing last night in the shower wife to be?"

"Not funny."

"Or what you were about to do when I stopped you?"

Faith shook her head and kissed him. "Ridge, you keep doing that, I swear..."

He kissed her again and she slid into his lap.

"What," he teased.

"You are so bad."

"And all yours."

"Oh, I know," Faith replied as she smirked. When her assistant knocked that it was time for her meeting, Faith shook her head and kissed him.

"Alright sexy. Get goin so we can get out of here," Ridge teased.

She got her laptop, her papers and her phone and made her way down to the meeting. Ridge logged into his email and saw a message from Kellen to call him.

"What's up," Ridge asked as he called almost instantly.

"There was a delivery this morning. Miss Faith didn't say anything about expecting a package or anything."

"What is the sender address?"

"I just forwarded it over to you. I didn't bring it into the house. It's on the driveway, but I wasn't sure." Ridge looked the address up and it was from the beach house.

"That's the address of the beach house."

"Then someone put it on there to throw her off?"

"Get in touch with the police and be on high alert at the house. Nobody in or out other than Faith and I."

"Done," Kellen said as he hung up. Why someone would go to all that trouble, Ridge didn't know, but he knew that one way or another it was gonna stop.

He went upstairs and talked to her dad's security while Faith was in her meeting. "I'll send security down to handle it."

"They put the house on lockdown as per my request. Nobody in or out."

"If you can send them updated information that Jeffrey Hamilton is on his way there to pick it up." Ridge nodded and came back down to Faith's office sending off an email.

When Faith made it out of her meeting, Ridge already had lunch waiting for her along with a sweet tea that he knew she'd want. "What's all of this," Faith asked.

"Lunch. You have to eat sometime beautiful."

"An in-office picnic. How cute," she teased.

He got up and sat on the sofa with her as they had their sushi. "How was the meeting?"

"Long. Got all the stuff for that author done. I have one other one then a little paperwork and a call I can take at home. Why do I get the feeling that the crap hit the fan while I was in the meeting?"

"Package showed at the house. Your dad's security is taking care of it." Faith looked at him almost surprised.

"The guys couldn't handle it?"

"It had the beach house as the return address. Not exactly a good sign."

"Why," Faith asked.

"Would you really have got some random person to grab something from the beach house when you and I could just go there and get it ourselves?"

"Nobody other than security is there to send anything."

"And now you understand why I involved dad's security."

She looked at him. "Ridge."

"You're safe here. He has more security in this building than in the dang white house. You're fine.

Barefoot Bodyguard

When we head back, we take a different route so nobody is following us. That's all." She finished her lunch and looked at him. He slid his arm around her and she slid into his arms.

"I get that someone is being an idiot, but screwing with me like that?"

Ridge kissed her. "I have it handled love. I promise."

"Why are you being so mushy? Aren't you..."

He kissed her. "Yeah I'm mad, but it's handled. Your dad had the same idea I did about who it is. It'll be handled. The police are there for a reason. I promise."

Faith looked at him. "So, in other words, the only time I'm actually completely safe is if we're here or we're in the house alone?"

Ridge looked at her. "That's what all of the security is there for. I promise that you're safe."

"There goes my good mood," she teased.

He kissed her and shook his head. "You're safe with me. If you want to go to your mom and dad's we can go. If you want to go down to the beach house for a few days, we can. Just tell me what you want," he said.

"Can we vanish into the sunset?" He smirked. "I don't know that your folks would be happy with that idea, but if you want to go away for a weekend, we can."

"And if I want another weekend with nobody around?"

"Where do you want to go?"

She looked at him. "What if we rented something and ran away somewhere?"

"Name the place," Ridge said.

"Seabrook."

"You want the Notebook to come to life?"

Faith kissed him. "I just need to be away."

"Myrtle beach."

Faith shook her head. "Kiawah?"

"It's all of 20 minutes from the house."

"What if we went to Blue Ridge," he asked. Faith shook her head. "Jekyll island."

Faith looked at him. "Resort?" Ridge nodded. "Can we get a private cottage?"

He nodded. "Well," he asked.

"Do it," Faith said as he slid his arms around her and gave her a hug.

"We can go this weekend if that's what you want."

She nodded. "You finish your meetings. I'll get it booked and organized." Faith kissed him again. "I'm bringing extra security. You're okay with that right," he asked.

"If you think we need it, sure," Faith replied as she got her papers together for the last meeting.

Ridge made a few calls and got a reservation for that weekend. They had two of her dad's security taking over the main house security and opted to bring Kellen and Leo with them. They made sure they had that settled and took a deep breath. He knew her meeting would be a while, and really the only thing standing in the way of them going was her dad losing his mind. He sent a quick message to her dad and within 2 minutes had a reply:

> *Perfect idea. She'll love it. If you need anything while you're there, let me know.*

It was a better reaction than he thought it'd be. He replied back with the full plan and made sure everything was booked. Ridge got a reply 2 minutes later:

You can take the plane. I'll get them to take you there and then back here when y'all are ready to head back.

He nodded. Everything was gonna work out. He was about to plan a few surprises when there was a knock at her office door. "What can I do for you," Ridge asked as her assistant came in.

"There's an officer here to talk to you and Miss Cartwright. Am I okay to bring him in," her assistant asked.

"Do we have an available meeting room?" She shook her head. "In here it is then," Ridge said as she went and brought the officer in.

"Mr. Sams," the officer asked.

Ridge nodded and her assistant brought in a pitcher of water and glasses for them. "Did you pick up the package from the house?"

The officer nodded. "Considering the issues that your team has come across, she must feel safe."

"She is for now anyway. What was in the package?"

"Black roses and a threat. I'm glad that your team called. We're adding officers onto the security at her house inland and the beach house. Just for backup. They'll be in unmarked vehicles, but they'll be there on 24-hour watch. I don't want anything else showing up that we don't find out about. I want her to feel safe."

"That's why I'm there," Ridge said.

"Alright. The fingerprints we came across on those devices were from someone that's known to the department. His son on the other hand is now in detention. He's not gonna be getting out. Luckily, and it still surprises me how, you managed to get him before he did anything else. The downside is that his father is out. He was just released recently. That could be what's pushing all of this on." Ridge's jaw was clenched. His hands were almost in fists. He was mad. Past mad.

"So, what is the next step," Ridge asked.

"If his father makes a move, we'll be there. We'll handle him. If we can't, then we have your team."

"I'm taking her away for the weekend to a private resort in Georgia. She needs a break from all of it."

"Understood. Who will be watching the house?"

"The security will be her dad's top-level security. They're guarding the house as I would. His personal security is keeping an eye on her inland house. The beach house is staying in the hands of the rest of my team. We're going for 4 days max."

"Alright. Keep me posted so I know that you two are both safe." Ridge nodded and the officer gave him a card and put his cell phone number on the back.

When Faith came back in and saw the officer heading out, she looked at Ridge. He took her hand, walked her back into her office and closed the door. "How was the meeting?"

"Ridge, why was the investigator here?"

"Went over everything we found at the house and the packages that showed."

"And what was in that package?"

"You don't want to know. There's no way it was Zack's kid. He's in jail."

"Great," Faith said.

"Babe, we're good. You and me and a private house in Jekyll island. High security and your dad's security is taking care of the house while we're gone so we can keep the house safe."

"You booked it?"

He nodded. "And your dad is flying us there and back. We're good baby." Faith wrapped her arms around him and he kissed her neck. "You're good. We're safe and we always will be," he replied.

Faith looked at him. "I love you," he said.

Faith kissed him. "I love you too. Thank you for this."

He nodded. "We're good. We go back and pack and we leave in the morning."

"You sure," Faith asked.

He nodded and kissed her again. "You ready to head home?"

Faith nodded. "I have one other call to do, but I'm doing it from home."

"Then we can go home and pack."

Faith nodded, got the last of her paperwork and her laptop and put it into her bag just as her assistant was coming in. "What's up," Faith asked.

"There's another author that your dad wanted you to look at. Are you able to take a look?"

"Email me over the info and I'll look at it. We're heading to the house to pack then we're taking off for a few days. I can always look over what the author has done so far," Faith said.

"I'll send it over. We have this so far," she said handing it to Faith.

"Alright. We're heading out. If you need anything, call me. Try to keep it limited contact while we're away."

Her assistant nodded and smirked. "Enjoy the mini vacation."

"Thank you," Ridge replied. She got all the paperwork she'd need and went through everything that she was gonna need to bring. They headed out and just as they were about to step onto the elevator, she saw her dad.

"Hey," Faith said as she gave her dad a hug.

"You excited about the holiday," her dad asked.

"Yes. I haven't got all the information from Ridge yet. Beyond that, I'm happy to be away from everything for a bit. How was the rest of your trip? I forgot to ask," Faith asked as they made their way to the parking garage. They got down there and her dad pulled Ridge aside.

"They'll be there tonight for a walk around with the team you already have. Keep my girl safe," her dad said.

"I will. Thank you again." He nodded and Ridge walked Faith to the SUV and helped her in, then walked around to his side and hopped in, making their way out of the office and off to the house.

Barefoot Bodyguard

When they pulled in, Ridge helped her out and they headed inside to get packed while Ridge went and talked to the guys, giving them the update on the plans. When he came upstairs, Faith was sitting on the edge of the bed. "What's wrong," Ridge asked.

"I love you."

"I love you back. What's wrong?"

"You know that he never stopped coming after my mom right?"

"Babe, that was your mom. Not you. We're good. We always will be baby. I promise." He hugged her and she wrapped her arms tight around him. "Tell me what you need."

"To stop feeling like I'm collateral damage to this psycho," Faith said.

He kissed her, devouring her lips. "We're getting away and being far away from all of this. The officers have the house covered as well as your dad's security. We're good. We can fly out tonight if that's what you want," he said.

"Will they let us," Faith asked.

He kissed her. "If that's what you want. Otherwise, we can have a movie night alone. Just us," he said.

Faith smirked. "Really," she teased with that look that said she was totally and completely game.

"We can leave after working out in the morning."

Faith smirked again and he shook his head. "Ridge."

"What beautiful?"

"Thank you."

"For what? Getting you into a better head space?"

She nodded and hugged him. "Babe, that's why I'm here. My job is to keep you safe and to make sure you're alright. You know that."

"Ridge, you shouldn't have to fight all of this." He kissed her again and held on a little tighter.

"Alright. Dinner tonight then we watch the movie. Beyond that, we do whatever we want to," Ridge said.

When she calmed a little, she looked up at him. "What," he asked.

"Thank you."

"Faith."

Barefoot Bodyguard

"For being here. For making me feel safe. For making me calm when I'm about to lose my marbles."

He kissed her again. "For fulfilling all of those fantasies from fifty shades," he whispered as he knew that the goosebumps were back.

"Better," Faith teased.

He kissed her neck. "Alright. Go get changed into movie attire. I'll figure out what we're doing for dinner."

"I was told seafood pasta. We could do steaks if you want," Faith said.

"I'll go talk to your favorite housekeeper. You get ready," he teased. He headed downstairs and saw her dad's security coming in.

"Right this way," Ridge said as they all walked into the security office.

"What are the details," her dad's security Calvin and Rogers asked.

"Full outdoor search, full inside search. Monitor the gate. We've found listening devices and cameras in the house before now. We're making sure it's clear. We'll be back Monday probably. So long as the house stays safe, we're fine," Ridge said.

"We're going with them," Kellen and Leo said.

"Alright. We'll do the hourly sweep and gate check. Beyond that, we'll keep you posted." Ridge nodded and the guys gave the security team their info. Ridge came out into the kitchen and saw the housekeeper.

"Steaks or seafood," she asked.

"Is there a surf and turf option if I grilled," Ridge asked.

"Sure," she replied. Ridge went and started up the grill and when he felt arms slide around him, he smirked.

"Feeling better," he asked.

"Yes. I guess we're having steaks?"

"Surf and turf," he said.

Faith smirked. "Love it. So, are we watching Fifty or the other one of that series that we watched the other night," Faith asked.

"That's up to you. Can you handle watching it?"

"We could watch both," she teased.

He knew she was almost hesitating. "Faith."

"Both."

Barefoot Bodyguard

He shook his head. "Alright, but the same rules..."

She kissed him. "We're watching it upstairs."

He shook his head. "Downstairs."

Faith shook her head. "Fine. If you can't watch it without anything, we're going in the guest room."

"As in your old dark room?" He nodded. "Ridge."

"That's the deal. You want to watch it in bed, you can't..."

She kissed him. "And if I just called it now that we wouldn't make it through it?"

"Then we watch the movies on vacation."

She smirked and kissed him. "Can you handle watching them tonight?"

"We start on one."

He smirked and wrapped his arm around her. "Done." The housekeeper came out and brought the food out and Ridge put it on the grill.

"I have your salad and grilled potatoes in the house when you're ready." "

Thank you. I appreciate it," Faith said.

"And the chocolate silk pie tarts are in the fridge whenever you're ready."

Faith gave her a hug and she headed in, leaving Ridge and Faith outside to grill. When he noticed what Faith was wearing, he shook his head. "You're just itching to watch that movie aren't you?" She kissed him. He shook his head again and they walked back into the house. He poured them each a glass of Jack and Cola and handed one to Faith.

"Already," she asked.

"You started it," he teased.

He finished with the seafood, plated the steaks, and took a few into the security guys, got a plate for the housekeeper and they sat down outside to eat alone. "Well," he asked.

"What," Faith teased as she slid her legs across his lap.

"How's the steak?"

"Almost as good as the lobster. How was yours," she teased.

"Good. You ready to watch the movie and admit that you can't stay apart," he teased.

Faith smirked. "Ridge."

Barefoot Bodyguard

He kissed her. "If you can get through…"

"Let's just say right now, it's not looking good on my end," she teased. He kissed her again, devouring her lips and went to take the dishes in when her housekeeper came outside and got them. "Thank you," Ridge said. She nodded with a smirk and he walked Faith in and refilled their glasses. "If you make it through the first half, you choose where. If you don't, we're going into my old room," he whispered.

Faith grabbed a blanket and they curled up on the sofa. "Blanket?"

She smirked.

He shook his head and they flipped on her movie first. "Ridge."

"What?"

"You sure you want…"

He kissed her. "Watch the movie. I've seen it a million times." She slid in tight to him and he shook his head. "I know what you're doing."

"I know you do," Faith teased.

"That's not exactly playing fair with this little game we have going."

She wrapped his arm around her and he kissed her neck. He poured them each a glass, handing hers to her. He took a gulp of his and Faith shook her head. "What," he asked.

"I still don't know how you drink this."

"I can always get the honey jack next time."

"Next time? What movie are you taunting me with next time," she teased.

"I have a bunch of them in my list," he teased. Faith shook her head.

They got to the end of her movie and she turned to face him. "What," he teased.

"Before you turn the other one on."

"Faith."

She kissed him. "Promise me something."

He shook his head. "What," he asked.

"Promise me that if you start feeling like something isn't right, you tell me."

"When we're away?"

"And when we're here. Even if it's a gut feeling."

He kissed her. "Watch the movie. We're good. We have 4 security guys here tonight. I told Leo he could bring wifey for a little mini work vacation."

"Good. He deserves a little break."

She hadn't moved from straddling him. "Faith."

"What?"

"You gonna watch the next one?"

She kissed him and he smirked. "Behave."

"Never." When he felt her try to undo his jeans, he stopped her.

"Giving in that fast," he teased. She shook her head and he could see in her eyes what she was thinking.

"Turn around and watch the movie. You don't get that until after."

"Mine," Faith said.

"I know. Behave and watch," he teased as she kissed him again.

"And if I said no," she teased.

"You admitting that I won?"

She shook her head. "Then watch."

He kissed her until he felt her get goosebumps. "We could just take…"

He kissed her again and turned her to face the TV. "You start that, we're gonna end up doing it on the dang sofa."

"And that's bad why," Faith asked as they whispered back and forth. He shook his head. "Watch the movie and finish your drink woman," he teased. He finished his, getting himself another glass and added some into hers.

He handed the glass to her and slid his hand under the blanket. "What," Faith asked.

"Nothin," he teased as his hand slid down her side.

"Ridge."

"Watch the movie."

"What are you doin?"

"Nothin," he teased as she felt the hem of her skirt slide up her leg. When his hand slid over her hip, she slid in tighter to him. When his hand slid between her legs, she paused the movie.

"Ridge."

"Put it back on." She flipped it back on and the taunting began. When her hand slid to his knee and almost white-knuckled it, he smirked and kissed the edge of her ear.

"Did you really think that I'd let you win tonight," he whispered almost purring in her ear.

"You are so not playing fair," she said as he felt her body almost throb around his fingers. "Ridge," she said.

"Mmm," he purred into her ear.

"Not fair."

"Yeah it is." He kissed her neck and she shook her head.

When he knew that she was about to explode, he pulled his hand away. "Playing with fire," Faith said.

"Back at ya," he smirked. When she shook her head, he smirked and took a gulp of his drink.

"What are you up to," she asked.

"Taunting you until you can't hold off for one more second. Taunting you until you are so hot and bothered that you drag me up the steps."

"Past it."

"Tell me what you want," he whispered.

"You know what I want."

"Say it." She paused the movie and turned to face him.

"What," he teased.

Faith kissed him and he smirked. "We watching the rest in bed?"

"If we make it that far."

He smirked, finished his drink, refilled his glass, and topped off hers, handing them to her. "What," she asked.

"Stop the movie." She pressed stop, turning it off and he picked her up, flipping her over his shoulder and carried her up the steps to his old bedroom. He slid her onto the bed, took the glasses from her hand, putting them on the side table and locked the door.

He flipped the light off and kissed up her leg. "Ridge."

"What," he asked between kisses. When he got to her inner thigh, he could feel her muscles almost trembling. "Faith."

"Come here." He pulled his shirt off and slid into her arms as she wrapped her legs around him.

"What you need baby?"

"I want you."

"Good. Feeling is mutual," he teased.

"Now."

His fingers took over the taunting and he kissed her. "You sure," he teased.

"Ridge, take the jeans off."

"Boxers too? Nah."

She shook her head." Ridge."

He kissed her, kissed down her neck and felt her trying to pull at his jeans. "Faith."

"Off."

He pulled her skirt off, slid her shirt and bra off and kissed down her torso, getting her even more hot and bothered. "You're so not playing fair."

"Oh, I know," he teased.

He kept going until she was about to try and grab him and drag him back to her. "Ridge."

He kissed her. "What," he teased as he nibbled at her breasts.

"Come here."

"What," he teased as he kissed up the front of her neck. When he felt his jeans slide down, he smirked. "That bad," he asked.

"Now. Take them both off." He kissed her, kicking them to the floor then his boxers.

"Now what do you want," he asked.

When she pulled her legs tight around him, he smirked. "Faith."

"I need you," she teased. He devoured her lips and before she said another word, or gasped for another breath, they were having sex. It started out hot, then went to passion, then intense, then harder when she dug her nails in. When she slid on top, he shook his head, as things got even more intense.

"Faith." He kissed her and slid her back onto her back, going deeper, harder. She linked their fingers and he made it more intense. He grabbed the little buzzing toy from his drawer and had her body almost humming.

"Ridge." He intensified it. "Crap. Ridge," she said again.

He kissed and nibbled her shoulder and his body was nearing that point. He kissed the front of her neck and he kissed her shoulder. "What," he teased.

When he felt her body tightening around him, he was a goner and he knew it. "Ridge."

"Baby," he said as he exploded into her and her body throbbed tight around him.

"Crap," she said. He kissed her and devoured her lips.

"What," he asked.

"I can't stop shaking." He kissed her and leaned onto his back, pulling her to him.

"Now, what were you saying?" She kissed him, devouring her lips until she finally stopped shaking. "We still have a movie to finish," he teased.

"I don't think I can move," Faith said. He kissed her again. He handed Faith her drink and she drank the entire thing in one gulp. He took a gulp of his and smirked. "I know that look," she teased. He kissed the tip of her nose.

"And," he teased.

"Yeah, we're not making it through the movie. I can barely move. My legs are still shaking."

"That was my plan beautiful," he joked.

"Hilarious." Faith kissed him and he slid her tighter into his arms.

"Faith."

"What handsome?"

He kissed her. "You sure you're okay," he asked.

Faith kissed him. "I'm alright. Promise," she teased.

"Are you ready to go tomorrow?"

Faith kissed him, devouring his lips. "I'm also 100% sure that we're never making it out of bed," she teased.

"We have a beach to go to. Just no going topless on the beach."

She kissed him. "Whatever you say handsome."

He kissed her, shaking his head. "When do you have to go to the doctors again?"

"Next week I think. It's a while off," she teased.

"A week isn't a while."

"Meaning?"

"We go to your doctor early then head there."

"Ridge."

"You want to run…"

She kissed him. "We're waiting until I'm back."

"Then we aren't…"

She kissed him. "Ridge."

"We're making sure." She nodded and he kissed her neck.

When he got way too comfortable, he almost started nodding off. "Where are the phones," Faith asked.

He kissed her shoulder. "What do you need?"

"Call the doctor."

He kissed her and got up, pulling his jeans on and headed downstairs, grabbing her phone and his from the table, made sure the doors were locked up and let the security team know they were heading to bed. When he walked back into his room, their glasses were gone. He smirked and walked into her bedroom, seeing her in bed, putting lotion on her legs. He shook his head, locked the door and walked over to her. "What did I say about that lotion," he teased.

"That it got you hot and bothered."

"And?"

"Doing it intentionally."

He shook his head, kissing her and leaned her onto the bed. "Phone," Faith asked as he handed her phone to her.

She made a quick call and the doctor offered to come over that night. "Are you sure," Faith asked.

"It'll only take a few minutes. Easier than you coming into the office before you leave."

"Thank you," Faith said as she went and slid her hoodie on with a pair of shorts.

"Now?"

She nodded. "She lives maybe 5 minutes from here. It's fine." He took a deep breath and shook his head, pulling his hoodie on and walked back downstairs.

"Sir," the security guys said.

"Her doctor is on the way over. Two minute thing. Just keeping y'all posted," Ridge said.

"Thank you," Kellen said. Ridge nodded and refilled his drink, sitting back down on the sofa.

When Faith came downstairs, he smirked and she walked over to him, sitting in his lap. "Faith."

"What," she asked as she leaned in and kissed him.

"Behave." She shook her head and kissed him. Just as she started attempting to taunt him, there was a buzz at the gate. The doctor having an office so close by was a bonus. She could grab whatever she needed and make house calls just like she had when Faith was in her 20s.

"Miss Faith, your doctor has arrived," Kellen said.

"Thank you," she said as she kissed Ridge. She came in and the doctor sat down with her. Ridge went to get up and give them privacy when Faith sat him back down with her.

"And you know for sure that you aren't pregnant yes," the doctor asked.

"I know that I'm not," Faith said.

"I need you to do the test then we can go ahead with the injection." Faith kissed Ridge and went and did the pregnancy test. Part of him was almost hoping that it came up positive. She came back downstairs, handed the test to the doctor and within a matter of a few minutes, she looked up at Faith.

"Well, it's still negative. Which arm," the doctor asked. Faith pointed to her left and she gave Faith the injection.

"I'll make the appointment for the next injection."

"Just shoot me over the details. Thank you for coming over here so late. We're heading away in the morning."

"Have fun on the trip." Faith nodded as she talked to the doctor as she walked her out.

Ridge walked upstairs and slid his hoodie off, packing what he'd need for the trip. He came back into the bedroom, kicking his jeans off, and slid under the covers. When she came back upstairs, she slid her clothes off and slid into the bed on her side. Within a matter of 2 seconds, his arm was around her and slid her to him. "And here I thought you were asleep," Faith teased.

"You still have half a movie to watch," he whispered as she got goosebumps all over again.

"You sure that it's a good idea," she teased as his hand slid to her hip.

"That mean you're giving up?" She went to turn to face him and he wouldn't let her.

"Depends," she teased.

He kissed up the nape of her neck as her body almost tensed and curled into him. "On," he asked as just the sound of his voice got her turned on.

"On whether we're watching it from the beginning or not," she teased.

"And you're convinced you'll make it through the movie."

She slid her hand on top of Ridge's as it started moving closer to the apex of her thighs. "Ridge."

He kissed and nibbled up the back of her neck. "Um hmm," he said as he kissed the side of her neck.

"And if I say that I give up?"

"Still watching the end Faith. That was the deal."

Chapter 13

Faith smirked and flipped the tv on. He locked the bedroom door, came and slid back into the bed and she curled right back up against him. "Now, where were we," he teased.

Faith smirked and leaned back, kissing him. "I love you," Faith said.

"Love you more," he replied as he kissed her shoulder.

When she felt his fingers start taunting her again, she shook her head. "You're seriously not playing fair," Faith said.

"And? Did you want me to," he joked. When he saw the smirk, he knew her answer.

"I don't even know why I'm packing clothes for the trip."

He smirked and nibbled her neck. "You have a point, but we are going out to dinner."

"Good point," Faith said as her heart started racing.

"We have to eat sometime." It was like everything he said just amplified the feeling she had. Her body craved him and his fingers taunting her and his kisses hitting just the right spot had her toes curling. "Faith," he whispered as the goosebumps came back.

"Yes," she said as he curled her tighter to him.

"Pause the movie." She pressed pause and went to turn over when they were having sex.

Her body against hers as he felt her body almost trembling with that fill of passion. The sex was even more intense. He nibbled her ear and her body almost exploded with pleasure. It was more than once, more than twice when he found his release. "Yeah that movie is staying on pause," Faith said as she tried to catch her breath.

"You sure?" She nodded and he kissed the back of her neck again, still connected to her as her body still throbbed around him.

"Ridge."

"What," he teased as he nibbled at her ear.

"I give in," she teased.

"I know," he joked.

"Meaning what?"

"I have the movie saved on my laptop," he joked.

"Meaning?"

"Rematch this weekend."

She managed to get up, put the phones onto the charger and shook her head. "What," he teased.

"I can barely move. It's all your dang fault," she joked.

"You started it." She smirked, leaned over and kissed him and went and cleaned up. He put his morning alarm on and got up, walking into the bathroom behind her. "Ridge."

"Sexy."

"What if we just did it while we were there?"

"You mean your dad killing me and feeding me to the sharks?"

"Ridge."

"We're waiting. We have all the damn time in the world. I'm not even talking about planning anything."

"You sure? We can do it on the beach."

He looked at her. "That determined to do it now?" Faith nodded. "Why?"

"Because we have to plan anything else early," she said as he leaned her against the counter. "Ridge."

He picked her up and sat her on the counter. "You really want to talk about this now?" She smirked and he shook his head. "Bed. You need sleep so those sexy legs quit shaking," he teased. He kissed her and she slid to her feet.

"Fine," she teased. He shook his head and she kissed him then walked back into the bedroom. He cleaned up, got the toiletries he needed to pack and came into the bedroom to see her in his t-shirt in bed. He smirked, pulled his boxers on, and slid into the bed behind her.

"Faith."

"Yes," she said as he slid his arms around her.

"Come here."

She turned to face him and kissed him. "What?"

"You want to really plan it?"

"Our folks are home. We have time."

"Faith."

"Everyone keeps asking when the wedding is and there's no answer." He lifted her gaze to meet his.

"We just got engaged. Hell. We were fighting about the ring this week. What's the rush?"

"If you could choose."

"Cypress. Away from everything and everyone. Just our folks and a friend or two."

"Church?"

"If you want. I just don't think either of us want the extra drama if we have too many people," Ridge said.

"What if we had the reception near the beach?"

"Babe."

"I know. I just want something that's us."

"There's one really good solution. Safe, secure, easy, and comfortable."

"What," Faith asked.

"Either here or at your mom and dad's."

"I doubt they'd want everyone over there."

Ridge kissed her. "We have time. We can do whatever you want. Just give it a little time. We can plan it when we're back or something."

She kissed him. "As long as we're there and happy, I'm good with it," she said.

"Good. Babe, I'd be happy just you and me on the beach. You're the eldest. Your folks and your brothers are gonna want to be there. Same as my folks." She kissed him.

They fell asleep talking it all through. "Your dad planned the wedding to your mom all on his own," Ridge said.

"And you'd want to do all of that? No," Faith teased as they were curled up together.

"I have a few ideas there wife to be." She kissed him and nodded off, curled up with him until he was completely out cold.

The next morning, she woke up and noticed he was still asleep. For once, she'd managed to wake up before him. She kissed his chest and had no idea that he'd actually woken up the minute her lips touched his chest. When he felt her hand slide down his torso, he shook his head. "I know what you're doing."

Faith looked up. "And?"

"Faith."

She looked at him with a smile. "Was going to surprise you," she teased.

"And?"

"Nothin." He flipped her onto her back.

"Tell me what you want Faith."

"I want it."

He shook his head. "Faith." When she managed to grab hold of what she really wanted, it was a turn on. "Behave yourself." Faith shook her head and kept going, rubbing until she knew that he couldn't really walk away. He slid her hand away and kissed her as her legs slid around his hips. Morning sex was an understatement. When she started almost digging her nails deep into his back, he just went deeper.

"Ridge," Faith said as her body tightened around him and throbbed deep into her core.

"More," he whispered as he saw the goosebumps.

"Aah." He kept going until his body couldn't hold back. He leaned to his side and Faith linked their fingers.

"More," he teased.

"Yeah, I don't think I can move."

"You started it," he teased as they both giggled.

"I made a decision," she said as her body still shook in his arms and he pulled the blanket over them.

"Which is what beautiful," he asked.

"Next summer. May."

"You sure," he asked.

"No. I'd say December if you wouldn't lose it."

He kissed her shoulder. "Are we seriously talking wedding plans right now?" Faith nodded with a little giggle. The same one he'd always loved. "We could just do it in January or before Valentine's Day."

"Ridge."

"Don't want to wait. I get it." She shook her head and he went to get up.

"Where are you going fiancée?"

"Gym." She smirked. "I know what that smirk means Faith. I'm getting a workout in before we leave. No distracting me." He went and cleaned up, slid joggers and a tee on and went to head downstairs when she slid her arms around him. "What's up sexy?"

"I'm coming with you." He smirked, turned around and kissed her and went and got warmed up.

She was a distraction alright. When she came downstairs in the shortest shorts he'd ever seen and nothing else but a sports bra, he almost tripped over his feet twice. "Faith."

"What?"

He shook his head. "That whole no distractions thing just went right out the window?"

She nodded with a smirk ear to ear. "Something like that," Faith said as she did her yoga. He shook his head, attempting to block his eyes from looking. He finished his run and stepped off the treadmill.

"Faith, you need to quit."

She kissed him. "I'm working out."

"In the shortest shorts ever," he teased. "You might as well have walked down here naked to do yoga."

"I considered it. Didn't think that my dad's security..."

He kissed her. "Behave. Tomorrow you can do whatever, but right now, please." She smirked.

They both finished their workouts and he went into the kitchen to see her housekeeper making omelets for them. "I can do this," Ridge said.

"Go and sit down. I have 3 more days off. I'm making you both breakfast. I appreciate it, but I'm cooking."

He smirked, thanked her, and sat down to see Faith intentionally taunting him all over again. "Woman."

She smirked and kissed him. "What," she teased as she had her breakfast.

"You don't quit, I swear."

"What," Faith teased as the housekeeper got a smirk. He shook his head and ate. They finished breakfast and went to clean up when her housekeeper brushed him and Faith both out of the kitchen. Faith kissed him and he picked her up, carrying her up the steps. He walked into the main bedroom, kicked his sneakers and joggers off and she smirked.

"Faith."

When she smacked his backside, he shook his head and did it right back, sitting her on the bathroom counter. "Ow," Faith said.

"Back at ya," he teased as he kicked his boxers off. When she motioned for him to come closer, he shook his head. "I know exactly what you're up to. Grounded," he teased. He flipped the water on and slid into the shower. She slid her clothes off, throwing them into the laundry, and stepped into the shower, walking towards him.

"What am I gonna do with you and your dirty mind," Ridge asked.

"You started it."

"Really? Seems to me that you started with the dirty mind this morning when you were taking full advantage of…"

She kissed him. "I had something else planned," she teased.

"I bet you did."

"Something I can still do when we're away."

"We talked about that." She smirked and grabbed her shampoo, sliding him out of the stream of water. She showered and he shook his head. "Faith."

"Mm."

"I love you, but you're seriously taunting. Like taunting a lion with food."

"Then you should probably get dressed."

He shook his head and he pulled her out of the water. "No more taunting."

"Then don't start it," she teased as he kissed her.

He devoured her lips and sat down on the bench as she slid into his lap. "What am I gonna do with you?"

"Marry me. Plan it," she teased as he pulled her legs around him and she slid him into her. "Mine," Faith teased.

"That's what you want?"

She nodded. "You sure?"

She leaned forward and kissed him as they started having sex in the shower. Body-shaking, so deep she could barely move and her body pulsating around him sex that had her mind forgetting anything and everything else there was. When she almost crumbled into his arms. "Wife to be," he said.

"Ridge," she said as her body stared shaking and her heart almost flew from her chest. "You sure I started it?"

She smirked and he kissed her again as he took a beat then got up. "I'm sure," she teased. He kissed her and rinsed off, bringing the hand shower to her and rinsing the conditioner from her hair. "Thank you," Faith said.

"Welcome beautiful." He kissed her again and put the hand shower back on the wall. He took her hand and walked her out of the shower, turning the water off as he wrapped her up in a towel and sat her back on the counter.

"You good," he teased as he slid a towel around his hips. Faith smirked and he shook his head. "When are you gonna behave?"

"Never." Ridge shook his head, devouring her lips with the toothpaste kiss. "I love you," Faith said.

"Love you back, but you know we have to actually get to the airport right?"

"I know. I just felt like a distraction," she teased.

He shook his head. "Then next time, I'm distracting you."

She shook her head and he kissed her. "Just remember you said you wanted a distraction."

She smirked. "Oh, I will sexy fiancée," Faith teased.

They managed to get dressed, double-checked what they'd packed and made their way downstairs before they got a call from her dad. "Sir," Ridge said as he walked into her office and sat down.

"The plane is ready and waiting. We were talking last night. What would you think about having the wedding at the house?"

It's like her dad had read his mind. "Well, we were considering it, but I'm determined to wait for a while. There's no reason to rush into it now."

"Partially, I'm glad to hear it, but her mom is determined to start planning asap."

"I'll get them together for a day to plan stuff when we're back. I'm getting her out to the airport now," Ridge said as Faith came into the office and saw him.

"Alright. Let me know if she agrees to it."

"I will. Thank you again for all of this."

"Most welcome."

He hung up with her dad just as Faith slid into his lap. "Faith."

"What?"

"Your dad wants you to have the reception at the house."

She smirked. "Go figure," she teased.

"Up. We have a flight to catch." She kissed him. "What?"

"Still stunned that you two are on the same level now. You were worried," she teased.

"And? Now we managed to find a way to fix things."

Faith kissed him. "This mean that you're gonna let me plan it?"

"When we're back, your mom wants to help." She kissed him and they got up and were about to head out when her dad's security stopped them. "What's up," Ridge asked.

"We have a car on the way to take you over. The security guys are coming in the second car. We have everything under control here. If you need anything at all, call," one of the two security guys said.

"Thank you," Faith said as they headed outside to see the car coming up the drive.

They handed over the suitcases and headed off with Leo and Kellen following in the other car. When they pulled into the private airport, Faith smirked. "What," he asked.

"Before we hop out," Faith said.

Barefoot Bodyguard

"What?"

She slid into his lap. "What else do you have planned while we're there?"

"A few things. The rematch. Beach. Sleeping. Dinner."

She kissed him. "Ridge."

"You'll see when we get there. Up."

She kissed him and they opened the door. He picked Faith up, carried her up a flight of steps into the plane and sat her on the sofa. He got the bags, made sure he had everything and went and got on the plane. "What," Faith asked.

He handed her bag and purse to her. "I'm glad you remembered to pack it," Faith teased.

"You said you wanted to make sure you were around if they needed you."

He kissed her and slid his laptop out of his bag. "What are you doin all the way over there," Faith teased.

"Emails then I'm all yours beautiful." She got up, put her bag beside his and sat down beside him as they put their seatbelts on. He double-checked his emails, made sure nothing important was happening and slid his laptop back into his bag.

When he sat back up, she slid her legs across his lap and typed through emails.

The guys hopped on, grabbing a seat, and stretching out. "Faith."

"What?"

"Really?" She nodded. She finished with the email she had to send, slid it into her bag, and slid in closer. He shook his head and she held his hand. "Don't start," he said silently.

The plane took off and he shook his head. "Probably a half hour flight. The car is there to meet you when you arrive to take you to the resort. There is an item that was delivered to the house that you'll be staying at. Beyond that, everything is at your disposal when you arrive," the attendant said.

"Thank you," Ridge said as he took the key and she handed the other two to the guys.

"Wifey is already down there. She went to Savannah with her friends last night. That alright," Leo asked.

"I just hope that y'all have fun. That's why we're there," Ridge said.

Faith smirked. "What," he asked.

Barefoot Bodyguard

She motioned for him to come closer. "What," he teased. She kissed him, devouring his lips. "I have a surprise for you."

He smirked and shook his head. "Wife to be, at least for now behave."

She shook her head. "Over-rated," she teased. He shook his head. In what seemed like a matter of 20 minutes, they were landing. He remembered driving it years before and it wasn't a 20-minute drive. It was hours in traffic on a busy highway. They stepped off the plane and put the bags into the waiting car then headed off. They got to the resort not long later and walked into the private house. It was still part of the resort, but private enough so they had space.

Ridge walked Faith down to their suite and when she saw the flowers, she looked at him. "What's this," Faith asked. "Look at the card." She took the card and opened it:

> *I love you. Never doubt it. I'm yours for life. Remember one thing. I'm never letting go. You had me at 2 days old. You always will.*

When she turned and looked at him, she had tears in her eyes. "And," he asked.

Faith walked over to him and kissed him. "I love you."

"Good." He kissed her. "You like?"

"The flowers I'd want," she teased.

"I know. Those have always been your favorite. I know you."

He kissed her again. "And what else did you plan?"

"You'll find out tonight. Right now, you in a bikini and going to the beach."

"Ridge."

"What?"

"Can we just relax?" He smirked and walked her into the bedroom. When she saw the rose petals in the shape of a heart on the bed, she smirked. "You went all out didn't you?"

He nodded and hugged her. "I wanted you to have time to relax and soak it all in. I want to show you driftwood beach."

"What?" He smirked. "You can't take any of it home, but it's really beautiful."

"And then what?"

"Dinner under the stars alone. I even got a fancy dinner for you."

Faith smirked. "Planning all of it out?"

"Late night thing." She shook her head.

"Ridge."

"Yes love."

"Thank you for all of this." He kissed her. One kiss turned into two, then they were making out in their bedroom.

"Bikini," he said. Faith nodded, kissed him again and went and slid into a bikini while he slid into swim shorts.

When she came back into the bedroom, she was in a pale pink bikini and he shook his head. "What?"

"String bikini?"

She nodded and kissed him. He shook his head, handing her the shorts. "Really?"

Ridge nodded. "And a shirt." She smirked and kissed him and he shook his head. If she knew what he'd planned, she wouldn't be complaining. She slid a sundress over the bikini and he smirked. "You sure you're ready to go?"

"Purse, beach blanket, towel."

"In the cart."

Faith looked at him." "And the cooler."

He let the guys know where they were headed, and headed off with Faith. They made it to driftwood beach and she was in awe. "Seriously," Faith said as she saw the driftwood. The trees were almost sandblasted and looked like sculptures in the sand. The twists, turns and beauty of them had her completely surprised. They walked through the pristine white sand and he smirked. "What," Faith asked.

"Like?"

She nodded and kissed him. "I needed this," Faith said.

"I know. Now, we're off to the actual beach," Ridge said.

"Meaning?" He kissed her and they made their way back to the golf cart and headed to the beach. When they got there, Kellen, Leo and Leo's wife were there waiting for them with the beach chairs and umbrellas.

"Oh really," Faith teased.

He kissed her and they came out to everyone. "Where did y'all vanish to," Kellen asked.

"We went out to driftwood beach. I wanted to show her," Ridge said.

"You haven't been out there in years. I should take you out there," Leo said to his wife.

"Y'all go and we'll hang here," Ridge said. Leo headed off with his wife and Kellen stayed with Faith and Ridge.

"It's fine. You can enjoy the beach," Faith said.

"I'll stay here," Kellen said giving Ridge a look that said there was a really good reason.

"Come with me," Faith said as she got up.

"Where," Ridge teased as he stood up. Faith took his hand and walked him out into the water, away from everyone.

"You like," Ridge asked.

Faith nodded and kissed him. "I'm getting a weird feeling. Something's not right," Faith said.

He kissed her, picking her up and wrapping her legs around him as he waded further out into the water. "Kellen has the same feeling. That's why he didn't leave our sides. It's alright."

"What if it isn't," Faith asked.

He kissed her. "Then Kellen and Leo handle it. My job is to keep you safe and I am." She kissed him and he shook his head. "What?"

Sue Langford

"You sure we're safe out here?"

He nodded and hugged her. "I promise you. Whatever it is, they're handling it. It something else happens, I handle it. Either way, you're safe."

She kissed him again and his hands slid to her backside. "What are you up to," Faith asked.

"Back to the hotel or we stay out here," he asked.

"If that feeling doesn't go away, back to the house."

He kissed her, devouring her lips until he felt her goosebumps come back out. "Better," he teased as they came up for air.

She smirked and kissed him again as he undid her bikini bottoms. "Ridge."

"You wore them."

"Not happening Ridge."

"Really," he teased. They were further out from everyone else and away from prying eyes.

"We're not doing this. Not out here," she said.

"House it is," Ridge replied as he retied the one side of her bikini bottoms.

"You were seriously gonna..." He kissed her again and walked back in towards the towels when Kellen flagged them in.

"What's wrong," Ridge said as they made it back in and Faith was almost white knuckling his hand.

"I saw someone watching a little too intently. Older. Dark hair. 6 feet."

Ridge nodded, handed Faith her sundress and they packed up and made their way to the other golf cart. Within a matter of 20 minutes, they were back in the house. "Kellen."

"I got a photo. I don't know who he is, but I'm gonna find out," Kellen said as he walked up to his room and started searching. Ridge let Leo know that they were at the house and he watched Faith almost start to pace.

"Babe."

"I told you," she said.

He kissed her and wrapped his arms around her. "You're good baby. I promise you are."

"Ridge."

"I know." He kissed her forehead and wrapped his arms tighter around her. When Kellen came downstairs and motioned for hm to come up the steps. He went to walk out of the bedroom and Faith wouldn't let go of his hand. "Two minutes," he said. Faith shook her head and went with him.

"And," Ridge asked as Kellen looked over at Faith. Ridge nodded and Kellen turned the laptop to face him. When Ridge saw the photo, he sat down.

"What," Faith asked.

He saw the one name that he'd hoped that Faith would never have to see. "Ridge."

"The guy who was with your mom before she got together with your dad isn't the guy. Not the one who was watching us."

"Who is it," Faith asked.

Ridge shook his head. "He's not after you. This one is after me."

"What," Faith asked.

Ridge shook his head and walked downstairs. "What does that mean?" Kellen stopped her. "Tell me," Faith said.

Ridge went down to the bedroom, got his handgun and changed into jeans and a t-shirt. When he walked outside, Leo and his wife were just showing. "What's wrong," Leo asked.

"Go inside."

"You get your backside in the house. What are you doing," Leo asked.

"He's here."

"Who?"

"You know who. Kellen saw him at the dang beach."

Leo dragged Ridge back into the house. "He knows better. That restraining order still stands. Especially here. He's not coming near you," Leo said.

"He's here. Last time, I ended up with one too many stitches for my liking. I'm not gonna put her through that," Ridge said.

"Put me through what," Faith asked as he turned and saw her coming down the steps.

Ridge shook his head and walked into the bedroom. Part of him was determined to pack up and leave. Get her as far from there as possible. "Ridge, tell me." He shook his head and Faith followed him into the bedroom and blocked him from leaving.

"Faith."

"Either you tell me what in the hell is going on or you aren't leaving this room."

When she looked at him, the playful guy was gone. Long gone. It was like he'd just been put into a box. Ridge walking with a loaded weapon on his hip was not a look that she ever remembered. "Talk to me."

"That idiot came after me when I came back to Charleston. I had to move twice."

"Who is he," Faith asked.

"This girl I dated. He's her brother. He's shot at me twice already in my life, both of which involved me and stitches. He tried to beat the crap out of me. He rammed my truck. Him being anywhere near me isn't permitted and he knows it," Ridge said as Faith saw the jawline of the man she loved clenched. Ridge going into protective mode. If he hadn't been so tensed up, it would've been kinda hot. Actually, really hot.

"Do you want to go back to Charleston?"

He shook his head. "Not when he already figured out that I was here."

Faith shook her head. "Stay here."

"Faith."

Barefoot Bodyguard

"Stay with me. Don't go doing something ridiculous."

He took a deep breath. "I don't want you hurt in the dang crossfire."

She kissed him and within a minute or two, he leaned down and kissed her, devouring her lips. "He doesn't know where we are. Just breathe. Please."

Ridge took a deep breath and Faith slid her arms around his neck. "Babe."

"Ridge, please."

He kissed her and wrapped his arms tight around her. "Just remember. If I'm not here, Kellen and Leo and his wife are in the other room."

"Ridge."

"I promise that I'm keeping you safe. I told your folks I would and I'm not…" She kissed him. She needed her Ridge back. The one that tripped over himself to make her feel the love. The one who taunted her until her legs could barely move.

"Ridge."

"Faith."

"Look at me." When he finally did, she kissed him. "Stay here with me. I don't want you to leave."

"Faith."

"I get it, but I want you staying here. I don't want you getting hurt." He looked at her and there was a knock at the door. He took a deep breath and went to answer when Faith stopped him.

"Faith," Kellen said.

She opened the door and sat Ridge down. "Everything okay," Kellen asked.

"He's worried that the guy is gonna show up here." Kellen shook his head.

"I'm not taking you to the dang hospital again. You're staying with Faith. We'll handle him if he gets anywhere near here."

"I don't want him coming close," Ridge said.

"I get it. We're here for security. Let us do it," Kellen said.

"He wants me and he's only gonna stop when he confronts me face to face."

"Then he can do it from his hospital bed when we cuff him to it," Kellen replied. When Leo came in, he knew.

Barefoot Bodyguard

"Tell me what I need to do," Leo said.

"If he comes near me or this house, I swear I will pulverize him," Ridge said.

"Stay here then. We'll keep an eye out. I promise you that we'll figure it out. Stay here with Faith. You keep her safe, we keep you safe," Kellen said.

"If I find him first…"

"Ridge."

He shook his head. "Faith, I have to do this."

"No, you don't," Kellen said.

When Ridge left and made his way out the front door, Kellen went after him as Faith shook her head. "This is insane. Completely insane. Where the hell did he go," Faith asked.

"Kellen will find him. It's alright. I promise you," Leo said.

"Then find him."

By the time that Kellen caught up to Ridge, he was on the beach, hunting the man down. "Ridge, you can't do that. You can't just hunt through a crowd," Kellen said. When Ridge's phone buzzed, he handed it to Kellen and saw someone he thought it might be. He looked and saw a message from Faith, following Ridge down the beach. "Dude, you need to call her. Stop hunting."

"Kellen, go back to the house and keep her safe. One hair on her head," Ridge said.

"Leo is good with Faith. Don't do something stupid." Ridge spotted the man and took off, grabbing him by the scuff of his neck. Kellen called the cops and pulled Ridge away from him.

"There's a restraining order for a reason. What are you doing here, and why are you watching him and his fiancée," Kellen asked.

"Why would she even want an idiot like you? She doesn't know that you murdered someone," the man said.

"Shoulder. That's it. I didn't murder anyone. I got him to drop the gun," Ridge said taking him away from any prying eyes.

"He died on the damn table."

"Not because of me. The judge said stay the hell away from me and he meant it," Ridge said. Kellen pulled Ridge off him and told him to go back to the house.

"You come near me or her again and…"

"Ridge, shut it and go back to the house," Kellen said.

"You..."

"Ridge." He shook his head and walked off. When he didn't have his cell phone with him, Kellen shook his head. He got the cops to handle the psycho and took off to try and find Ridge.

Faith shook her head, pacing the room. "Faith, he's fine. Kellen is with him," Leo's wife Kate said.

"This is insane. What the heck was he thinking?" Kate got her a drink and Faith walked off, went back into their suite, and went and showered off the salt water. She slid into jean shorts and a tank and dried her hair. She put on some makeup and all of a sudden got a horrid feeling in the pit of her stomach. She'd known Ridge long enough to know deep down when something was wrong. She sat down on the bed and called his phone. When Kellen answered, she almost snapped. "Where is he," Faith asked.

"I'm getting him to the house. It's fine. I promise."

"Kellen."

"I know," he said as he hung up.

Faith paced and shook her head. She checked over emails, tried to message him and came up with the one and only way that she knew she could reach Ridge. She knew his watch had something in it where she could send an SOS. She did it and heard his watch buzz. She looked in his bag and saw it. "Crap," she said as she took it out of his bag. "Come back Ridge. Come on. Please. Don't do this," Faith said like a prayer.

When it started to get dark, she heard someone walking up the front gravel drive. She ran out of her room, ran down the stairs and Leo stopped her. "What," Faith said.

"Stay inside."

"Get out of my way," Faith said pushing him aside. When she saw Kellen, but not Ridge, she almost snapped on him. "Where is he?"

"I have no idea. I had him and he vanished," Kellen said.

"What? What are you saying," Faith asked.

"I can't find him. I went everywhere trying to track him down," Kellen said.

Faith shook her head and sat down on the steps. "Faith."

"Don't. You lose Ridge somewhere on this stupid island. This is insane. How could you even let him vanish?"

"Because I was handling things. I needed to keep him safe from being an idiot," Kellen said.

"And I gather it takes more than one person to do that?"

Kellen nodded. "Today, yes."

Faith sat there and even when food came for them for dinner, she didn't move. "Faith, you have to eat. Come inside," Kellen said.

"Not until I see him."

He walked over to her, took her hand and walked her back inside. "Eat. It's right here. We're right by the door," Kellen said handing Faith a plate of lobster pasta. She ate and still had that gnawing feeling. She watched the door like it was sprouting polka dots. When she finished eating, she walked back outside with a glass of Jack in hand for him and a second for her that she was taking sips of while she waited. When she saw someone walking up the drive, she looked, squinting.

"Ridge."

There was no reply. She got up and looked. The person was coming closer. "Ridge, please tell me it's you," Faith said. She put her drink down and the minute she was out of eye shot, the guys ran out behind her. She saw the person and realized that he was injured. "Ridge? Baby. Are you alright," Faith said.

When she looked and saw him, she wrapped her arms around him. "Where the hell have you been," Faith asked.

"Ow."

"What happened," Faith asked.

"Ow." The guys caught up to him and helped him inside. Faith grabbed the glasses and they went up to Faith and Ridge's suite.

"What in the hell happened," Kellen asked.

"Ow." Faith undid his shirt and he wouldn't let her.

"Seriously? You vanish without a damn phone, leave the watch here and disappear and I can't..."

"Out," Ridge said.

"No." Leo's wife walked Faith out of the room and topped up her drink, handing it to her while they sat on the steps.

"Give them a few. It's a stupid guy thing," Kate said.

"That's my fiancée."

"I know Faith. They will handle it. I promise."

"Has this happened before?" Kate didn't say anything but Faith saw her looking at Leo and him motioning not to say anything. "I'm going in there," Faith said as she got up.

She walked into the room, pushing Leo aside. When she saw Ridge with bruises, she shook her head. "You're not 20 years old Ridge. What are you doing?"

"Faith, go."

"No." What happened?"

"Faith."

"Don't you dare kick me out of this damn room," Faith said as Kellen tried to get her to leave. "Tell me what's going on."

Ridge shook his head, got the guys to leave and went and showered. When he stepped out, Faith was sitting on the bathroom counter. "You aren't leaving this room until you tell me what happened. You know that right," Faith asked.

"It's fine."

"No, obviously it isn't," Faith said.

"Faith, leave it. I'm fine. Sore, but fine."

"Then tell me who the guy was." He looked at her. "You're my fiancée Ridge. Say it."

"His son came after me for breaking up with his sister. When he didn't back off, I had no choice but to defend myself. I shot him in the shoulder so he'd drop his weapon and the cops took over. Something happened while he was in the hospital and he passed. His dad has been coming ever since. I have a restraining order against him. He showed up on the damn beach, watching us."

Faith shook her head. "And you couldn't have told me about this before why?" He looked at her, put arnica on the bruises and went to leave. "You're not done," Faith said.

"Meaning?"

"Where did the bruises come from?"

"Bar." She shook her head.

"Lie to my face. Good move," Faith said.

She went to walk out of the bathroom and he grabbed her wrist, pulling her back to him. "Ow."

"Someone made a comment and I snapped. Obviously the wrong person. The cops arrested him."

"And left you there?" He looked at her. She shook her head, pulled away and walked off.

Chapter 14

Faith walked into the bedroom and grabbed her bag. "What are you doing," Ridge asked as he slid on his jeans.

"Packing. I'm going home."

"Faith."

"Then tell me the damn truth. You could've asked to use their phone. Do you realize how…"

He kissed her, devouring her lips. "I shouldn't have left."

Faith shook her head. "No kidding," she replied.

He wrapped his arms around her. "Ow."

"Did someone throw a dang punch?"

"That too," Ridge replied.

"I'll get ice." He shook his head and kissed her.

"I am not about to lift that bag," Ridge said.

Faith put it back on the luggage rack and sat down with him. "You need food."

He nodded and Faith went to get up. "Where are you going?"

"To get you food." She kissed him and went and got the seafood, warming it up. She came upstairs, handed him the plate, and gave him the drink that she'd made for him before he'd vanished.

"Faith."

"Don't. You disappeared. You shouted out a dang order and vanished. Then you took off on Kellen without your cell phone. You literally disappeared. I didn't know if you'd even make it back."

"Babe, I needed to handle it."

"I get it. Next time, keep your phone on you or I'm gonna have to attach a dang AirTag to your head."

"Faith."

"I'm not joking. You do that again and I swear I'm whooping your butt myself."

Ridge finished his dinner and Faith took the dishes to the kitchen. When she felt arms slide around her torso, she turned. "What," Faith asked.

"Come," Ridge said as he took her hand and walked her back into the bedroom.

"Ridge, leave it."

"Come." She shook her head and he walked her up to their suite, closing and locking the door behind them.

"What?"

He kissed her. "I'm sorry."

"It's not enough Ridge. You can't vanish. You said that you were protecting me, but you can't do that if you vanish."

He pulled her into his arms. "Ow."

"Then stop trying to be Romeo and just lay down and rest and let me get ice for you." He shook his head.

"Faith, I'm fine."

"No, you aren't."

He looked at her. "You scared the crap out of me. You know that right?"

"I know. I was out of my damn mind. I couldn't help it," he said. Faith shook her head and got up. "Faith."

"Don't. You scared me. You vanished for hours. Hours Ridge. I didn't know if you were gone if you were hurt or if you drowned in the damn ocean. Don't."

Barefoot Bodyguard

"Faith, please." She shook her head, went and changed into pajamas and came and sat down on the bed, grabbing her laptop.

"Put it away."

"No." "Faith, put the laptop away. Please."

"No." He grabbed her laptop, put it in his suitcase and walked back into the bedroom.

"What are you doing?"

"I love you. I screwed up today. I get it. Don't shut down because you're pissed at me."

Faith looked at him and he saw the tears welling up in her eyes. "I snapped. That's all," Ridge said.

"Then don't snap on me and walk off. I love you, but you can't do that."

He looked at her. "Baby, I love you. I needed to find him so he didn't come near you. I didn't want anyone coming near you and harming you. I love you too much."

Faith shook her head. "Nobody was gonna get near me. He wants to look for you, let the guys handle it."

"Not when he was gonna come near you. I'd do anything to protect you baby. Anything."

"Ridge, don't. You weren't protecting me when you ordered me to stay here. I'm not an employee. You don't get to tell me what to do either. You vanished and practically locked me into the stupid house. What do you want me to do," Faith asked.

"I wanted you to stay here so you didn't end up shot. Last time he did something, I ended up in the hospital with stitches from a gunshot wound. One I don't want happening to you," Ridge said.

"And?" He shook his head and kissed her. He cradled her face in his hands and snuggled her to him.

"I'm not letting one hair get harmed on your head. That's why I said to stay. I don't know that he wouldn't hurt you to get to me."

Faith shook her head. "Ridge, just stop." She got up and went and sat down on the sofa in the main sitting area.

Ridge took a deep breath, did his best to hold back the ow's and walked down to the sitting area. "Faith."

"What?"

He put a hand out. "No. Go away."

Barefoot Bodyguard

He grabbed her hand, pulling her to her feet and walked her back up the stairs to their suite. "Ridge, leave it."

He walked in, sat her on their sofa and locked the door. "What," Faith asked.

"That man is the only person in the damn world who could make me lose it. The only one. I love you more than you'll even know, but you have to know that I had a life and a past before we got together. I said stay because I knew you'd be safe."

"And then handed your phone to Kellen."

He took a deep breath. "Not my finest moment."

Faith shook her head. "No it wasn't," Faith replied.

He kissed her. "I'm sorry." She nodded and he slid into her arms. "Come to bed."

Faith shook her head. "Not after…"

He kissed her again, grabbed her hand and walked her into the bedroom. "We have a movie to watch."

"Ridge, bad timing."

"Not that one Miss Potty mind."

"Which one," she asked.

"Come lay down with me."

"Ridge."

"You have to get sleep anyway. Come."

She went with him and they curled up together on the bed. "What movie," Faith asked. He grabbed his laptop, put it on the bed between them and flipped play on the movie. Instead of Fifty shades or 365 days, it was old home movies that his friend had digitized for him.

"What's all of this," Faith asked.

"When we were little, our moms did this every dang holiday that we were together. It's like the minute we were separated, we gave everyone a headache."

"Still do," Faith teased.

He smirked and tried to wrap his arm around her. When it got to the video of their prom, her mom got video of them talking outside alone. "I don't even remember what all of this was about," Faith said.

"I remember every damn word. You'd found a way to get into the champagne, and were miserable. Your date said he wouldn't make it on time. You were upset because it'd mean walking in alone. I told you that I'd be honored to walk in those doors with you. I hadn't got a date because I'd wanted to ask you. Your idiot boyfriend invited you first. I barely made it past asking if you'd got a date yet. I walked through those doors with you and felt like I'd won a billion dollars. We got pictures that our moms took, but the one we got at the prom is still in my wallet, even now."

Faith looked at him. "What?"

He grabbed his wallet and handed her the photo. On the back of it, there were three words that she knew were in his handwriting. "My future wife," Faith asked.

"I knew then."

She looked at him. "Really?"

He nodded. "Babe, I always wanted you in my life. The fact that it took me walking in as your bodyguard was just a bonus. It's one very sexy body to protect," he teased.

Faith shook her head and kissed him. "And then what," she teased.

"I promise I won't vanish. Not without a note or telling you what's happening." Faith nodded.

"Good. I meant what I said about kicking your butt." He smirked and leaned into her arms trying to ignore the nagging pain.

"Now, are you still mad," he teased.

"Yes."

"Mad enough to kick my bruised body onto the floor?"

"No and I'm still getting…"

He kissed her again, devouring her lips until he felt her legs slide around his hips. "You sure that you're not too sore," Faith asked.

He shook his head and kissed her. "All I know is that I want you. I want the woman I've loved since the minute I was born," he said as he kissed her again. When he slid her shirt off, she knew they were alright again. At least he hoped they were. She slid her shorts off and went for the button of his jeans. "Faith."

"Ridge," she said as he kissed down her neck. When she managed to get the button undone, his phone buzzed.

"Leave it," he said. Faith shook her head and kissed him, grabbing the phone. When she saw the police name on the call display, she handed it to him.

"Sir," Ridge said as he answered.

"The man that you notified us about has been released."

Barefoot Bodyguard

"What?"

"He was told that if he didn't stay away from you and your fiancée, he'd be in jail period. He was released into his daughter's custody. They are out of the state now."

"Thank you, but this isn't the first time. He's done this more than once."

"Understood sir, but it was not our choice. That's what the judge chose."

"This is insane. Fine. If he comes near me again, I can tell you that he's not gonna be doing it to shake my hand. He starts while I'm here, I'm handling it." Ridge hung up and Faith kissed him.

"You sure you don't want to just go home," Faith asked.

He kissed her, devouring her lips. "I promise you, if I see him…"

"You're gonna let Kellen or Leo handle it period. I don't want you hurt even worse."

He nodded and kissed her. "Alright."

"I mean it," Faith said as he kissed her neck then trailed the kisses down her torso. "Ridge." Just as she said it, his taunting started all over again.

"What," he teased. She shook her head and he kissed her again.

"I know what you're doing," she said.

"Good," he teased as he kissed her hip and trailed the kisses up her torso until he leaned into her arms and devoured her lips all over again.

"What," she asked.

"You're stuck with me. You know that right," he teased. She nodded and undid his jeans, sliding them off with her feet as he kissed her again and they had sex. In no way was it as insane as they'd had at home, but she didn't care. Being with him was all she wanted and had wanted since he walked in the door. The hotter things got, the more she wondered how she ever managed to live without him.

Even bruised, every inch of her was throbbing around him and he knew that she wasn't about to say no. She wasn't about to refuse anything. He devoured her lips and just as she was about to explode in his arms, her phone buzzed. "You touch that phone and you won't be walking," he teased. She kissed him and he kept going, making it more and more intense despite the bruises. When she climaxed not once, not twice, but three times, he smirked and kissed her again, letting his body release all the tension he'd held onto. He exploded in her arms and held on even tighter.

"Shit," Faith said as he almost left handprints in her backside. One more kiss and her body was shaking in his arms. "Faith."

"Sexy." He kissed her again.

"What else did you want to do tonight," he teased.

Faith kissed him. "Nothing. You sure you're okay," she asked.

"Can't feel anything."

Faith shook her head and he kissed her again, leaning onto his back and wincing. "You need ice," Faith said.

"I need you and only you. Just you," Ridge said.

Faith shook her head and curled into his arms. "You sure you're okay?"

"Nothing that sleep won't fix," he teased. Faith curled her leg around his and fell asleep in his arms. He kissed her forehead and wrapped his arm around her, pulling the blanket up.

When Faith woke up the next morning, he was sitting on the chair beside the bed in his joggers out cold. Faith smirked and looked over, seeing the ice pack. She looked over at him and he was literally unconscious. She gently got up. Walked over and was about to walk past him when his arm slid around her waist. "Where are you goin," Ridge asked.

She smirked. "Bathroom." She leaned over and kissed him and he smirked. "What," she asked.

"Did you really think that you could do what I know you were thinking about doing without me stopping you?" Faith nodded and kissed him. "Nice try though beautiful," he teased. She shook her head and walked into the washroom to freshen up. When she came back out in nothing but her satin robe, he was on the bed with the ice.

"You know that you could've told me that you needed ice right."

"I'm fine. I had a sore spot," Ridge said.

"And did you actually sleep or just pretend to sleep?"

He kissed her. "I slept. I woke up like an hour and a bit ago."

"Ridge."

"What?"

"You sure you're alright?"

Barefoot Bodyguard

He nodded and pulled her to him. "Come here."

Faith smirked and slid into his lap. "What?"

"Are we okay," he asked.

"Depends on whether you decide to vanish again."

"Not leaving this room. Breakfast then I'm putting you back to bed."

"Oh really," Faith teased. He nodded and kissed her.

She slid into his lap and he untied the satin robe that she had on. "Ridge."

He kissed her again, devouring her lips. "Yes sexy fiancée," he said.

"What would you think about breakfast in bed," he teased.

"I need to be able to move," she joked. He kissed her again and she slid out of his lap. She re-tied her robe, and they went into the kitchen.

Ridge threw the ice out and they started making breakfast. When the chef came in, Ridge shook his head. He handed Ridge another ice pack and made lobster benedict for them both. "Special breakfast," Ridge asked.

"Since you missed dinner sorta," Faith said.

He kissed her. "And," he asked.

"What?" The chef headed out, leaving them alone in the kitchen.

"I was thinking," Faith said.

He kissed her. "I bet you were sexy," he said.

Faith shook her head. "We're not going to the beach."

"Good."

"We have two other options. We go to the pool..."

"Or we stay in bed," he teased.

Faith kissed him. "Or we go shopping for a bit."

"Oh fun. Spending money neither of us need to spend," he teased.

"Or I can look for a dress."

"Since I know you want to do that with your mom, no. Pool, but I swear, if you walk around with that tear-away bikini, you're gonna be really..."

She kissed him. "Unless you want to go to the beach."

He kissed her. "Eat first, then we negotiate," he teased.

Faith smirked and he shook his head. They finished breakfast and he kissed her hand and went to walk her back into the bedroom. "What are you doin," Faith asked.

"Come with me," he said.

He closed and locked the door and leaned her against it. "Ridge."

"What?"

"Bruises. Pain. The ice…" He kissed her and picked her up and devoured her lips, wrapping her legs tight around his hips. "Ridge."

He pinned her hands against the door. "Faith, trust me."

She nodded and he kissed her again as he kicked his joggers off. "Aah," she said as he slid inside her like a hand into a perfect fitting glove. He undid the robe and slid the belt out of the loops. "What," Faith asked. He smirked, leaned her onto the bed and tied her hands with it. "What are you up to," Faith asked. He smirked, slid her legs around him and kissed up her body. "Ridge."

He kept going until she was almost squirming in his arms. Taunting her continually was completely unfair. when he leaned in, he kept going until her body was bursting and climaxing over and over. When he finally climaxed, he barely managed to untie her hands. "Faith," he said.

"Yes handsome."

"Beach."

"You sure," she asked still trying to catch her breath.

"You wear that bikini again and I'm taking it off in the water like it or not."

"And then what," Faith asked.

"That shot won't be enough to prevent you from getting pregnant."

"Really," Faith teased. He nodded and devoured her lips. "Ridge."

"Mm."

"You sure you don't want to get married while we're here?"

"Positive." She kissed him and he smirked, linking their fingers and pinning her hands back down. "Now, do I get to pick the bikini or are you actually gonna wear a one-piece?"

Barefoot Bodyguard

"Or I just go naked," Faith teased.

He shook his head and kissed her again. "Woman, you wouldn't dare. You're gonna have sand in places you aren't gonna want sand."

"Promises, promises." He kissed her again and she leaned in. That kiss that she loved deepened until the goosebumps started all over again.

By the time they finally made it out of bed, they got semi-dressed and went and checked on the guys. "Where we heading," Kellen asked.

"Going to try the beach again. See if maybe we can't have a less-stressful day," Faith said.

"You sure," Leo asked as his wife linked their fingers.

"No fights, no vanishing. If he shows up, you take care of it, and I stay with Faith. Otherwise, she's dragging me home in a body bag," Ridge teased.

"Literally," Faith replied.

"Alright. This time I'm bringing sneakers," Kellen teased.

They got their things together and headed back out. Faith barely let go of Ridge's hand the entire way there. "I'm not going to vanish Faith. I promise you," Ridge said. Kellen found a spot with a private cabana, away from everyone else, and any chance of the random stranger finding them and ruining all of the fun.

When their feet touched the beach, Faith almost felt like she was home. Ridge walked her to the chairs then slid his shirt off and walked her into the water, away from everyone and everything so they had two minutes of complete and utter privacy. He went up to his neck in the water, wrapping her legs around his waist. "What are you up to," Faith asked as he kissed her neck then her ear.

"Taunting my woman. Why do you ask," he teased.

"Ridge."

"What? We're away from everyone, nobody can see what I'm about to do, and…"

She kissed him. "I love you, but for once, try and behave."

He shook his head. "Never," he teased as his hands slid to her backside.

"You sure you're okay?"

"I'm sure. I also know that you wore the dang bikini. Not my fault what happens to it when we're under the water."

Barefoot Bodyguard

"Don't you even..." He kissed her, devouring her lips until her toes started to curl and his hand slid under the front of her bikini bottoms. "Ridge," Faith said.

He smirked and continued taunting her until she shook her head. "Still want me to stop," he whispered as he almost purred into her ear.

"You're taunting."

"And," he said as the taunting intensified and she felt the sides of her bikini come undone.

"Ridge." He tied them to the back of her bikini top and she felt him.

"We can't do this out here," Faith said quietly. He smirked and they moved so they were completely out of sight to any onlookers. He devoured her lips intentionally hiding any moans or toe curling moments. "Crap," Faith said as her legs started shaking. It just got hotter. It always had, and being out in the water was making it more intense. When her body climaxed more than once, he knew. He re-dressed, slid Faith's bikini bottoms back on and they dunked under the water. She kissed him again and shook her head. When they surfaced, Faith was almost laughing. "What," Ridge asked.

"I don't know that I can even walk back to the chairs."

"I can solve that problem," he teased.

"I bet you can," she joked. They made their way in closer, and he carried her to the chairs, leaning her onto hers and sitting down behind her, wrapping his arms around her.

"You two are ridiculous," Kellen said.

"Why?"

"Inseparable. I mean really."

Faith smirked. "It's called finding your person Kellen. When you meet the right one, you'll know," Faith replied.

Ridge smirked and kissed Faith's neck. When his phone buzzed, Faith looked at him. "What," Ridge asked.

He looked at it and smirked. "Hi mom," he teased.

"And how's my baby boy?"

"Good. Down in Jekyll. What's up?"

"Well, I was talking to Faith's mom, and we were wondering when y'all were thinking about having the wedding," she asked.

"We haven't even decided. We have time."

Barefoot Bodyguard

"I understand. I guess she'd mentioned to Faith that you two could have it at their house."

"Mom, I love you, but we're on vacation for a weekend. We can talk about it when we're back."

"Then let me talk to Faith." He shook his head, handing his cell to Faith. When she went to get up, he pulled her back into his lap.

She talked to his mom for what seemed like hours. When he finally got his phone back, Faith was almost laughing. "What," she asked.

"And I gather you planned everything out?"

Faith nodded. "She wants to go look at dresses with me and my mom. Honestly, it's almost cute."

"You know, you can't really look at dresses until you have a date," Leo's wife said.

"We have a general idea of a date. Opposing choices, but a general idea," Faith teased.

"Since when," Ridge asked.

Faith turned and kissed him. "Before Christmas."

He shook his head. "That's less than 6 months off." Faith nodded. He shook his head. "We'll finish that conversation when we're at the house alone."

Faith kissed him and grabbed a drink from their cooler.

By the time they got back to the house, it was almost dinner. Ridge could smell the barbecue and the steaks on it. "What's for dinner," Faith asked.

"Surf and turf with crab legs, grilled asparagus and roasted potatoes. We have wine or the Jack Daniel's special batch. Up to you," the chef said.

Ridge smirked, took Faith's hand and walked her back up the steps to their suite.

"What's wrong," Faith asked.

"Christmas? Really?"

She nodded and kissed him. "We talked about it."

"But in the flipping cold?"

She smirked. "Suit without sweating, no stress about anything and on top of it, we have it somewhere we can control security. Isn't that what you said that you wanted to do?"

He nodded. "I didn't mean this year Faith. We have time. We can wait until next…"

"No. Ridge, I love you. I have since we were kids. There's no reason to wait. It's not about getting to know each other better, since we already know everything there is to know. You know more than my parents do."

He smirked. "Can't we wait until Valentine's or something?" She shook her head. "Please." He shook his head and looked at her.

"Here's the deal. We do it then, we still wait on the kids so we can go and enjoy ourselves. I don't want this issue we have to still be a problem when we get married. I don't."

She kissed him. "So, we do have a date?"

"Before thanksgiving?"

She nodded. "November 16th?"

"Faith, that's less than 5 months. You can't even get a dress..."

"Yes, I can handsome."

"If you think it'll all be done by then, fine," he replied realizing that they were really doing it. They were really throwing caution to the wind and getting hitched in the dang winter in Charleston. He almost said a prayer hoping that a hurricane wouldn't get in their way. She had so many ideas, and every single one of them said she wanted the wedding of her dreams. Her mom and his would be in heaven. It also meant he only had a matter of months until the stalker was going to be handled one way or another. He shook his head and Faith looked at him. "What," she teased.

"You know that this whole thing is gonna end up being a massive 600-person event right?"

"Not when it's us."

He looked at her. "Babe, my mom, and your mom put together? Right. It's gonna be a..."

She kissed him, silencing his complaining. Silencing the worry and getting his mind back on what was really important. "Ridge."

"What?"

"You do realize that all that really matters is us. That's all I want." She kissed him and he sat down on the bed.

"Babe, I get it, but I just..."

She slid into his lap and kissed him. "Just what?"

"Tell me that this isn't gonna be a circus."

She smirked. "No circus. Fairy lights instead."

He shook his head and kissed her. "Promise me."

"What?"

"That it's about you and me. That if we can't catch whoever is really behind all of this, we hold off."

Faith kissed him and he leaned her onto the bed, wrapping her legs around him. "You know we're gonna be fine right," Faith asked. He nodded and kissed her.

He leaned over and kissed her again. That kiss deepened until he felt her goosebumps. It was the one way that he knew she still wanted him. "Faith."

"Mm," she replied.

"We're gonna be late for dinner." She kissed him and he linked their fingers, pinning her arms to the bed. When he saw the grin, he knew that she was thinking the same thing he was. "Now, where were we," he teased.

"Not funny," Faith joked. He kissed her and peeled her bikini off, peeled off every inch of clothing between them and devoured her lips. "What," Faith asked.

"All...mine," he teased as he kissed down her torso and started taunting her all over again.

"Ridge." His hands slid down her silky skin to the one place that would have her body throbbing, toes curling and heart racing in seconds. His breath against her skin was enough to get her turned on. The taste of her skin got him beyond hot and bothered. Letting her see that wasn't happening. Taunting was her only option. Intense until her nails dug into his skin was just a dirty memory in his mind, but when it happened again, he intensified it. "Crap." He nibbled in the one place that she couldn't resist, and the one place that would make her forget everything he'd ever done wrong.

She melted into his arms. That's what she wanted, that's what she craved at that exact moment. She didn't care about food, air, oxygen or anything else except the man that was making every inch of her hot, bothered, turned on and horny for him. Just him. The sex was indescribable. She could barely even think about breathing. Nothing had felt like that ever. The only thing that was even close was that first night after the movie. The first night that she thought that her body had exploded from the inside out. That was the only thing even close to how that moment felt. He kissed her as their bodies found a rhythm together and it just got even more intense.

"Faith," he said as she kissed him.

"Don't stop." He shook his head and kept going until he could barely breathe. They exploded together until her toes were curled into triple knots and her body was tight against his.

"Faith."

"Yeah."

"You good?" "I'm not gonna be walking for the next 6 hours, but I'm good. How's my man," she asked.

"Good," he teased as he kissed up the back of her neck.

When they finally made it out of bed, she could barely move. "What else did you want," he teased as Faith kissed him.

"Food." He smirked, kissed her and got up, pulling his jeans on. "Where are you going?"

"To get dinner so we can be alone in here and eat."

"I'll come..."

"Faith." She looked at him, got up and grabbed her sundress, pulled it on, and they went into the kitchen. Faith's arm was around his waist, and they sat down.

"Bruises healing," Kellen asked.

"Getting there," Ridge replied.

When Ridge's phone went off not 2 minutes later, Faith slid it from his pocket and saw the name of her dad's security guy. "Why is he calling," Faith asked.

He kissed her, answered and left the room. "What's wrong," Ridge asked.

"The guy you thought was part of it is, but he's not the ringleader. We got more information off the cameras. It's someone that Faith knows. Someone she knows personally. That she dated."

"Who," Ridge asked.

"Holden Whittaker."

"The dick she dated in high school?"

"The guy she dated 2 years before you two met up again."

Ridge shook his head. "And?"

"She needs to come back. He has a house on Jekyll."

Ridge shook his head, walked back down to the kitchen and finished dinner with Faith. "What's going on," she asked.

"Nothing."

Kellen looked at him and saw the look in his eye. "I'll go pack," Kellen said as he finished his last bite and headed up to his room to pack up.

Barefoot Bodyguard

"Meaning," Faith asked. They finished dinner and Faith looked at him. Leo and his wife finished, headed up to pack and Faith looked at Ridge. "Meaning what," Faith asked.

"We're heading home tomorrow."

"Why?"

"We can talk about it upstairs."

"Now," Faith said starting to get irritated. They finished eating and he poured them each a double shot of Jack and took the drinks upstairs. "Ridge."

"Holden."

"What about him," Faith asked as she slid her sandals off.

"He paid them to add the cameras to the house after you bought it. The microphones were his. The bedroom cameras were his."

Faith looked at him like he'd sprouted a horn and became a unicorn. "He what?"

"And he has a house on Jekyll."

"Lord help me. Meaning we're vanishing back to Charleston?"

He nodded. "I don't want him near either of us. Especially now."

Faith kissed him. "He's not gonna do anything if we're here."

He looked at her. "I doubt that," Ridge replied. Faith shook her head, and her phone went off. Yeah, it was the worst timing ever, but it did.

When Faith looked at it, she dropped the phone on the floor. "Who," Ridge said.

He grabbed her phone and saw Holden's name. "Holden."

"I thought I called Faith."

"You did. What's up," Ridge asked.

"I was gonna see what y'all were up to. I'm down at my place in Jekyll. Did y'all want to come down and hang out," Holden asked.

"We're actually heading to Blue Ridge for a few days. Thanks though," Ridge said intentionally lying to him about where they were.

"Well, when I get back, I'll let you know. We can go do guy time," Holden said.

"Sure," Ridge said planning out exactly what he'd do if given the chance. They hung up and Faith looked at him.

"We're going home. Tonight," Ridge said.

"Can we not just have one last night?"

"Baby."

"One last night. Alone."

He kissed her. "We're going home. I don't want him finding out that we're here."

She kissed him. "Movie night."

He shook his head. "Babe, I love that you're trying to get me naked again and in bed so you can try taking advantage, but we have to."

"And if I say no?"

He kissed her. "We're still going."

"Ridge."

"Babe, I'm saying that we aren't safe. I'm doing my job and getting you as far out of it as possible. I need to get you away from here."

"Then we go somewhere else. I don't want to go home."

He looked at her. "Faith, I love you. I do. We need to go."

"Then pick somewhere. Anywhere."

He kissed her. "And if I choose somewhere you don't want?"

Faith kissed him. "Blue Ridge. Hell. I don't care if we're in a submarine. I just want you without the stress of being home."

He kissed her and gave her what she wanted. One more night in Jekyll. When she nodded off, he booked a cabin by the water in Bluffton. Away from home, high security and privacy even if it was only for a night or two. He let the guys know, let the hotel know that they were checking out early and packed their stuff up. He called the pilot, got the plane ready, got the hotel in Bluffton to let them in when they arrived and got the car to come get them and take them to the airstrip. He showered, got dressed and came into the bedroom to see her still asleep. He slid her into his hoodie and her shorts, handed off the bags and laptops to Kellen and picked her up, carrying her out to the car waiting to take them.

By the time Faith woke up, they were already on the plane back. "Where are we," Faith asked.

"Plane. We're going to Bluffton. Away from home, but safer and higher security. Kellen is coming, but Leo and his wife are staying in the hotel in a suite."

"And where are we staying," Faith asked.

"The main house. They're in the gatehouse. Their choice," Ridge said.

"And?"

"We're staying until Monday or Tuesday and heading back." He kissed her.

"Had to do this in the middle of the night?" Ridge nodded and the plane landed.

They stepped off the plane and the car took them to the resort in Bluffton. Faith was practically asleep the entire way there. When they got to the cottage, he carried her up the steps to the main bedroom leaned her onto the bed and grabbed the bags, quietly thanking the driver. Kellen made sure they were settled, went to his room on the other side of the cottage and got some sleep. Leo and his wife got settled in the gatehouse, leaving Faith and Ridge alone.

He got undressed and slid onto the bed behind her, noticing that the hoodie and shorts were both gone. "Faith," he said.

"Get in bed," she replied.

He smirked and slid in, wrapping his arm around her.

She turned to face him. "Had to leave at…"

He kissed her, devouring her lips. There wasn't another word muttered between them the rest of the night. The sex was so intense that her legs were shaking, and he fell asleep with his head on her chest.

Chapter 15

They woke up the next morning and she wasn't in bed. He shook his head and saw a note:

Breakfast is coming. Back in a minute.

He shook his head and went to get up when she walked into the bedroom in lingerie. "What are you up to," Ridge asked.

She kissed him and slid into his lap. "Why did we leave in the middle of the night," Faith asked.

"Because I wanted us safe and as far from him and his stupidity as possible. I wanted you safe. The minute he offered for us to come to Jekyll is when we had to leave and get as far away as possible."

"We couldn't have left this morning?"

He kissed her. "I love you, but no. You were tired. You wanted to sleep, so I got you here as fast as possible."

"Ridge."

"What?"

"Next time, wake me up first." He kissed her and she leaned into his arms. "Now, I had another idea," Faith said.

"Which is," he teased. She kissed him and kissed down his chest. "Faith."

"What?"

"I know what you're doing."

"And?"

He shook his head trying to pull her back up and she shook her head. She kept going, heading towards the one thing he wasn't willing to let happen. "Faith, don't." When she did anyway, he shook his head, leaning back as he sucked in a breath.

He shook his head as she took him in deep. Part of him was enjoying it and the other wanted her to stop. "Faith."

She kept going. Finally, he managed to pull her back up his torso and pinned her to the bed. "That's what you were up to," he teased.

Faith nodded and kissed him, wrapping her legs around him. "That's what you want? Just that?"

Faith shook her head. "I want every inch of you. All of you. Good, bad…"

He kissed her and made one very large decision. "Roll over," he said.

Barefoot Bodyguard

"Why?"

"Faith," he said as he nibbled her lips. She did as he asked and he leaned behind her, pulling her against him as they had sex. Deeper. More intense. Her body trembled in his arms, and he kept going. "Tell me what you want," Ridge asked.

"All of you."

"Faith, you already have it."

"More." He shook his head and taunted her in ways he'd never dared to. Her body trembled and crashed around him more than once until she was determined to get her way. One hand taunted, the other held her tight enough that she could feel every breath. "Ridge."

"What," he asked as he nibbled at her neck. His body crumbled and hers throbbed tight around him as they slid to the bed. "You are one heck of a good morning," he teased as Faith smirked.

"At least I know now how to wake you up," she teased.

"Not happening again Faith. I told you."

"Yeah it will," she joked.

"Meaning?" When he saw the grin come across her face, he shook his head. "I created a monster. Great," he joked.

"Am I not allowed to want to taunt you back," Faith asked.

"No. My job." Faith smirked and he pulled the blankets up, wrapping her up in the comforter of the bed.

"Ridge."

"What?"

"You mad?"

"Depends. You mad about me carrying you onto the plane without you being awake?"

"I know why. All I asked was that next time you wake me up first." He kissed her shoulder and she smirked. "Where are we?"

"Montage Bluffton. Resort that has enough security that the guys can have a break."

"This also mean we can have an actual vacation?"

"If that's what you want." She slid out of bed, and he shook his head. "Now what," he asked. She kissed him and walked off. He could hear the water running. He got up, walked into the bathroom and saw her stepping into the shower. He grabbed towels, putting them on the counter, and slid in behind her.

Just as she was washing her hair, his fingers took over and she smirked and leaned into his arms. "Thank you," Faith said.

"Welcome beautiful," Ridge said as he leaned her under the stream of hot water. He kissed her and she smirked as she reached for him and leaned back into his arms. "What," he teased.

"I love you."

"Love you back sexy. Always." She shook her head, and she slid him under the water. He washed up and leaned his head back in the water. It felt too good. Way too good. He could finally have a few moments of no stress.

"Remember that idea of doing whatever we wanted," Faith teased.

"Don't even think about doing what I know you're thinking about. I mean it."

"Doing what," Faith asked.

He shook his head, picked her up and sat her under the stream of water. "Don't you dare," he said.

Faith smirked. "Woman, finish washing your hair and cut it out." He kissed her, stepped out and wrapped a towel around his hips. He dried off and she stepped out. He wrapped the other towel around her and went and got dressed. Just as he pulled his jeans on, Kellen knocked. "What's up," Ridge asked opening the door.

"Breakfast showed. You guys good," he asked. Ridge nodded and he followed Kellen downstairs.

"She mad," Kellen asked.

"She got her payback," Ridge teased. Ridge got their breakfasts and made coffee. He was about to bring it upstairs when Faith came down in her sundress.

"How'd you sleep," Kellen teased.

"Good. Did you get any sleep," Faith teased.

"Not exactly. I was up going through background on that Holden guy. Why on earth did you ever date a sleaze like that," Kellen asked as he ate his bacon.

"You have a really good point. I kept bumping into him when I'd go into the city or when I was at the beach. We sorta started hanging out as friends, then he wanted more when I was in no way ready or willing to do that. When I turned him down, he sorta vanished for a while until I saw that he'd bought the house a few doors down from mine at the beach." Ridge looked at Kellen and nodded.

"What," Faith asked.

"That explains a whole lot. I'll tell you that," Ridge said.

"Meaning?"

"Nothin."

Faith looked at him like she was waiting to hear the ridiculous comment. "Just say it," Faith said. Ridge shook his head, opting to eat his Eggs Benedict instead of comment what he wanted to. "We sorta just say hi in passing until that time he tried talking me into drinks and you showed up," Faith said.

"That wasn't a coincidence by the way," Ridge said before he stuffed another mouthful of the delicious food into his mouth.

"Alright. That's it. Say whatever it is that you're gonna say. Spit it out," Faith said.

"You don't think it's odd that first he bumps into you all the time, then moves into a house near you, then magically knows where you are at all times," Kellen asked as Ridge gave him a look.

"It's not like it's a big city. It's Isle of freaking Palms. There aren't that many nice places out here."

Kellen looked at Ridge and Faith turned and looked at him. "Say it, Ridge."

"Did he give you a business card at all? Anything like that?" Faith got up and grabbed her purse, handing Kellen the card. When he felt through it, there was one little bump in the middle. One that wasn't gravel or dirt. One that was the same size as a microchip on a pet. Kellen grabbed his lighter, walked outside and torched the card, destroying it completely.

"What in the world?"

"Microchipped. Probably a tracker of some kind," Kellen said. Faith looked at him, then at Ridge.

"Seriously?"

"I knew there had to be a way somehow," Ridge said.

Faith took a gulp of her coffee. "You seriously think all of this is Holden?"

"He does IT. Not that hard to access whatever devices he leaves behind. According to your dad, some of those were there when your mom dated that Zack guy. All he needed to do was hack the system and add more of whatever he needed when there was an open house to buy it. He could've rented it for the weekend and installed them to blackmail whoever rented it," Kellen said. Ridge was silent.

Faith looked at him. "You aren't saying anything," Faith said.

"It was a thought I had. I didn't know he'd bought the house two doors down until you said so."

Faith shook her head, finishing her breakfast. "So, what do we do now," Faith asked.

"Relax for today. Tomorrow, head back to Charleston without the tracker in your wallet," Ridge said as he finished the last of his food.

"And what are we doing today," Faith asked.

"I'm getting work done. Y'all can do whatever. I heard the pool was nice," Kellen teased.

"Why is this funny," Faith asked.

Ridge's hand slid to her leg, and she shook her head. "You do still have another bikini in that bag from what I remember when I packed it last night."

"And what are you gonna do," Faith teased.

He smirked. "Get you back for this morning."

Faith smirked and finished her breakfast and cleaned up, putting the dishes into the washer.

"Really?" Ridge nodded as he walked over to her, picked her up and carried her back upstairs to their room.

"Ridge, put me down."

"No." They walked into the bedroom, and he leaned her onto the bed. "Now what were you saying?"

"You wanna stay inside all day?"

"No. We can go over to the pool if you want. It's a little easier knowing that he isn't here."

"You really think that he's gonna do all of this?"

"He could just be helping whoever it is, but it's something. Why didn't you tell me that he was around?" Faith shook her head, got up and went and changed into her bikini, sliding her shorts on and a t-shirt. "Faith."

"If you're coming with me, you should probably get changed. Did you want some assistance," she asked as she came back into the bedroom and walked up to him.

"You sure you don't…" She kissed him and undid his jeans. "Faith."

"What?"

Barefoot Bodyguard

"I know what you're doing."

"And what might that be," she asked as she undid the button of his jeans.

"Woman, stop."

"Stop what," she teased as she unzipped his jeans. He grabbed her hand and leaned her onto the bed.

"You seriously start that, and I swear, you're gonna need a car to take you to the pool." She kissed him and slid his jeans down. She smirked and he devoured her lips. She was gonna have no choice but to behave. If he could've, he would've tied her hands so she didn't do what he knew she wanted to. "What is wrong with you? Pawing at me," he teased.

"You started it handsome."

"And how did I start it?"

She smirked. "Yesterday after dinner."

He shook his head and slid into her arms. "By the way, you aren't making it to the pool."

"Really?"

He smirked and shook his head. "And?"

"What am I gonna do with you?"

She smirked and kissed him. He leaned into her arms, devouring her lips and she slid him onto his back. "Faith."

"What?"

"You aren't doing what I think you are."

She smirked, pulled his jeans and boxers off and slid into his arms. He untied her bikini bottoms and grabbed her hands. "What are you up to," Faith asked.

"Like I said, not doing what I think you're up to."

"I still don't understand what the big deal is," she teased.

"Meaning what," he asked.

She kissed him and he shook his head. "I told you."

"And I don't think there's anything wrong."

He shook his head. "Faith, are you gonna pick a fight about this all day?"

"Until you let me without fighting me on it, yes."

He shook his head, got up and pulled on swim shorts. "You seriously have to quit. You trust me don't you," she asked.

"Not the point."

"Ridge." He came back in with shorts and a tee on, slid his flip flops on and took her hand seeing her fully dressed again. They grabbed their laptops and phones, grabbed the house key, and went down to the pool. Kellen followed as Leo and his wife were already there. They got to the pool and saw 3 chairs set aside for them. Ridge put the laptops down, grabbed towels and sat down by Leo. "You guys alright," Leo's wife asked.

Faith nodded. She slid her shorts off and he saw the string bikini. If they'd been at the beach, the bikini bottoms would've been gone, and he would've been taunting her under water.

"I know what you're thinking," Faith teased as he kissed her hand.

"Which would be," he teased.

Faith got up, pulled him to his feet and slid into the warm saltwater pool. He slid in behind her and came up behind her in the water. "What," Faith asked.

"We good," he asked.

"Depends."

He shook his head. "You starting that again?"

She nodded and kissed him. "Faith, I love you and I always have, but leave it be." She shook her head and kissed him, sliding her legs around his hips.

"Come back to the house," she whispered.

"I thought you wanted some sunshine?"

"We have a screened in porch and a balcony. I'm good," Faith teased. He shook his head, leaning her against the wall of the pool.

"And why are you so determined to get me back into bed," he asked.

"Because I can," Faith teased.

He kissed her, devouring her lips. "And I'm telling you that if we end up back at the house, you won't be walking to the car tomorrow." Faith smirked.

"Promises…" He kissed her again and she felt his hand near her inner thigh. "Ridge."

"What?"

"You aren't doing…"

He kissed her, nibbling her lips. "You want to start this then be prepared wife to be. I can taunt until you forget your name," he whispered as she got goosebumps all up and down her body.

Barefoot Bodyguard

"I know. One of my favorite things about you husband to be," she whispered as he devoured her lips all over again.

"House or stay," he asked.

"Depends on whether you can keep your hands to yourself," she teased.

"Are you gonna behave?"

"Maybe," she teased as she kissed him and dunked him under the water. He shook his head, hopping out of the water.

"An hour or two then you're mine wife to be." She smirked, splashed him and he went back over to the chairs. He dried off and went through emails.

When he managed to get the emails done, he saw one from Holden:

> *Thought I'd see what you were up to. Did you want to grab a drink on Shem creek?*

Ridge's skin almost crawled. "What," Kellen asked.

"I'm so not in the mood for this stupid crap. Does he think I'm an idiot," Ridge asked as he showed Kellen the email.

"What do you want me to do," Kellen asked.

"I swear, I'm whooping his butt to the moon when we're back," Ridge said.

"Did you read the email I sent you," Kellen asked.

"What?"

"He's working for someone."

"Meaning what?"

"Meaning Holden is number two. Not number one."

Ridge looked at him. "Meaning what?"

"Meaning we still have work to do. We need to go home."

"We will tomorrow. Give her another night." Kellen nodded and Faith splashed around with Leo's wife. She'd at least made a friend through the insanity.

They hung out for a while and when Faith finally made it out of the pool, he handed Faith her towel and she sat down in his lap. "Faith."

"What," she asked.

"Had to sit here?" She nodded and leaned into his arms. "Faith."

He kissed her neck and Faith smirked. "What were y'all talking about," Faith asked as she grabbed her laptop.

"Trying to determine how all of this insane crap started. It's like the closer we get to figuring it out, the more insane it gets," Ridge said. Faith slid backwards even more, and he knew what she was doing.

He kissed her shoulder, nibbling on it. "Hungry," Ridge asked.

"Why," Faith asked. They all ordered lunch and got it at the pool. Simple and easy. Sweet tea, grilled cheese, fresh fruit. All of it was what she'd craved, and what he wanted.

They finished lunch and Ridge was now being taunted in public by his fiancée. Faith sliding closer and closer to him was almost ridiculous. "I'm gonna head back to the house. Get some actual work done. Are you coming," Ridge asked as Faith smirked.

"I guess," she said.

"We'll be at the house if you need us," Ridge said grabbing the bag and walking her back down to the house.

"What," Faith asked as he shook his head.

"Had to taunt and tease didn't you," he replied.

"One of the things you love about me." He shook his head, and they headed inside. He locked up behind him and they headed upstairs. "Faith."

"Husband to be," she replied.

"No more taunting in public."

"That include the beach?"

He shook his head, closed their bedroom door behind him, locked it and saw her walking into the bathroom. "Faith."

"What?"

"What are you up to really?"

She washed her hands and came out. "Meaning what," Faith asked.

"Meaning you keep taunting like that and that shot isn't gonna do you any good," he said.

"Sounds like a challenge," she teased.

"Faith." She came back into the bedroom in her satin robe and nothing else. "Seriously," he said.

"Alone. Just you and me in the house. Nobody to complain."

Barefoot Bodyguard

He shook his head. "And you need to stop or that belt on your robe is gonna end up tying your hands so you keep them to yourself."

"Really. You don't say," she joked.

She walked towards him, and he shook his head. "Faith, seriously. Why," he asked.

"Why what? Why do I want to taunt you back after all the taunting you've done already," she teased.

"Why me? Of all people that you could've chosen, why..."

She kissed him. "Because I do. Ridge, you showed up at my house not knowing anything that had happened since we were in high school. I told you and you didn't run, you didn't leave, and you didn't walk away. You stayed and made me want to be with you. You saved me from stupid..."

He kissed her, devouring her lips. "And," he asked.

"You saved me from his stupid crap. From the date that I seriously didn't want to go on."

"That's all?"

She kissed him. "You saved me from myself a million times over. I wouldn't known about any of it if you hadn't been honest and told me."

He slid his arms around her and kissed her. "And," he asked.

"I've never stopped loving you. When we were kids, you were my best friend. You still are."

He kissed her and picked her up, wrapping her legs around his hips. "What," Faith asked.

"Wife to be." She kissed him and he leaned her onto the bed. "You sure about that whole idea of taunting me," he teased.

"I still don't know what the deal is. I'm not gonna hurt you."

"Faith."

"What?"

"Just leave it. I said no and I meant it." She undid the drawstring of his swim shorts.

"Not happening," he said as he backed away and went and slid boxers and his jeans back on. He sat down on the chair in their room and opened his laptop, seeing two emails from her dad:

> *Thank you for getting her out of there. Hotel is covered. Do you need anything else? They're bringing the SUV over to the resort for you and for your team. Hopefully bruises will heal. Come by when you're back.*

Barefoot Bodyguard

My daughter told me about the issue in Jekyll. He's been handled. Rest easy.

Ridge shook his head. "You told your dad about what happened in Jekyll?"

"I was scared that something happened to you. What did you expect," she asked.

"Faith, in future, leave your dad out of it please."

"Then don't vanish."

He went through emails, getting confirmation that the SUV's were there, and Kellen had the keys. He took a deep breath and Faith looked at him. "What," she asked.

"Nothing."

"I got a few emails. Work stuff, but I kinda have to be home to do any of it," Faith said.

"We're going tomorrow."

"Meaning tonight's the last night of vacation."

He nodded and Faith put her laptop away. She got up, walked over to him and slid his laptop out of his lap. "What are you doing," he asked.

"If we have one night left alone without anyone around, then I'm taking advantage of it."

"We still have dinner Faith."

"Dinner in bed. I don't know that you'll be able to move," Faith teased. He shook his head and she slid into his lap.

"So determined."

She kissed him. "Taking full advantage of my man," Faith teased.

He shook his head and Faith kissed him again. "Can't behave?"

"Not around you," she said as she went for the button of his jeans.

"Faith, leave the jeans alone."

"Off."

"No."

"Ridge."

"I said no. You want…"

She kissed him. "I want you. All of you."

"Faith."

"What? What's so wrong," she asked.

He shook his head. "I love you. I do. Faith, we can't keep doing this."

"What?"

"We can't keep ignoring all of the crap getting in our way. I love you. Always. I just…"

"Come lay on the bed with me."

He shook his head. "I have work to get done."

"And we're on vacation. Come lay down with me."

"Faith."

"I swear." He kissed her and laid down on the bed with her. When she went for the button of his jeans again, he stopped her.

"Ridge."

"Breathe. There's more to a dang relationship than screwing around a million times a day," he said.

"And what has you in such a crap mood?"

"Emails. Ones from your dad praising me."

"And that's bad?"

"If he knew what we've…"

Faith kissed him. "Stop acting a fool. He knows what he needs to. I'm safe, in one piece and happy for once."

"Then what," he teased.

"Ridge, we love each other. That's what matters to them."

He shook his head. "And I know that I'm not good enough for you."

She looked at him. "We've been together, inseparable, since you walked in my house and you're saying that now? Now that I have your ring on my finger? Seriously Ridge." He got up. "Where are you going?"

"Downstairs."

Ridge opened the bedroom door, walked downstairs and sat down on the screened in porch. He needed to clear his head. Something was really off. Way off. He didn't know what it was, but it had to get out of his system and fast. He took a deep breath and leaned back in the rocking chair when she came outside. "What are you doing out here," Faith asked.

"Thinking." Faith sat down on his lap in his hoodie and her shorts.

"What happened? We were fine. We were laughing at the pool and having fun. What's going on?"

He shook his head and picked her up, sitting her on her own chair. "Ridge."

"I need to think straight. I can't do that when you're determined to rip my clothes off every two minutes."

"What are you worried about?" He took a deep breath and ran his fingers through his hair.

"I don't know who Holden is working for. I don't know who's causing all of it. Cameron and his dad were low on the totem pole. We know that now anyway. I don't know how to protect you from something that I don't even know to look for."

She took a deep breath, waited a moment and got up. "What," he asked.

"Come inside."

"Faith."

She took his hand and walked inside. "Seriously." She walked into the house, closed and locked the door behind them and sat him on the sofa.

"What," he asked.

She slid into his lap and looked at him. "I love you. I get that you're worried that the wrong thing is gonna happen and that you won't be able to protect me. I get it. Try to remember one thing alright? I chose you because I wanted you in my life. We can figure it out. Whoever is coming after us isn't getting near us. I promise you. Whatever happens, I'm not letting you go Ridge. I'm not leaving just because we figured it out. Either are you," Faith said.

She kissed him and his arms slid around her. "No more doubts. Promise," she asked. He kissed her, picking her up with her legs around him and carried her back upstairs. He locked the door behind him and leaned her onto the bed. "What," Faith asked.

He slid the shorts off, and she undid the hoodie. He leaned into her arms and devoured her lips. "Ridge."

"What?" She went to undo his jeans and he stopped her.

"You're..." He kissed her and the kiss went from soft to deep to getting her turned on to the point that she undid his jeans without a second thought. Her legs slid around him, and the taunting began all over again. Whatever she'd said that hit him just right was enough to get him out of the mood, or so she thought.

She slid his jeans off along with his boxers, and he leaned into her arms. "Ridge," she said as he nibbled down her torso, taunting her.

"What," he asked.

"Please." He shook his head and kept going until he could see her toes curling into pretzels.

"Come here," Faith said.

He shook his head and nibbled even higher up her thigh until her body was beyond turned on. Every inch of her wanted him however she could. His fingers continued taunting until she ran her fingers through his hair and tried to slide him up her torso. "Ridge, come here."

He kissed and nibbled his way back up and kissed Faith as he plunged himself into her. "Aah."

"And what did you want," he teased as he kept going and deepened the simple kiss until he was muffling her moans with the kiss. Her body pulled him deeper until he couldn't hold back. When his body crashed into her, it's like a wave had hit them both and neither could let go. She wouldn't move and he couldn't let go. He slid to his side and Faith wouldn't let go.

"I love you," Faith said as she kissed him.

"I love you too." Just as the words passed his lips, his phone buzzed:

> *Back from pool. Can y'all keep it down up there. Lol. We ordered dinner. Simple and easy. Y'all are having steak. We're hanging outside if you want to come out of the nest.*
> *– K*

Ridge smirked and kissed her. "What," she asked.

"They're back. They even ordered us dinner." Faith kissed him as he leaned onto his back, and she curled up resting her head on his chest.

"Are we okay," Faith asked.

"It's insane. Sometimes I wonder why you're even with me. Holden has money and so did half the idiots you dated in high school. I'm not in that league."

"Ridge, I need you to hear this. Please. I don't care how much money someone has. I never have. The guy that treats me right and makes me happy is what I wanted. You do that even when you worry me to death. There are guys with money who are idiots and horrid people. Guys I'd never even consider dating. Then there are the unicorns that treat me right. That love me the way I want. The guys who love a picnic as much as a fancy restaurant. The ones that come to my office and make sure I eat something. That love my addiction to Starbucks. Those, my fiancée, are the ones that I never ever let go of. That's why I said yes when you proposed. That's why I was worried about you. I'm not losing the unicorn." He smirked and kissed her, snuggling her to him. "Now, if he'd stop being ridiculous about the things I wanted to do, it'd help."

He shook his head. "Behave. For once in your life Faith, behave." She kissed him and they nodded off.

If almost felt too good falling asleep in his arms. She'd become addicted to that feeling of being surrounded by his arms. When she woke up a half hour later, he was still out cold. She smirked and made one last attempt to do the one thing he'd never wanted her to. When he woke up to her between his legs, he'd shook his head. "Faith."

"Mm."

His body almost trembled. She kept going until his fingers slid into her hair and down to the nape of her neck. "Come here."

She shook her head and took him deeper. "Shit."

"Mine," she teased as she came up for air. He pulled her on top of him and then flipped her to her back, fast, deep and almost like he was replacing the feeling that was negative with her. They had sex again and when he climaxed, Faith's body curled into him.

"Crap," Faith said. Her body was throbbing around him, and he couldn't stop it. "Holy crap," Faith said as she caught her breath.

"No more," he said. She kissed him and he flipped onto his back. She slid into his arms, and he looked at her. "What part of don't didn't you understand," he asked.

"Did I hurt you?"

"No."

"Definitely didn't break anything."

"Faith."

"It makes me feel good."

He looked at her. "What?"

"That I can do that to you and get you all turned on like you do to me."

"That's why?" She nodded. He kissed her, tasting himself on her lips. Fine. When she did it, it was hot. Only her. They got up a half hour later, he slid joggers on, and Faith slid her shorts and his hoodie back on and they headed downstairs.

"Good timing. Dinner just showed," Kellen said as he handed Ridge and Faith their dinner. Ridge grabbed the Jack and poured them each a glass.

"You do know that you're driving tomorrow right," Kellen teased.

"I know," Ridge replied. They sat down with everyone and it's almost like they were waiting to hear Ridge say they were heading back. "We have to head back tomorrow. No early morning stuff. We're gonna head back around 9 if y'all are good with it," Ridge said.

"Sounds good," Leo said.

"Then we're gonna find this guy who has it out for Faith."

"I mean, could it have been someone coming after her dad through her," Leo asked.

Faith looked at him. "Really," Faith asked.

"Could it be that," Kellen said.

"He did say he'd been getting threats for years. This could just be part of it," Ridge said.

"All of you are freaking me out," Leo's wife said.

"If that's true, then mom and dad are in just as much danger," Faith said.

"Exactly," Ridge replied. Faith looked at Ridge. "Finish dinner then we talk."

They all finished dinner, cleaned up and went to their rooms to pack. When Faith and Ridge walked into their room, she sat down on the bed and her hands started shaking. "Faith, your dad has more security than the president. He's safe and so is your mom. Nobody put two and two together about this. Not until now. We'll get home, talk to him and his security and tell them everything we figured out. We're alright."

She hugged him. "Promise me that this isn't gonna ruin everything," Faith said.

"There's nothing for whoever it is to ruin. We're fine. Your mom and dad are good. We'll figure it out."

"Promise me."

He nodded and kissed her. "Let's pack before you decide that you want round 952," he joked as Faith threw a pillow at him.

TO BE CONTINUED.......

Coming Soon

Barefoot Bliss – The Charleston Series Book 6

The continuing story of Faith and Ridge

Made in the USA
Middletown, DE
02 April 2024